Messenger

REFUGEE

PART I

MICHAEL POLOWETZKY

ISBN: 978-1-63950-014-7 (sc)
ISBN: 978-1-63950-015-4 (e)

Writers Apex

Gateway Towards Success

8063 MADISON AVE #1252
Indianapolis, IN 46227
+13176596889
www.writersapex.com

To: E

CONTENTS

IN A FAR COUNTRY

....

"*It's* going to be awesome!" exclaimed the young traveler to her three special friends with similar unbounded teenage enthusiasm. "No! It's going to be *really* awesome!"

"So it'll be for you, Pascale-love!" responded her companions, all-as-one. "It's going to be awesome, *really* awesome! We only wish we could come, too!"

Pascale Kedari was so excited about embarking on a ten-day trip to Paris. "*Twelve*" she swiftly amending, "if also counting arrival and departure dates!"

"Such an awesome opportunity it's going to be, my loves!" she told Pierrette, Francoise and Agnes Haidar. All three insisted on accompanying her to the military airfield to see the traveler, off.

This cute teenage quarto was seldom physically divided.

In a far deeper, more transcendent way, its members never ceased viewing themselves as a single spirit from the moment first introduced to one another at a mutual friend's sixth birthday party. United through common high intelligence and remarkable untutored-artistic gift, they also each possessed the same abundant black hair, were each less than five-feet-tall.

Each girl wore an identical wide chapeau, short, sleeveless pattern dress, white gloves and socks, white high heels with strap fastened at side. All sported identical big leather handbag cast over left shoulder. All, used the same color lipstick, each dabbed her neck with same subtle

1

fragrance. No surprise, many mistook these four miniature young ladies as deeply-affectionate, near-inseparable sisters, or, upon observing this eager team, expressed sympathy for parents raising quadruplets.

"What a grand, tremendous, awesome experience it's going to be!" continued Pascale—teenagers are given to hyperbole."And so how only appropriate for my dearest pals in all the whole wide world, coming to see me off! Magnificent! Paris! Yes, I'm going to Paris! Such a marvelous chance I've been given at last to possibly find romance, maybe even at last have true adventure!"

An hour earlier, Pierrette, Francoise and Agnes Haidar made their globetrotting buddy take a solemn oath with her right hand placed on the Bible, promising: *I'll relate every last detail about Paris when I return.*

Pascale put both hands on the Bible to further symbolize unmatched-sincerity.

"I swear to God I'll tell you about all that happens to me, my three dearests friends in all the-whole-wide-world!" she guaranteed as the compatriots neared gate leading to the airplane. "I'll tell all and each of you every last detail of the odyssey when I come home. In fact, you'll soon hear me jabbering-on so incessantly about how awesome—*really* awesome—Paris is, that you'll even become tired hearing it—even pray for me to shut-up!"

"Let's all hope it'll be just so, Pascale-love!" declared Pierrette, oldest of the four chums. "Let it be you've so much fun, it'll actually be boring to yet again hear about all your magical experiences!" She gave the voyager a warm, supportive hug and affectionate peck on lips. "*There*! That's to show that wherever you travel, Pascale, our own hopes and dreams and hearts and minds are always with you!"

"Still, it'll certainly be difficult making me tired of hearing about romance and adventure in Paris" commented Francoise, wistful, she too providing the voyager a supportive hug and affectionate peck on lips.

"It'll be terribly difficult making me ever-tired of hearing about romance and adventure in Paris!" reiterated Agnes, following application of own embrace.

Pierrette gave a final inspection to the voyager's passport and other papers. As her smile indicated, all was in order.

"God bless you all!" cried the voyager as happy tears raced her smooth, unblemished, adolescent cheeks. "Bless you Pierrette-love! Bless you Francoise-love! Bless you Agnes-love! I'll never forget the concern you always show for me."

"It's no more concern than you always show for each of us Pascale-love!" assured the others, no less happily teary-eyed.

"All-for-one-and-one-for-all!" cried the little musketeers. "It's all-for-one and one-for-all! That's for now-and-ever-more!"

The friends broke into treasured, precious sobs. They embraced long, close and memorably tender. Four separate hopeful, idealistic bodies and souls welded into one deathless, feminine spirit.

At last, a flight attendant politely signaled it was time for the plane to depart.

"Goodbye Pierrette, Francoise and Agnes. I love you! Each and all of you!" called-out Mlle. Kedari, sniffling, waving, as she scurried-up the steps leading to the aircraft front door.

"Goodbye Pascale! We love you too!" waved the Sisters Haidar. "We can't wait for you to return."

The plane departed.

THE PROFESSOR

....

"$\mathcal{I}$ can hardly believe Father finally granted me permission going on this trip!" reflected his daughter as the *Air France* jet began descending from a porcelain white and turquoise sky. *Charles de Gaulle International Airport*'s dark brown and battleship-gray tarmac was still miles away. So far, the earth viewed from passenger window betrayed no hint of approaching frantic, self-absorbed, urban sprawl. There was to be seen only peaceful, soothing, amber, green and yellow checkerboard farmland meandering to the horizon. "Father finally permitted me to be alone with my thoughts—at least temporarily." ***Permitted me***— was a phrase so often in this *Army Brat*'s speech, she long ago stopped noticing.

The young voyager was sure to take plenty of reading material to help occupy the cramped, uncomfortable hours of a several thousand mile flight. A journey made longer still, by the necessity to change planes in Frankfurt where a wild-cat baggage-handlers' strike delayed transfer of luggage until evening.

Surprising only those unacquainted with Mlle. Kedari, she chose not a fashion magazine, detective story, or scandal-sheet to lazily peruse, idly thumb-through but instead, a favorite *Nineteenth Century*-novel. It, rightfully demanding complete attention. This was one of those great pieces of western literature who's title and plot everyone claiming to be "sophisticated" knows intimately, spends regular occasions in heated-debate over the work's true historic, cultural and political significance.

4

Yet also a book, few of even its most fervent admirers and bitterest critics, actually read. The soldier's daughter in contrast, was today reading the novel a fourth, time.

"I'm very impressed with your taste in *light fiction*–your choice in–*summer reading*–Sweetheart!" interjected an attractive lady in her early-thirties seated beside, speaking in French. She wore white running shoes, blue-jeans, a gray pull-over sweatshirt bearing left-wing social commentary logo written in German. Her long brown hair was tied back under a *Yankees* baseball cap. "I'm most impressed! It's not what people usually take to read on airplanes. I see you're a serious sort, an intellectual."She paused. "I can see you want to mount the battlements!"

"Thank-you kindly, Madame" replied Pascale, touched. Incapable mastering the fine art of *Chit-Chat,* she learned-the-hard-way not making another fumbling attempt. This current neighbor however, instantly struck her as prepared discussing more than just the weather, sports, or sexually-ambiguous *Pop*-singers.

"This is one of my favorite novels" added the young bibliophile, inexplicably assured she elaborating on a subject of great interest to a fellow-spirit. "I find this novel awesomely moving each time I read it, Madame. I can't help crying reading one of the chapters. Not *Scatterbrained Woman*-tears but tears in humble recognition of the author's greatness. I often wish I could somehow climb inside the pages and participate. I say to myself: 'Oh, if only I'd written it!' 'If I'd accomplished nothing else in my entire life but written this single novel, I'd be awesomely satisfied."

"It's the quality of your accomplishments that counts, Dear" promised the attractive lady with *Yankees* cap, "Not the mere quantity. Some writers publish a large number of 'successful' books. Ones, which along with their author's name are soon erased from all human recollection! It's the quality that counts. Writing a single masterpiece is an infinitely greater achievement than cranking-out a legion of mediocre works."

"So right you are, Madame."

"And the same holds true for all worthwhile human endeavors!"

"Father tells me I was born in wrong century."

"The present one is terribly overrated! I've at least *six million* reasons!"

"Father's right" admitted *Chere Petite*. "I'd prefer the Eighteenth or early-Nineteenth."

"Were it not for typhus, cholera, chamber pots, corsets, no plumbing, no refrigeration or dentistry," commented new friend, "I might prefer living then, too."

"So grand those days were, Madame!"

"When were your favorite eras, Dear? The ones, during which you'd especially enjoy being alive?"

"The latter part of the *Eighteenth, Century* Madame" responded Pascale, dreamy. "And also the first quarter of the *Nineteenth Century*—I wish I was in the French Revolution–with the British *Lake Poets*–alive during the start of the *Romantic Age*—I'd like to storm the Bastille. I'd like to be at *The Oath of the Tennis Court*, to proclaim the *Declaration of the Rights of Man and the Citizen*.'—Liberty! Equality! Fraternity! No more feudalism, no more class privilege! Out with the aristocrats! No more tyranny, justice for all!"

She hummed *La Marseillaise*, her seating companion enthusiastically joining-in.

"Who was it, Madame?" questioned the cerebral youngster after the duo completed humming stirring national anthem. "Was it Wordsworth or Goethe who wrote of 1789: 'I knew the world when she was in her springtime.' 'I saw the morning of the world.' How did Wordsworth describe Dorothy in *Tintern Abbey*? Oh yes, "A mansion for all lovely forms, a dwelling place of all sweet sounds and harmonies.'"

"I've visited Tintern Abbey."

"AWESOME"

"I've visited Lake Grasmere, too."

AWESOME"

"I've seen where Wordsworth met *The Solitary Reaper* and contemplated *The Daffodils*. I've seen where Wordsworth experienced: 'splendor in the grass' and realized: 'the child is father of the man.' I've seen where he went: 'trailing clouds of glory.'"

"Goodness, gracious!"

"Just last week," added Matilda, "I also located the spot on the winding Alpine road where Mme. de Stael first encountered Benjamin Constant! Remember, Sweetheart? Mme. de Stael ordered her carriage to halt, threw open the door and demanded she immediately become the object of Benjamin Constant's unbridled passion."

"–And even though Benjamin Constant never met Mme. de Stael before, or had the slightest inkling where she was going, what she was-up-to" giggled Pascale, finishing the famous story, "he instantly jumped in! He let Mme. de Stael whisk-him-away to parts unknown! Little did Benjamin Constant realize, he wouldn't be free from Mme. de Stael's possessive-hands and smothering-affection for years to come! Once, he tried escaping in the middle of the night. Mme. de Stael promptly instructed her bodyguards to recapture him, tie him up and bring Benjamin Constant back. And so in no time they did! She next, placed her antsy-lover under permanent watch lest he ever again flee the object of his unbridled passion. Mme. de Stael wasn't the needy, submissive type. She didn't believe it's the man who makes all the decisions!"

"We forgot about the novel you've read, Sweetheart."

"Ah, yes, Madame" the teenager conceded. "Hollywood tried making a movie but failed utterly. The movie isn't at all like the book! No one takes off his or her clothes in the novel but Hollywood of course adds 'the mandatory sex-scene.' Father was horrified he permitted me seeing it."

"Indeed!"

"The principal male character, Madame, a fool in the novel, is portrayed in the movie as wise. The heroine: a brave, skillful, redhead in the novel, is a *Scatterbrained Female* blonde in the wretched movie. In the novel, she doesn't need a man rescuing her. She's the one who gets *him* out of trouble! It's all reversed by Hollywood. Women with brains scare the wits out of American men. They often make American men develop collective cold sores and fidgets, become intellectually-constipated. Of course, that's just my personal opinion."

"I fully agree, Dear!" encouraged the lady wearing a pull-over sweatshirt with left-wing social commentary logo written in German.

"You're most insightful! You could be one of those television pundits. Although, I don't think your views—*our* views—are currently in-vogue."

She pushed back the heavy, sinuous locks obscuring Pascale's face. "You've certainly got a lot of impressive hair."

"Thank-you, Madame. I'm so proud of it."

"But don't let it hide from the world your pretty face."

"This is one of those novels" informed Pascale, "which just doesn't translate into film. That's my personal opinion."

"I'm glad you told me. I'll save money and time not seeing it"

"Of course I'm only giving my personal opinion of the film, Madame!"

"Don't worry, Dear, I trust the word of someone who mounts the battlements."

Pascale wore white shoes with strap, white socks, a sleeveless pattern dress, a light green open cardigan. Her jet-black mane fell below her shoulders. If grateful being thought a *serious sort* and *intellectual,* she wasn't sure these appraisals were deserved. Of her ability 'to mount the battlements,' however, the girl was in no doubt. "Mount the battlements!" she mused. "Like *Tosca,* after I've rid the world of the evil Scarpia. Like *Tosca!*"

"Oh yes indeed, dear?" endorsed Professor Matilda Eisenberg, her voice and gaze protective. "The day will come, I'm convinced, when you too mount the battlements. I pray that chance somehow allows me to see it happen!"

"Like Tosca!"

"Be careful! Don't forget Tosca hurled herself from the battlements so as not to be captured by evil Scarpia's flunkeys."

"So she did" conceded Pascale. "But Tosca's story is still so awesomely romantic! It's hard to find how a girl could have as awesomely, awesomely romantic a life as Tosca! She also didn't suffer from tuberculosis like Mimi or was abandoned like Cio-Cio San. Sometimes I wonder, Madame, if considering all Tosca got to do, that hurling herself from the battlements wasn't worth it!–And Tosca could stand up for herself! She got to make her own independent decisions!"

"Yes darling, *Tosca* is as you say 'awesomely, awesomely, romantic.' Her life and deeds are far more uplifting than those of *Manon Lescaut*."

Pascale nodded with a wide, affirmative, teenage grin.

Kindred-spirit acknowledged with her own broad adult Smile. "But I was being figurative about you wanting to mount the battlements, darling. I meant to say you're a very highly intelligent, gifted, noble, idealistic child. A type of person today's Americanized, instant-gratification, materialist world is all far, far, too often, sorely lacking. The world needs more idealistic young adventurers like you."

Matilda paused.

"You're a precious little creature. One, who I'm somehow absolutely sure will at last be justly cherished, honored, respected! I'll be far, far from alone in appreciating you! In fact, I'll find a particular joy in knowing I was the first! 'Isn't it an honor to look upon the noble dear, Mattie? Isn't the girl an inspiration?'—I'll be asked repeatedly. 'So indeed,' I'll answer, 'so indeed. And I was the very first to know she is the Divine Child, to understand she's the Messenger!'"

She kissed Pascale's unblemished cheeks, pressed the girl's shoulder loving. "Just mark my word!, Dear *One* day, sooner than we both think, I'll be reading about you in the newspapers, seeing clips of you on television!"

If the two had never met before, Matilda still felt a deep responsibility for her chance traveling companion. Rather than questioning this notion's validity, pondering how a sense of motherly-devotion emerged within someone unmarried, never pregnant, she preferred instead to relax and enjoy. Simply, *relax* and *enjoy* the previously unknown warmth, contentment, rightful pleasure, responsibility for another's welfare now caused to run throughout her entire mind and body.

"I'll try my best to succeed, Madame."

"Don't worry, I know you'll succeed."

The *seat-belt* sign turned on.

Female voice over intercom instructed passengers to return to seats.

A flight attendant scurried down aisle.

"Good lord!" Matilda chided herself, grimacing. "What's suddenly come over me! I've never behaved like this before! I'm acting like one of those charlatans on American television claiming to possess the secret to obtaining a fortune! –I sound like a Bible-thumper!--I've never before chattered such pseudo-religious gobbledygook!--Maybe I'm getting *Alzheimer's Disease*!"

Reaching into her *Coach* handbag, she took out a pair of reading glasses. Next, she took a long, furtive look at this unique young companion with a fondness for the *Romantic Age* and Puccini opera. "Fascinating" whispered the professor, evaluating neighbor from academic's perspective. "Fascinating!"

Pascale radiated an uncanny, invisible but increasingly-persuasive mental power. She emitted a mysterious, captivating aura. Initially restricted to her own four-foot-ten-inch body, this girl's peculiar, charismatic glow steadily expanded outward until bringing observers too within its curious, magnetic diameter. Hers was a *power, force, aura* as easy to appreciate as it was impossible to define, as immediately apparent as also, unseen. Still more unusual was that the girl possessed of this beguiling attribute remained totally, unaware.

"I never chattered such pseudo-religious gobbledygook until sitting down beside this special *Little Dear,*" whispered Matilda.

She pondered further. With each succeeding moment, becoming less uncomfortable with her *charlatan* statements.

No, it wasn't "chatter," "pseudo-religious gobbledygook," or *Alzheimer's Disease*. Rather, this was first stammering words of a positive philosophy, constructive worldview. A concept of life, the current speaker would have instantly scoffed before embarking on this trip. Half-Jewish, that side of family murdered at Auschwitz, herself, a lapsed-Roman Catholic cruelly betrayed by the political party she sought to make up for lost faith and deceitful lover, Matilda was skeptical about the future. Nevertheless, she instinctively understood her dark pessimism couldn't survive confronting this girl with mane of jet-black hair who daydreamed of jumping from the battlements like Tosca.

The professor beamed with delight at discovery–*revelation*–sounded too hocus-pocus. She inhaled deeply of her companion's welcoming mental force. Happily, she allowed herself be drawn into this special child's magnetic personal aura. "Something tells me the day will come when I'm far from the only one recognizing your splendid value" Matilda promised. "How, why am I certain? I don't know, still, I know it to be true!"

"Thank-you for the encouragement, Madame" answered Pascale, demure.

"I read that novel too but didn't enjoy it as much as you" apologized Matilda, ashamed she not appreciating the book to same degree as new friend.

"You didn't enjoy the novel, Madame?"

"I read it in secondary school when too young to appreciate it. The instructor was also the Jungian-archetype of *Unmitigated Bitch*—oops! Please forgive my bad language!—I'm sure a combination of these factors let the literary aspects of the book fly over my simple head."

"I insist you reread it, Madame," urged Pascale. "I'm sure today you'll find the novel delightful, thought-provoking—personally inspiring! There'll be no Jungian-archetype of unmitigated—that *bad word*—souring the experience, now. You'll easily understand too why the movie was so atrocious, so unworthy of the book. You'll easily understand what I mean about how many aspects of the novel just don't translate onto the screen."

"Yes, I'm sure I will."

"It's an awesome novel, Madame. No, it's a *really* awesome novel!"

"I promise I'll reread the novel," pledged soul-mate in sneakers, blue-jeans, and pull-over sweatshirt with left-wing social commentary logo. "As a matter of fact, I'll reread it as soon as I get home! I've got ten days before returning to work. I'll devote them to reading and learning to better appreciate that *really* awesome novel."

"Good, good. I'm so excited for you, Madame."

"And I'm so excited knowing I'll make you happy, Sweetheart!"

Matilda pushed-back the thick jet-black tresses again obscuring Pascale's face. "Mi! I'm acting just like Mama! She insists I always look *proper*! I was born in St. Clothilde. That's an industrial center on the French side of the Rhine. Mama—her name is *Brendel*—came from Breslau in Upper Silesia. Today, it's called *Wroclaw* and belongs to Poland. Mama was orphaned during the war and evacuated to St.

11

Clothilde when the Allies liberated the death camps. Despite all that happened to her in the war, Mama still considers herself German. She speaks only German at home, reads only German newspapers, listens only to German-language radio. Mama insists Goethe, Mann and Kafka are really only understood if read in the original German. Not surprisingly, I grew up bilingual."

"St. Clothilde regularly had a bunch of unpleasant-characters in the streets after dark" Matilda elaborated, "pimps, prostitutes, dope-pushers, hooligans. Mama insisted I always be home before sunset. I promptly received a spanking and was sent to bed without supper whenever I disobeyed. Mama also wouldn't allow me to *date* or *hang-out*. She said: 'You must deserve wearing a white dress at your wedding.' I often grumbled about how Mama was so *strict, old fashion*. But today, I understand her concern was well-founded. Her *strictness* and *old fashion* notions of child-raising—especially *daughter*-raising—were entirely an expression of her deep love for me."

"Hadn't it been for Mama's Breslau-notions of raising girls" reminisced her offspring, taking amber-shade handle hairbrush from her *Coach* handbag to straighten Pascale's mane, "I'd never accomplish all I have. Without Mama keeping stern watch over me in rough-St. Clothide, instantly smacking me on fanny whenever I disobeyed, she, keeping me away from boys—instead of a professor today, I'd be either—working the cash register at my philandering, alcoholic husband's grimy shop; putting an unclean needle in my arm; punching bolts into gadgets on a factory assembly line; or maybe become a prostitute spreading AIDS."

There" proclaimed, Brendel's Daughter when work on Pascale's tangled-mane complete. "*There*. You look even more lovely now, my little Tosca! I can't let the world be left any longer unaware of your splendid face!"

"So kind of you, Madame"

"I confess, Dear" revealed her new admirer with growing emotion, "until meeting you, I never felt the *maternal urge*. However, it's now come on me all at once. Just as Mama understood I possessed a gift and dedicated her life to making sure I fulfilled that gift, so, I somehow know I've got a not dissimilar obligation for you, Little Tosca. Just as Mama protected me from the pimps and drug addicts, so, I've got a not dissimilar obligation keeping track of you—making sure you don't go unrecognized, or leap from the battlements before slaying your own evil Scarpia—"

"Good lord!" cried Matilda, flustered. "I sound like I've just escaped from a madhouse! Who, must you, think you're now needing to put-up-with!"

"I'm not 'putting-up' with anyone, Madame! I think you're a very nice lady."

The plane landed at *Charles de Gaulle Airport.*

Slowly the craft advanced toward terminal gate.

"The instructor at your lycée" observed Matilda, "did a far better job engendering in her students a love for great literature than that—*bad word*—odious Mlle. Charlotte Guérin, did at my own."

"I learned of the novel on my own, Madame. I don't go to lycée."

"Ah, I see. Your parents send you to Catholic school."

"No, Madame. I learned at home. I don't attend school."

"*Don't attend school!*" gasped Matilda, horrified, instantly taking the magical girl's hands tight with both Older, protective, own. "A so brilliant, gifted child as you doesn't attend school!"

Pascale looked away ashamed.

"Well it's not your choice" Matilda swiftly consoled, trying to think of a solution to the problem before the airplane reached terminal gate. Finding none, she instead offered a business card. "How long are you going to be in Paris, Sweetheart?"

"Ten days, Madame."

"I realize we hardly know one another and I'm being terribly presumptuous. Still, I somehow feel responsible for you! How long again, will you be in Paris?"

"Ten days, Madame."

"If at all possible, contact me or leave a message with my secretary at *this* telephone or fax number. I'm someone of significant influence in certain circles. I guarantee I can get this matter of your neglected-formal education rectified. It's not only in your best, deepest, long term interest, it's my sacred duty!"

"I promise, Madame" assured the girl beneath a mane of jet-black hair. "I'll either contact you or leave a message with your secretary in the next ten days if at all I possibly can!"

"Yes, yes, I know you'll do all you possibly can to contact me." answered Matilda. Tears racing her cheeks, she pressed Pascale close. "I just hope the people in-charge of you permit it!"

Two pair of eyes linked.

Exchanging, a message requiring no words.

Matilda embraced Pascale.

For a moment, individual bodies, separate souls, united.

Two become one.

They parted.

I

Following Customs and retrieval of luggage, Mlle. Kedari traveled the congested, multilane freeway uniting *Charles de Gaulle Airport* with downtown Paris. She was transported in a shiny, sleek, stretch-limousine Father previously arranged to pick-up his *Chere Petite*.

Notre Dame, the Louvre, Eifel Tower, Arc de Triomphe were still miles away. For nearly thirty minutes, save language employed on fast retreating sexually-suggestive billboard advertisements, or printed on quickly-passed water towers, this busy, serpentine traffic artery might be linked to any piece of urban sprawl on the planet.

Rolling-down the window in the vehicle's second row, the young traveler closed her deep, gray-green eyes. Next, she lay back on the beige leather seat to enjoy sensation of wind massaging her mane of jet-black hair.

The girl recalled how her recent flight companion so admired the teenager's thick, sinuous locks, lovingly stroked them, insisted on protectively brushing those same heavy tresses. Remembering too, a television science program in which the learned hostess explains a personal *DNA* sample is left on all a human being touches, Pascale stroked her voluminous hair thoughtful, pensive. "I can feel the airplane lady's hand even now! I can feel that fabulous lady's hand even now!" Grown contemplative, she meditated on the novel friends just discussed.

In one episode, the gifted, strong-minded heroine, exhibiting her usual untamed heart, turns-down a wealthy suitor's proposal. Boldly, she rejects the safe, prosperous but also intellectually-mediocre, spiritually-unproductive future still often considered a woman's supreme desire. Instead, she seeks infinitely grander, nobler yet not at all guaranteed accomplishment located somewhere in the uncharted societal *Great Unknown*. By the novel's conclusion, it's abundantly clear the heroine made the wise choice. Not until allowed making their own decisions, charting their own destiny, insists the author, will women ever truly succeed, fully express their individual potential.

Youngster debated.

Could she too follow the heroine's independent path?

Did she too share the heroine 's free spirit?

Might this particular dreamer also summon the strength of character to reject mediocre convention and all the material blessings it seductively offered?

Was Father's daughter brave enough to achieve far grander, nobler but not at all guaranteed success in the perilous, uncharted, societal Great Unknown?

No guts no glory!

No pain no gain!

Pierrette, Francoise and Agnes would be ever-so proud of their fellow musketeer! Now that their comrade was in France, no one back home could interfere.

Checking passport for second time, Pascale discovered an absent-minded Customs clerk stamped a six months visa.

"Awesome!"

Maybe miracles really do happen! Or at least terrific, unexpected opportunities. "Romance" and "adventure" in *The City of Light* could perhaps actually be at hand. True "romance" and "adventure," not merely the afternoon daydream variety. As might say Father in his usual military phraseology, Pascale was now in a position to launch a "major expedition, "primary campaign," "pincer movement." She was given a marvelous chance to established a real "bridgehead," secure her very own "deep salient."

Pascale once more read the business card.

Matilda-Gisela Eisenberg

Department of Political Science, Department of History

University of Paris I (Panthéon-Sorbonne)

Office No: –

Rue Saint-Jacques

Tel: – Fax: –

"Ooh! That's awesome! Mme. Matilda's *really* distinguished! She's not just any Lisa, Wendy or Sue! Mme. Matilda will help me!"

Words from the conversation on airplane sounded vividly in adolescent consciousness. Mme. Matilda possessed an especially gentle, melodic, genteel voice. Hers, was the voice of the most loving, understanding of benefactors.

My Little Tosca
The day will come Dear, when I'm far from the only one who recognizes your splendid value.
It's not only what you rightfully deserve and were so wrongfully denied, it's my own sacred duty.
I feel terribly responsible for you.
I'm a person of some influence in certain circles of Paris
I know you'll do all you possibly can to try and contact me

Pascale felt once more safe in another's sheltering arms, sensed her smaller body again brought securely to omnipotent Professor Eisenberg's comforting, own.

"Oh my God!"

Air pressure created by the limousine speeding freeway sucked THE business card from loosened fingers. Carrying it, out an open passenger window. Frantic, the girl scrambled about the second row beige leather seat to peer out the back. Only to find the spot of the disaster already several hundred meters behind. The business card, if still lying somewhere along the freeway was now crushed under the wheels of heavy traffic.

"Well, at least Mme. Matilda won't suspect I'm just another *Scatterbrained Female*. Mme. Matilda will believe I was somehow prevented quickly contacting her!"

Snatching a *Michelin* guidebook from her handbag, Pascale rapidly searched for the section on the University of Paris. What was the precise address printed on the card? She'd forgotten. However, she did remember it was definitely located somewhere on the Rue Saint Jacques in the *Latin Quarter*.

"Stop that!" Pascale reprimanded herself moment later, casting guidebook aside. Often when alone, debating future course of action, she spoke to and of herself in *Third Person*. "Stop that Pascale! Don't be stupid!"

Only partially did speaker believe those words.

"Remember Pascale, you'll never succeed in challenging your relatives' wishes! They'll cut-you-off, label you a family-disgrace. You'll be called the ungrateful, disloyal, conceited, self-consumed *Prodigal Daughter*. Everyone back home except Pierrette, Francoise and Agnes will sympathize with your parents. Then, after France deports you, you'll go crawling back on hands and knees begging your parents' forgiveness—humbly begging they let you do exactly what you fled the country claiming you'd absolutely never do!—What a *Scatterbrained Female*!–Pierrette, Francoise and Agnes wouldn't behave this way!"

"Don't make a fool of yourself" she added, "especially in public! You must get used to it. This is a *Man's World* like-it-or-not! A girl spending too much time concerned with something she can't change anyway only leads her to more gloom and anger. Worst of all it leads to—*self-pity.*"

"There're few personal qualities lower, baser, more squalid than *self-pity.* Don't worry, Pascale. You'll eventually learn to put-up-with-it. Pierrette, Francoise and Agnes will also soon need to up-with-it. At least you've got this awesome trip to Paris, first."

She paused.

"Besides, how many other girls have no alternative than to marry a rich husband?"

FATHER

··

 $\mathcal{N}$ ext month, Mlle. Kedari was supposed to wed Father's longtime army colleague. Graduating from military academy in same class, frequently serving together in various theaters of operation over subsequent decades, the two soldiers were the closest, most trusted of friends. Both were highly-decorated officers renowned for bravery under fire, each possessing a natural sense of leadership, innate ability to obtain the devotion and best performance of troops under his command. Whimsical luck proved slightly more generous to Father's comrade in providing situations to win visible distinction, be photographed in newspapers. That disparity in career success failed engendering jealousy. This lack of bad feeling was a further mark of the strong emotional bond the two men created when just teenage cadets. Their families, also grown intimate over the years, fervently supported the match. Only the bride was unenthusiastic. In truth, she dreaded the prospect.

So why did thought of her approaching wedding cause the bride to lose sleep? And then, after she finally dozing-off near dawn from utter exhaustion, experience unnerving dreams? Several times she imagined being on the debarkation ramp at Auschwitz chosen by the *Selector* for the showers. Why, as her wedding neared did the bride suffer during daytime from bouts of shortness of breath, develop a nervous twitch in neck, even periodically stammer?

Marie-Emmanuelle-Pascale, or, simply *Pascale* as she preferred, was resigned to Arranged-Marriage. Born in a country, raised in a culture and social environment where it was traditional, she long accepted this ancient practice. All the Arranged-Marriages in the extensive Kedari clan, in those of her friends, neighbors, acquaintances seemed functioning well; these carefully negotiated settlements providing each spouse both communal happiness and individual fulfillment. If admittedly not as romantic a form of union as practiced in the "more enlightened" West, neither did half of these non-love matches decline into infidelity, estrangement and bitter, acrimonious divorce.

The prospect of entering brokered-matrimony didn't especially trouble Pascale. Rather, her uneasiness arose from the knowledge she must afterward consent to frequently being kissed, touched, held close by a man other than Father. Receiving a different male's embrace, even if he a relative or longtime family friend, instantly consumed both Pascale's mind and body with indescribable but all too real, physically-palpable, terror. Like most dreamy, romantic, teenage girls, she much enjoyed the idea of becoming object of an aristocratic gentleman's devotion, of exchanging with faithful knights and noble champions endless letters of passionate courtly love. She simply didn't want her heroes to touch.

Were Father informed even at this late date, he'd immediately cancel the wedding. Tender, protective, parent's sympathies always rested with his daughter. As for being "cut-off," "disowned," *Chere Petite* could assassinate Pope Francis, Bob Dylan, Nelson Mandela and the Dalai Lama but Father's affection would remain unbroken. "The child didn't understand what she was doing, the poor impressionable *Little Thing*"–would plead Father to the court. "She fell under the influence of rough company who took advantage of the *Darling's* well-meaning character. It was my fault. As the *Precious Creature's* parent, I take full personal responsibility."

Nevertheless, so embarrassed was *Daddy's Little Girl* about "my shameful, unnatural, improper, sinful weakness," she divulged it to no one.

The ill-suited couple already met on several occasions. First, when the young lady was a child, accompanying Father to a government function held within the lovely, well-kept *French Style*-garden surrounding the royal palace. Was it a dinner for a visiting foreign head of state, gala fireworks display or concert performance by a world famous pianist? Was it during a celebration of the Regent or his consort's birthday? Today, Pascale wasn't certain. It occurred more than a decade ago.

Several aspects of this original crossing-of-paths, she did vividly recollect. The most haunting, was of feeling Field Marshal Chamoun's large, heavy, right male hand caressing entitled (or so, Pascale couldn't but help sense *entitled*) her own head. The soldier's large, strong masculine fingers running proprietary (or so, Pascale couldn't but help sense *proprietary)* through her even back then multitudinous jet-black hair.

If that initial experience nowhere near as existentially-threatening as later ones, even the first sensation of Field Marshal Chamoun's touch gave Pascale *The Creeps*. It a *The Creeps* made endlessly creepier because she found its unsettling nature, root-cause, impossible to define. In addition, her tormentor was unaware his touch provoked such inexplicable dread. "It makes me feel so terribly guilty" she confessed. "*That Man* doesn't mean any harm. Likely, he's shy, lonely. He doesn't know how to relate to women. He's simply starved for affection. He wants to be loved. Even more, he wants to express his love. Unfortunately he's so clumsy, awkward."

"I really should be most honored and pleased to receive the attention," Pascale thought. "However, I'm not. I hate it! I so hate it when he touches me! Being touched by any male except Father instantly gives me *The Creeps*."

The service friends were soon in animated discussion about something of burning concern to ambitious army leaders in a politically-unstable Middle Eastern country. An issue, of tremendous interest to adults perhaps, but beyond the intellectual grasp of a child. Especially, one, just torn-away from her favorite *Bugs-Bunny* cartoons so Father might appear to photographers as a champion of *Traditional Family Values*. For the little girl, her elders' multisyllabic gobbledygook sounded like a long-dead, totally indecipherable, foreign language.

After the army chiefs, both wearing dark glasses, shined-cavalry boots, jodhpurs; each, with athletic chest covered in gaudy cordons and medals, gold epaulets and braids running wide shoulders and muscular arms, imposing semiautomatic side-arm at belt, pursued heated shop-talk for what to a five-year-old seemed interminable hours-on-end, Pascale, all the while standing silently beside, soft but earnestly tugged on Father's tunic.

"Goodness, gracious!" he exclaimed, "my poor Little Commander!"

Father cut-short his conversation with army friend. Swiftly, at jackknife-straight attention, clicking heels of brightly-shined cavalry boots, he delivered Pascale a formal salute and great ceremonial show of loyalty and appreciation; next, supplying daughter a warm kiss and hug. Finally, he lifted her far above with single easy motion of his powerful, athletic, paratrooper's male hands and arms.

"Ooh! Ooh! Ooh!" madly-squealed Pascale, happily. "Ooh! Ooh! Ooh!"

Father was six-feet-six-inches tall. For the child held atop outstretched arms, the earth seemed far below indeed.

"Ooh! Ooh!" madly-squealed *Chere Petite* at top of lungs. She experienced the same glorious emotional, physical sensation each time Father lifted her in the air. Nothing approached the delight consuming the girl's entire mind and body whenever Father's powerful hands clutched *Chere Petite's* narrow waist and soft, smooth, unblemished skin.

"Ooh! Ooh! It's so-exciting up here, Father!" daughter third time squealed. She, no less exhilarated by the dynamism surging through mind and body whenever held in grip of Father's powerful hands and arms.

"Please, forgive me, my poor Little Commander" begged Father, gazing up lovingly. "Please forgive my inattention. An officer is also supposed to be a gentleman. And a gentleman is always of assistance to the ladies!"

"Oh but of course my **Big Commander!**" child replied, giggling. "Of course I forgive you, my *Big* commander!"

"Bless you, my Little Commander!"

"After all we're a special set aren't we, you and I, my *Big Commander?*" laughed Pascale, held securely by little waist high above the earth.

'So we're a special set, you and I, *Chere Petite!*" acknowledged parent. "We're a special set and always will be!"

"I love you, Father!"

"I love you too, *Chere Petite.*"

"And I love no man but you, Father!"

"A day may come you love other men as well" advised Big Commander.

"No, no!" pledged loyal sidekick, earnestly. "I swear to love for all my life no other man in the whole world but you! Only you!"

"Time will tell, my fervent little darling."

"Yes, time will show!"

"Father won't be upset if his *Chere Petite* finds a second man to love one day" assured Big Commander. "Father will much enjoy lifting a granddaughter up in his arms like this too."

"No, no, Father! I'll love no man but you! No man will ever possibly enter my heart but you, Father!"

"Well, we'll see as time passes, *Chere Petite.*"

"Yes my dearest, dearest, Father!" guaranteed the miniature idealist, still held far above, her arms extended like an eagle in bold, confident flight. "Just watch me! Just watch me and see how I'll love no other man in all my life but you, Father!"

Placing daughter back on ground, Father signaled a subordinate fetch the pony he purchased for his "Little Tsarina."

"Yes, a pony! A real pony!" as its mistress was often fond of recalling. "A pony!" The most desired-longing, the most cherished-possession of her entire *Army Brat* childhood! Even today she still treasured that loyal, gentle animal named *Penelope.* She cared for Penelope in the little steed's own private stable and grazing field as if the creature was her own child. According to observers, Pascale was destined to be the most loving and tender of mothers. What started as a tedious, later, frightening affair, when she torn-away from favorite television cartoons so Father could appear before the media as *A Family Man,* concluded as one of the happiest days in *Chere Petite's* yet short life!

What additional memories did the bride retain of her first confrontation with future groom? None! From moment lifted into

Father's protective arms, *Chere Petite's* attention shifted elsewhere. Over a decade was to elapse without she even once hearing Field Marshal Chamoun's name. Given the tumultuous intellectual, physical and emotional growing experiences of even a sheltered childhood and adolescence, that chance meeting passed completely from Pascale's active consciousness, easy recollection. Yet one memory of that earlier incident she never forgot or veered from in steadfast loyalty—her pledge to love no man but Father. His, was also the only male physical touch *Chere Petite* could tolerate.

I

Then, following passage of eleven years without the lightest communication, Marie-Emmanuelle-Pascale Kedari and Auguste-Théophile Chamoun again, crossed paths. This time, the Field Marshal appeared not as Father's army friend but in quite another capacity. He now spoke directly to the young lady and in a language she was old-enough to clearly understand. Also, instead of at crowded public function in capital with *Chere Petite* clutching hem of Father's tunic, the pair met alone in the ornate first floor *Directoire* furniture parlor of the Kedari family's sumptuous, redbrick, enclosed, wooded-country residence. Rather than product of mere chance, this latest meeting was both mutually-expected and one for which two families meticulously prepared.

"It's a great honor seeing you once more" insisted the hostess in formal diplomatic voice, somewhat stiffly ushering distinguished guest into parlor. While Father an imposing six-feet-six-inches tall, *Chere Petite* was just four-foot-ten-inches. Still, she more than made up for diminutive stature with a charming face; pleasing teenage bust, Greek sculptured-little physique and excellent legs. "It's a great honor learning I've been selected to become 'Mme. Chamoun.'"

"I'm so delighted meeting you again, Mlle. Pascale" replied Field Marshal Chamoun clad in bright, multicolored, parade ground regalia including ceremonial sword at belt. No girl's heart, guarantees ancient tradition, can resist a man in uniform. "I'm so pleased we can at last know one another much better."

"Let it-so-be, Field Marshal Chamoun" fiancée answered, evasive.

"That's such a lovely frock, Mlle. Pascale."

Her dress, was white: to contrast with mane of jet-black hair; sleeveless: to display girl's fine, sculpted arms; short: so as to instantly draw attention to wearer's splendid legs. "Thank-you very much, Field Marshal. You're quite a dapper gent yourself."

"From first I saw you as a child, 1 wished we might be better acquainted" explained the soldier. H, bowing gallantly before placing himself beside Pascale in a white-upholstered, over-stuffed *love-seat*. "Now, thanks to your great and noble father, that day has at last arrived."

"Yes, so it appears we'll now get to know one another better, Field Marshal."

"Please call me–*Auguste*."

"*Auguste*"

Just as eleven years before in the palace garden, Field Marshal Chamoun stroked Pascale's thick, sinuous, jet-black mane, proprietary. She again cringed in silent terror. Memory of their earlier physical contact thanks to passage of time securely exiled from daily recollection, now rampaged anew throughout consciousness.

Pascale barely avoided urinating in her panties. *Goose Bumps* covered her legs. The girl's arms stiffened; teeth chattered; heart raced; lungs throbbed. She felt at once bitterly cold and suffocating hot. If an unsettling experience when a child, receiving *That Man's* unsolicited touch today, gave Pascale God-only-knows how much more than *The Creeps*. It was a God-only-knows how much more than *The Creeps* made yet "creepier" still by the fact the fear produced couldn't be defined and her tormentor unaware his touch caused such inexplicable dread.

"It makes me terribly guilty feeling this way" Pascale scolded herself. "He means no harm. He's clearly a very nice person, anxious to demonstrate his sincere affection. He's a bit clumsy but means well. All the same I can't help it! No matter how guilty I feel, and know it's wrong of me to act this way about him! Being touched by any man but Father gives me *The Creeps*!"

"Is anything wrong, Dear?" entreated Field Marshal Chamoun, concerned at his bride's violent agitation. "Are you ill? Perhaps I should've come on another afternoon? I'm told you've a delicate constitution." Releasing bride's long, thick, jet-black hair, he pressed her soft, smallish quivering right hand in his two large, calloused, firm, own. "Please call me *Auguste.*"

"No Field Marshal—I mean yes I will *Auguste*" begged Pascale, voice choked, thoughts scrambled. "No I—Sorry, I mean yes, yes, yes!—no, no! Excuse me–I'm all confused." She paused completely flustered and breathed as deeply as her throbbing lungs would allow. She also prayed her groom wouldn't notice the *goose bumps* on her legs, the cringing of her hands and arms. Everyone knew only fear produced such instant and involuntary reactions. Luckily, it appeared no one observed.

"I'm alright, *Auguste*" insisted Pascale. "It must have been the effect of a draught. Father has such a lovely old house and estate out here in the country. It's where I keep my pony Penelope. But like most lovely old houses in the country it has draughts."

"Don't worry Dear" assured Chamoun. "I'll fix that in no-time."

He stood up. Removing torso-encasing cordons, next unbuttoning his heavy, medal and ribbon covered-tunic, he placed it around fiancée's shoulders.

"*There.* This will make you feel nice and warm. What you said is absolutely correct. No matter how lovely old country houses are, they still often possess unsettling draughts. You'll find the same thing plagues my own estate. Pardon me, soon *our* estate!"

"I know how much you adore your pet" Chamoun added. "When we move to my, *our* estate I can provide Penelope an entire barn and pasture all to her pony-self."

"How so kind of you, Field Marshal." replied Pascale.

"I'm just a rough, unsophisticated soldier. One, not all worthy being husband to a young lady as refined, pious and well-raised as you" explained Chamoun. He, once more pressing bride's soft, smallish right hand gallant but too tight in both calloused middle-aged own. It was clear from tone and cadence of voice he was delivering phrases long prepared. "I've not nearly the wide knowledge and unique understanding you possess for Italian opera and *Nineteenth Century* literature. Those are subjects which will be forever above my own gauche head. Literature, music and philosophy aren't taught at the military academy."

Chamoun paused.

"Still, as I swore on the Bible to your noble father, both as an officer and as a gentleman, I shall undertake every effort to show myself at least a halting-degree near worthy to be your husband. Your slightest artistic-wish and cultured-hope is always my duty to fulfill. I swore on the Bible to your great and noble father, doing so both as an officer and as a gentleman, that I shall protect his only child, love her, keep her, honor her, support and cherish her all my life!"

He paused, again.

"I naturally don't expect you ever truly loving me–I mean loving me in a *romantic* way–Our ages, tastes, our personal skills and life-experiences are so different"

Chamoun kissed his betrothed on forehead, too hard. "But I'm confident we can soon come to regard one another as close, trusted– what do the Brits call it?"

"*Chums*"

"Yes indeed, Dear, we can be–chums. And from personal experience over the years and across the campaigns and battles I've fought, there's nothing more dearly to know you possess, more precious to understand you have and can always depend upon, as a –chum! And a pretty friend, as well!"

"Let's pray it may be just-so, Field Marshal?" suggested Pascale. "I promise I'll do all possible to be your obedient, loyal, supportive spouse and special chum. I'll also teach myself to call you–*Auguste*."

"God bless you my sweet, precious darling!" exclaimed the soldier, taking his bride's head by both cheeks with own two powerful not-Father's-hands; delivering her three much too-hard wet kisses on forehead with own not-Father's-lips. "I've yearned to hear those words or similar ones since first we met in the garden at the royal palace! I've long dreamed of a time in which I can cherish, hold, protect and provide for you. I've long wished to do so for you and for you alone, Pascale my very own!"

He released the girl's head. Moment later, violently embraced her again, squeezing ever-so hard. "God bless you my little treasure!"

"Ouch!"

"Please find it in your heart for us to be *chums*"

"I'm glad my words make you so happy, Auguste" responded Pascale anxiously when at last released. The soreness inflicted by her admirer's crushing arms would take several minutes to wane. Yet even after soreness abated, the girl's heart continued to race, lungs throb. Goose bumps still covered her legs. Whether received tight or gentle, long or short, the reaction was the same. Being touched by a man gave Pascale *The Creeps*.

"And so those wonderful words certainly do make him infinitely happy, declares *your* loyal and trusted and supportive spouse and friend!" cried Field Marshal Chamoun effusive, tears of love in eyes. Once more, he pressed bride's soft, smallish teenage, feminine right hand too tight in both larger, calloused, middle-aged masculine, own. "Remember, darling, I mentioned before that the slightest artistic-wish and cultured-hope you express, is my duty to instantly fulfill?"

"Yes, Field Marshal"

"Let me guarantee that following receipt of those kind words, my own little Marie, your *big* Auguste will fulfill his duties not merely because it's proper but for the joy it brings him!"

"Well, then your 'little darling' has the *wish* and *hope* her own *big* Auguste won't always place her on a pedestal?" ventured bride hesitantly, in forced-giggle.

The groom's assurance he would provide unstinting, lifelong, personal devotion, never-tiring daily assistance, struck his prospective female mate as more than a trifle ominous. "Ladies don't *wish* living only on pedestals, Auguste! Sometimes they want to climb down to walk the earth on their own power—a chance to launch expeditions of their own!"

"That's a pointed-observation, darling!" chuckled the amorous soldier without supplying question a straight answer.

This maladroit couple met three additional times, always in the first floor parlor of Father's enclosed, wooded-country estate. The encounters lasted exactly a half hour. On each, Field Marshal Chamoun in dress uniform, upon glancing at his gold *Louis Vuitton* wrist-watch to observe exactly thirty minutes passed, instantly rose to feet in single, uninterrupted, gentlemanly motion. Next, as if performing drill on military parade ground, he clicked heals, provided "Mlle. Pascale" a deep bow. Then, issuing gallant apologies, he departed. Making sure while exiting parlor, he never turn his back on "my dainty, little queen."

Yet although wishing to marry "my dainty, little queen," the Field Marshal clearly possessed no intention serving "her majesty" as mere acquiescent consort.

"If I've taught you to enjoy *Russian Caravan*" he assured his fiancée after introducing her to the soldier's favorite blend of tea, "I'm confident I'll soon teach you to enjoy doing other things with me, as well."

II

"Please God" prayed Pascale, "help me get through it. Please make it not as dreadful an experience as I think it's probably going to be. Please God don't let *That Man* hurt me too much! Or maybe better still, if it's not asking too much of you God—and I know it really is—please God, make it somehow possible this doesn't need to happen to me at all!"

Then abruptly, next morning, as if in answer to her supplication, Pascale was summoned into Father's private study. Seated behind the *Directoire* writing table at which he answered official correspondence, Father announced: "*Chere Petite,* I'm granting you permission to command a special reconnaissance mission. I'm aware that as the D-Day of her life approaches, my deeply pensive, thoughtful child could benefit from a few days of *R-and-R* alone."

TOURIST

....

PARIS

$\mathcal{M}$lle. Kedari began her latest drawing with a swift, bold stroke across sheet of white paper using piece of azure chalk.

Later, she provided detail to developing image through softer, more delicate applications of brown and gray chalk.

Next, skillful adolescent feminine hand employed red and ivory.

An additional bold stroke across paper was made with original azure.

The picture, was judged complete only after it given subtle touches of amber, rust, orange and yellow.

A second splendid sketch was initiated with the use of black pencil.

That finished, yet a third beautiful creation took shape in green pencil.

Fourth museum-quality work of the afternoon was drawn in mauve, crayon.

As much as she enjoyed Nineteenth Century-literature and Puccini opera, Pascale could do more than simply admire the achievements of others. She early-on exhibiting a unique gift for illustration, relatives encouraged the young lady developing her aesthetic ability as far as possible. Over time, with their warm support, Pascale expanded her field of expertise from illustration to engraving and woodcuts.

No one was a more enthusiastic booster than Father. He arranged for his daughter a private studio. She was amply supplied with all the art materials she needed—not merely ink and paper, but also: wood sheets; aluminum, brass and steel stock templates; carbide cutters, blades; hammers and chisels; printing presses. Giving a guided tour of his daughter's studio, became for Father, a hallowed ritual on any occasion guests arrived—even on one special day, the Prince and his Consort.

"*Chere Petite,* is another Durer, another Daumier, Goya, or Hogarth, Your Majesties!" exclaimed Father proudly. "My child isn't just another pretty face—although she certainly has one of those too! I'm a rough, humble soldier, but my daughter is a modern Durer, Daumier, Goya or Hogarth! In my office I've got framed-examples of *Chere Petite's* masterpieces all over my walls. Someday, I promise, Your Majesties, my child's pictures will be on the walls of every great museum in the world! She's a gifted *Little Thing,* more gifted than the industrious *Creature* knows herself! One day, when the rest of the world recognizes my darling is another Durer, Daumier, Goya or Hogarth, I'll be able to tell all humanity and history—I knew it first!'"

Few guests taking Father's hallowed tour did so out of more than politeness, nor, aside from: the Prince, his Consort; Field Marshal Chamoun; Pierrette, Francoise and Agnes Haidar–possessed any idea who Durer, Daumier, Goya or Hogarth, even were! Few other than: the Prince, his Consort; Field Marshal Chamoun; Pierrette, Francoise and Agnes Haidar, troubled stopping longer than a courteous four or five seconds to actually look at the newest engravings and woodcuts this girl wrapped in an apron too big for her small size, produced. Just a meager handful, realized that an exceptionally creative mind and gifted soul dwelt among them. Still, Father wasn't discouraged. As he was so fond repeating: "One day, when the entire world recognizes my *Chere Petite* is a genius, I'll be able to say—'I knew it first!'"

Rather than buying postcards or taking photographs, Pascale recorded her visit to Paris in elegant, hardbound, cloth-covered sketchbooks.

"I wish I could draw so beautifully, Mademoiselle!" declared one captivated aristocratic Parisian gentleman, halting to observe the new pictures.

"You really like my scribbling, Monsieur?" the young artist replied, modestly. None of the guests Father escorted through *Chere Petite's* workshop aside from the Regent and his Consort, Field Marshal Chamoun and the three musketeers in knee-socks, ever displayed such genuine interest in her drawings.

"Yes indeed, *Cherie*" reiterated the aristocratic Parisian gentleman. From the learned tone and cadence of his address, confident motion of elegantly dressed body, he was without doubted an individual of expert judgment. It was champagne flute glass-clear this nobleman was immensely and properly respected in his most genteel, scholarly community. The cavalier's personal opinion on the merit and quality of works of art was rarely if ever challenged.

"Could he" wondered Pascale, "be a noted critic or possibly even a distinguished artist himself?" It was more than reasonable guessing so.

This afternoon, Pascale sat upon a green wooden bench in the garden situated at the center of the Place de Vosges. It was a picturesque location found in the secluded, historic Marais District on the Right Bank. The gray and brown facades of the neighborhood's centuries-old buildings and quiet, sinuous, narrow, cobblestone streets were hardly changed since 1789. On all sides, ran Italianate *Renaissance* and magnificent French *Baroque* Mansard-roof townhouses. Victor Hugo once resided in the impressive mansion Pascale last sketched.

"You really, truly like my picture, Madame?"

"Very much so, *Dear*!" insisted a pretty, finely-dressed aristocratic lady in early-thirties, she too, stopping to inspect the talented girl's drawings. "How do you get perspective? I never understood. If I draw anything and it always looks flat. Light and shadow too! It's so difficult for me to have it look realistic. You make it seem so easy! And how did you get started?"

"How did I start, Madame?" answered Pascale, tremendously honored receiving yet another heartfelt compliment eagerly-volunteered. "I can't explain exactly. Since I was tiny, drawing caught my imagination. Perhaps that's just the way it happens. I started with stick-figures like everyone else. I don't know why Father continues having those funny creations framed on the wall in his office! Anyway, each time I drew a new picture I wanted to make it finer than last. Eventually, my family claimed I was a—*Artist*. 'Our little girl is—*accomplished!*' They trotted-me-out each time visitors came for dinner. 'Guess what she can do?' Finding yourself saddled with such a forbidding reputation, you need both to live-up-to-it and prevent those loving you from looking-*Silly!*"

"Well, again, very nice. Keep at it!" encouraged the lovely chatelaine, she taking a moment to fondly-adjust the angle of the Child Prodigy's own chapeau. "Your—*interpretations*—is that the proper term, Sweetheart?—aren't simply accurate. They've got some—extra, special, unique, I-don't-know-what to-call-it!"

"I'll try, Monsieur, Madame" promised Pascale her two admirers, demure.

"We all know you'll succeed, Dear!" wise adults assured, protective. "Soon we'll see your work in the big galleries! We promise!"

"I'll do my best. Monsieur, Madame."

"We know you will Sweetheart. We're all so proud of you."

"Thanks again, Monsieur, Madame"

"First, straighten your socks *Dear*! A gifted artist like you should always keep her socks straight."

"Yes, Monsieur, Madame. I promise to keep my socks straight!"

"Paris is everything people, books, movies and songs claim," thought the girl with delight. "It 's even far much more!"

Save for the mishap with Professor Eisenberg's business card, Pascale would return home with oodles of *really* awesome stories. Fabulous tales, Pierrette, Francoise and Agnes Haidar would over the coming years frequently beg she recount yet again, and Pascale fondly, eagerly, comply. This brief interlude of colorful independence granted in Paris was sure to provide countless soft, tender memories. Recollections, the soon-to-be *Madame Chamoun* hoped could provide consolation. Consolation: during, all the coming nights she lay prone, naked, at the total mercy of a much larger, panting, hairy male, pressing insatiably down from above; forcing her to spread her legs so he might rudely shove his unsolicited large cylinder up her own most intimate passageway.

33

I

Then, on the sixth morning of her "major expedition," "primary campaign," an incident occurred. One, unfolding far from Paris, not of Pascale's own making, or, given her restricted upbringing, an event not even of the girl's wildest imaginings.

"Is that you, Father?" asked the soldier's daughter upon receiving a telephone call in her third story hotel room. A quiet, elegant, welcoming, old fashion establishment in *Baroque* townhouse, *La Nouvelle Heloise* was situated off the usual tourist's hectic, camera-snapping, beaten track. Foreign visitors could obtain a far more accurate, intimate feeling for Paris and the Parisians here, than by staying at some exorbitantly-priced, unfriendly, far-less aesthetic, celebrity hotel.

"Yes, it is, *Chere Petite*"

"Is anything wrong, Father?" questioned Pascale seated elegantly on a large, antique, oak, canopied-bed, her attractive legs crossed right to left. The base of the telephone into whose receiver at end of long cord she spoke, was atop a waist height *Queen Anne Style* cherry wood chest-of-drawers nearby.

"No, not at all. I simply wanted to tell I've extended your trip a few days."

"Awesome! Thank, you so-very-much!"

"Father knew you'd enjoy that."

"What decided you permitting me stay longer?"

"A nuisance back here needs to be dealt with.'"

"A *nuisance needs to be dealt with,* Father?"

"Don't be concerned, *Chere Petite*. It's only one of those dull, sordid, dreadfully-boring *Men's Issues*. Something, far too knotty, convoluted for ladies to understand. Even trying, will only upset you—divert you needlessly from your splendid artistic pursuits."

"Do you mean, politics?"

"Yes, *politics*"

"Ick!" exclaimed Pascale, grimacing. "Politics! Ick! **Double**-ick! How gross! That's one of the main reasons I'm glad I'm not a man! I'll never need to worry about politics. If men are so fascinated by that cutthroat business and insist keeping it all to themselves, that's perfectly fine with me! They also make it so complicated, confusing—'knotty'— as you say. Even if I could vote, I've not the foggiest notion *who* or *what* to vote *for*. If I'm not supposed to think about this *nuisance,* Father, I promise I won't."

"Perfect! Now is the best behaved daughter in the entire world having fun? That's the only subject for me or her that's important."

"More fun than I even imagined!"

"Just, as Father hoped! Just as he knew! Been shopping?"

"Once" reported Pascale, wearing a white blouse, short skirt, heels with straps, all just purchased with Father's credit card.

"You only went once? Doesn't Father, wish his daughter to always have pretty things to wear? Is she worried about the price? Is she frightened Father mightn't approve of her indulging in what makes ladies most happy? Nonsense! Starting tomorrow, Father orders *Chere Petite* to go purchase all the dresses, skirts, blouses she wants—a few new hats and a purse, as well. Does she need any more makeup, too, or shoes? She mustn't trouble herself a minute about the cost. Father will take care of it all. It's his responsibility making sure his daughter has a good time."

II

"Did you change your mind, Father?" questioned Pascale anxiously when same white and gold rotary-telephone rang again unexpectedly three days later. "Do you want me coming home now? Are you angry with me? I did just as instructed and went shopping. Perhaps I purchased more than you expected? Girls do that sometimes."

Several abundantly-filled shopping bags and large hatboxes sat nearby. Elegant but sturdy, the hatboxes could be of more use in future than for only carrying chapeaus.

"Not-at-all, *Chere Petite*!" was tender, protective response. "It's good to know everything is well. Good for Father to know Favorite isn't distracted by the goings-on."

"What kind of: *Goings-on?*"

"Never mind"

"I've been doing some drawing too, Father."

Completed pictures were always placed in wide manila folders for safe-keeping. Carriers were marked with subject and date. Each was tied at the top with a piece of black flannel string.

"What a talented child, Father has! One day, when the entire world recognizes *Chere Petite* is a great artist, Father will proudly say, 'I recognized it first!'"

"I hope I'm not *a too expensive* one" interjected daughter, meekly.

"Oh, yes. Forgive me not telling you this first," the caller continued after moment during which movement of chair, rustling of papers atop desk was heard. "Your wedding is being put-off."

"Is that so!" responded Bride-to-be, not-at-all upset.

"A situation has arisen" explained Father, cryptically.

"A *situation has arisen?*"

"The Prince instructed Field Marshal Chamoun to step-down as head of government and leave the country. His Majesty instructed Field Marshal Chamoun to transfer his office to me. I'm now Premier."

"But Father" observed Pascale, "you're already both army Chief-of-staff and Minister of Defense!"

"So Father is. However, as a soldier he's accustomed to hard work."

"Is Field Marshal Chamoun, excuse me, I mean my *fiancé*, ill?"

"No, he isn't ill, *Chere Petite*. The Prince simply believes it's best at the present time for Field Marshal Chamoun to resign and go abroad until the current situation is resolved."

"Is Field Marshal Chamoun coming to visit me, Father?" queried Pascale, discomfited. Free hand running through long, tresses of thick, jet-black hair, her gray-green eyes turned to *French Window* with green chintz curtains. Beyond them, undulating mansard, black tiled-roofs stretched unhindered to leaping, sensuous, coffee and cream-colored medieval spires in distance. Above the city, a clear delft blue sky provided yet additional touch to image of boundless, hopeful motion. "Is my fiancé coming to join me, Father? Does he want me to be with him?"

"No, *Chere Petite*. Your fiancé is going to Rome."

"I see"

For Pascale, view beyond chintz curtains became grander still.

"I don't think you'll be seeing your fiancé any time soon," Father added. "Better in fact, put complicated things like weddings aside for the time being."

"So I *won't* be marrying Field Marshal Chamoun after all?"

"Hush, my blessed *Chere Petite,* hush!" answered Father, in especially comforting voice. One, indicating he now comprehended the reason his daughter sought time alone in Paris. "Hush! No need we ever speak of weddings again. No need either, you feel ashamed or ever fear disappointing me! I understand everything. You will never be forced to touch any man against your will!"

Two days passed without the telephone ringing.

Knowledge the wedding was off, made them quite artistically-productive.

On third day, with lime, ivory and black chalk; scarlet, turquoise, canary yellow pencil; mauve and amber crayons–alternating in her skillful right hand, Pascale brilliantly interpreted on paper yet more figures and objects. Sketching at leisure pace atop blue-painted wooden bench near Left embankment, she soon observed crowds collecting in a wide public square across the way. Arriving first from one direction, then, opposite, finally, approaching similar destination from third path, the increasingly larger number of overwhelmingly adult males, milled about.

Intent on making their presence felt, they forced all vehicular transport to a standstill and blocked passage to pedestrians. The crowd's animated expression of opinion also persuaded wary shop owners and restaurant proprietors to close doors. The demonstrators appeared more interested in gaining public attention than reaching a specific geographic goal. Angry speeches were vehemently delivered, banners enthusiastically waved.

"Nothing remarkable about street protests in Paris!" reflected Pascale. "Here, people are always irate about something."

She went back to drawing.

Still, Field Marshal Chamoun's abrupt removal from office, sudden cancellation of their wedding, and most important: Father's intimate, loving revelation—could only serve to generate suspicions. Pascale set down her colors and sketchbook and decided taking a better look.

Moving hesitantly within safely-retreated earshot range and accurate visual detection, she heard slogans called, observed protest signs lofted, cried, written not merely in French, but in her own native language. Paris, a world as well as national capital, major events held locally, were sure to be reported far-away.

After contemplating yet closer investigation, the agitated, fiercely masculine composition of the crowd soon convinced Pascale to retreat. If possibly just imagined, she thought the crowd turned to–look at her, judge her, and not in a favorable manner. Co-nationals: likely university students, day-laborers—all were clad in experienced blue-jeans, tested running shoes, old sweatshirts and hand-me-down jackets. Standing noticeably apart, conversing strictly among one another, they appeared separated by intention from larger community about. Voluntary-segregation seemed to represent double-statement of displeasure –hostility shown toward hosts no less than native land.

Whether real or mere artistic conjecture, the eyes of the crowd in unison appeared to cast Pascale a sinister, contemptuous glance. Appearing to observe her– fashionable, distinctly French clothing; refined feminine gestures; makeup; eager embrace of a culture not of her birth—the crowd seemed to denounce its fellow citizen as a traitor, condemning her as a co-instigator of their own misfortune and unhappiness.

Beginning at usual step but quickly, steadily, increasing pace, Pascale returned to the hotel.

Should wise, all-knowing Father be contacted?

"Yes, definitely!"

"Or," on more mature consideration, "perhaps not."

There was little sense in Pascale becoming more worried than she was already. She didn't want to act like a *Scatterbrained Female*! Indulgent as Father was, a possibly alarmist, totally unnecessary collect-call would be frightfully expensive. Offspring's shopping expeditions already amounted to a considerable bill!

As so frequently in this girl's life, a man made the decision for her.

"Is that you calling me, Father?" asked Pascale, lifting the telephone receiver.

"Yes, it is, *Chere Petite*."

"I was thinking I should speak with you, too, Father."

"See!" he responded warmly. "I always know when my little girl needs me!"

One moment of silent mutual-understanding passed, then a second.

"Is all this same icky-*politics* happening at home, Father?" asked Pascale frantically praying she be disabused.

"Yes. That's why I first began telephoning" parent answered in sober confirmation.

"Has all this same icky-*politics* been happening for almost a week, Father?"

"Yes, *Chere Petite*, increasing each day."

Across the telephone line, Pascale recognized a particularly wise, authoritative masculine hand taking-up a fountain pen atop a familiar *Directoire* writing desk in an equally-familiar study. The next random sounds detected—words and numbers scratched on paper; desk drawer opened, closed; shifting of high-backed, leather, swivel armchair (the one when she was seated in it her feet didn't meet the floor); pet parrot squawking—all, until now given little thought, suddenly took on profound importance. Each random noise came from a specific home far away, each, a vivid remainder of loved ones the young listener might possibly never see again.

Pascale's breath sped, body grew tense, face grimaced.

"I'm wiring a certain sum to our family account in Paris, *Chere Petite*" explained Father. "Hopefully, it won't be required. However, as your parent and legal guardian, I shouldn't be remiss in these matters. The money isn't to be used lightly or touched for the time being."

"I promise Father not withdrawing any money until you first instruct me."

"That's my *Darling*"

"What's causing all this?" Pascale stammered. "Why are our citizens living abroad too, so up-in-arms?–People seemed perfectly happy at home when I left. I saw no icky-*politics* then. No protests–No demonstrations. No strikes–Nothing on television or in the newspapers mentioned anyone opposed the Prince or his government–Last month I sat with you at that parade near the Royal Family–Everyone cheered the Prince, you, Field Marshal Chamoun and the other cabinet ministers–Everyone cheered the soldiers, sailors and airmen–What went wrong? Why are people suddenly so angry?–It frightens me! I feel as if it's directed at me! –I'm scared, Father!"

"Don't worry *Chere Petite*. This affair has nothing to do with little girls. Politics is complicated. It can often be as you said–quite *icky*."

"Stop that Father!" retorted Pascale, much surprised at previously unknown assertiveness. "You don't push me in a pram anymore!"

She heard a sigh of reflection on the other end of telephone line.

"The n the crowd is entitled to be angry" said Father at last slowly, deliberately. "Were circumstances different I would've been out there among them—I thought it was my duty to shield my daughter from certain unpleasant realities, certain unpleasant realities I believed *Chere Petite* wouldn't ever need deal with anyway—Our Regent and his government chose to shield themselves from these same realities too long, as well!"

"Remember when I finally gave you permission to travel?" he confided.

"Yes, Father"

"I detected signs of dissatisfaction among the General Public for some months. Until recently, I believed the protests could be safely contained. That's why I suggested to the Prince he stage all those nationwide cultural festivals and big sporting meets in order to distract, mitigate, canalize, the growing discontent. Unfortunately, in the last few weeks, I became convinced some kind of major, possibly quite-bloody, confrontation in the streets was impossible avoiding. I still believe the Regent and his government retain enough authority to contain the demonstrations. Nevertheless I want to make absolutely sure my precious, darling child is safe."

"And so you finally gave me permission to travel" said Pascale with foreboding "because you decided this *confrontation* was about to happen?"

"Yes. So it's happening. *Chere Petite.* But don't, fear. I still think you can come home to me. Now that Field Marshal Chamoun is out of office, the opposition may be satisfied."

The next two days in Paris renewed normalcy.

Demonstrators believing their point made, disbursed.

Vehicles re-embraced comforting congestion.

Pedestrians surrendered troublesome individuality.

Irritating distinct sounds gave way to peaceful metropolitan dull roar.

Delightful smell of freshly-made crepe was in the air.

Crisis passed?

Only tempest in a teapot?

Pascale thought it best not inquiring. She kept the radio and television off, avoided newspaper kiosks. She even breathed gentler when a new telephone call proved to be a wrong number. Returned to drawing, all the subjects of her selection were safely excluded from the present controversy.

She sketched a wide, historic staircase; a lofty tower; graceful river span. Next, employed colors and paper to interpret the curves of an ancient alley; the flying buttresses of a cathedral; some birds, boats and flowers—all, at least for today, far from the twisted reach of crazy sorrow. If one couldn't change human events, Pascale concluded, one could at least temporarily put them out of mind.

As on all earlier occasions, passersby expressed deep admiration for the teenager's artistry. One of those praising her drawings several days before, even returned for a second, no less approving inspection. "Has *Robin Redbreast* considered showing her pictures to the public?" inquired the same lovely aristocratic lady in early-thirties first encountered in the Place de Vosges. "Truly-truly, *Bunny Rabbit!* This isn't meant at all in jest!" insisted the grand dame, she once more adjusting the angle of the girl's headgear to suit own fashion-setting preference. "Simply contact–**Duchess Charpentier, No. 4 Rue Marina Tsvetaeva**–and all will swiftly be arranged!"

If lost Dr. Eisenberg's business card, Pascale remembered her new friend's office was situated somewhere on Rue Saint-Jacques, near the Sorbonne. Tomorrow morning, armed with a *Metro* map and *Michelin* guidebook, she'd go and locate the professor. Certainly, obtaining information on the hereabouts of a distinguished scholar within the confines of that academic's own university, wouldn't be difficult!

She'd take her sketchbook and colors along, too. The historic, narrow, serpentine Medieval streets and beautiful *Romanesque* churches of the *Latin Quarter* were sure to provide an artist inspiration for many pictures.

Yet as much as Pascale tried placing the crisis back home out of her mind as well as sight, dread over its possible bad outcome, festered. The next morning, while preparing to visit Matilda, the telephone rang again. Understanding Father's concern she be safely abroad when the troubles erupted, daughter instinctively knew the message she was about to hear.

"It's from your Papa, *Darling*" explained the hotel owner as she transferred the telephone call from front office. "Papa has something important to tell you. Don't worry, I won't be listening-in."

A painful, sickening sensation gripped Pascale's abdomen; her entire body experienced scalding-cold, bounding-weakness. Her mind knew only loneliness, emptiness, nakedness, hunger.

"Father?" she murmured into telephone receiver, not sitting down on the bed this time but remaining rigid on her feet.

"I'm here for you, *Chere Petite*."

"Well?"

"You can't come back."

Tears came to the girl's eyes, raced her cheeks.

"You wouldn't want coming back" said Father, soothingly. "There's nothing coming back *to*. What we love is gone."

Choosing to be strong, *grownup*, Pascale instead cried into the receiver. Suddenly once more feeling as a very young child completely at the mercy of adult whim, only tears could express her sense of total helplessness.

"No crying!" insisted Father. "You're in Paris, not the dark side of the Moon! Many people you've read about found themselves in this same situation! Think of some of them–Chopin, Turgenev, Stravinsky, Pavlova, Joyce, Hemingway. You used to talk to me for hours about how romantic exile in Paris seemed. Here's your opportunity! You'll be in very good company, too!"

Pascale could still not speak coherently.

"Stop that, foolishness!" again Father insisted across the line.

The girl tried with only partial success. She, desiring but to be held in loving arms, surrendering to the comforting guidance of a wiser, more powerful other.

"Stop that!" repeated Father, in softer, reassuring voice. "Most of us never get beyond daydreaming. *Chere Petite* in contrast, will become one of the few who actually turns idle talk into action. She'll get to *Seize the Moment*. She won't be just a *silly*, tiresome *Chatterbox*. One day, she'll write a noteworthy book about the experience–make a famous set of frescoes and engravings recording her adventures exhibited in the world's finest museums! I've always said you're another Botticelli, Durer, Daumier, Goya, Rivera and Hogarth! Oh, yes, let's not forget Giotto! Your story will also probably get turned into a movie."

"Imagine!" mused Father, "*Chere Petite* a movie! Actresses will fight tooth-and-nail for the right playing my daughter! A multi-*Oscar*, too! Crowds will camp-out all night in front of the theaters in order to see the debut! Scalpers will get-away with charging obscene prices for extra tickets! It'll come out on *DVDs*! Not just regular *DVDs* but also pirated ones from China! Makes a parent proud! I must've done something right in raising you! You'll be famous and look back on this day, frightening as it may seem now, as the start of your brilliant career!"

Pascale wept.

Tears raced cheeks; gray-green eyes reddened, burning. Her vision was obstructed; nose and sinuses congested. Once more she wished to flee into a greater, stronger compassionate being. Attempting to speak at last, Pascale could only manage hurried, garbled noises.

"The line is about to give-out," Father warned after pause. "I must go away."

"I understand, Father" answered Pascale, at last, halting tears.

Static grew over the connection but a comforting, shielding voice far away was still just made out.

"Remember Father arranged for his *Chere Petite* to escape to Paris."

"So you did, Father" she answered, sniffling, "you arranged my escape to Paris!"

"And you never disobey?"

"No, Father!" acknowledged Pascale, nodding strenuously. "I never disobey."

"Good! Then when Father commands *Chere Petite to* succeed in leaving a lasting, beautiful, noble mark on the entire world, Father knows he'll be obeyed!"

END PART ONE

THE KINDLY LADY

⸱⸱⸱

The telephone connection went dead.

"And I didn't ask about Pierrette, Francoise and Agnes!" cried Pascale. "I didn't ask about Pierrette. Francoise and Agnes! They're still back there! Father got me out of the country but they're still there! How horrible of me! How could I be so thoughtless?"

She imagined her chums as figures in a *Medieval* cathedral relief. One, depicting souls suffering in hell. They being clawed, bitten by lustful demons until the end of time. Each victim, begging pathetically for a mercy never to come. Pascale's artistic mind visualized the pain and suffering even more dreadful. Recalling how much the sisters longed to accompany her on the trip, were so eagerly awaiting their buddy's return so she might recount endless stories of grand adventure, Pascale felt especially guilty. Sensing, the entire disaster and all the suffering her friends might endure was own fault.

"Pierrette, Francoise and Agnes my dearests!" cried their globetrotting-comrade. "Please, forgive me! I didn't mean to hurt you! I love all three of you so-so much and always will!

At least this painful stab of undeserved-guilt distracted the girl's thought from her own situation—*marooned in a foreign land, home eternally far away*. Yet it could distract just briefly. Gone: like Pierrette, Francoise and Agnes, were all her loved ones—family, friends, her pony *Penelope*. Gone: were all the places, objects, fragrances, sounds, tastes, colors and other reminders of cherished memories, aspirations, successes, even failures. Everything animal, vegetable, mineral serving until this point in life molding a certain distinct individual, unique personal experience was gone, never to return. As if Mlle. Kedari and her entire world prior to this moment, never existed!

Exile—romantic, heroic, nostalgic; subject for British poetry and nineteenth century Russian novels—was an existence much less appealing when actually lived. Besides, unlike her insecure, teenage, near-penniless female self, dynamic adult males like Byron, Shelley and Turgenev could well afford being driven from birthplace.

So what next?

Even if, as Father claimed, *Chere Petite* was the modern Durer, Daumier, Goya, his daughter's work destined for all the world's great museums, she also must support herself in a cold, self-absorbed, often cruel world.

Besides equipment for art studio, Pascale also required: food on her plate, clothes on her body; enough money each month keeping a roof over her head. In addition to advancing her artistic career, she must henceforth confront—utility bills, taxes, investments, mortgages, complicated forms, overcharges, pushy-salesmen, faulty-products, home repairs, car breakdowns, stolen credit cards, doctors, attorneys, stalkers, uncooperative police, pompous mid-level bureaucrats, bigots, criminals, men who won't accept *no,* gropers, heavy-breathers, stolen-packages, lost-receipts, missed-payments, critical appointments forgotten, dry cleaners refusing responsibility for ruined-clothing, bounced checks, stolen-identity, important mail sent to wrong address, prying neighbors, nasty rumors no amount of evidence can disprove—And, she must do so, *alone!* Previously, these and similar tawdry but unavoidable matters were taken care of by Father. If Pascale married Field Marshal Chamoun next month, responsibility for all such worrisome issues would shift seamlessly to a powerful, influential husband.

Wasn't she also a bit young, unworldly, traveling unchaperoned? Especially *abroad* and considering she a girl from a male-dominated, conservative society?

In normal times, definitely! That was why Pascale's request for permission taking journey was so long refused. Permission, Father firmly denied yet again just days before mysteriously reversing himself and arranging *Chere Petite*'s almost immediate departure. Only, it was now discovered, his wish she escape revolution against a regime the Kedari family were key leaders, persuaded that government's final Premier, longtime Minister of Defense and Army Chief-of-Staff to ever release his daughter from paternal authority.

A restricted, closely-regimented, semi-cloistered yet at same time privileged, lovingly-shielded, warmly-protected *Army Brat*-childhood, was over. Not once signed a check, negotiated with tradesmen, or allowed contact with *undesirables,* Pascale was abruptly out on her, own. If Father confident *Chere Petite* would succeed, he was now forever far away.

She looked-about the room.

Closets shut, drawers closed, faucets tightened, television and radio were turned-off. Once appealing high ceilings, now seemed purposely withdrawn from contact. Once lovely view from window, displayed no longer grand possibilities but rather, unconquerable burdens. That pretty duchess so admiring of the young artist's drawings would certainly offer eager aid. Unfortunately, amidst all the fear and confusion, Pascale forgot the grand dame's name.

Panicking, she raced outside. Open air brought no relief. Wide long boulevards; traffic congestion; faceless, self-contained pedestrian mass only reinforced a sense of loneliness and anonymity. Spires, palaces and battlements no longer majestic, now intimidated with vast size and heaviness. Their interiors, once fascinating places to be investigated were become sources of community to which this girl was barred. In a city of millions, she felt alone in the universe.

Running back to the hotel, kicking-off heels, Pascale jumped on bed, closed her eyes tight and rolled into ball. How long she remained clutched in fetal position—long, thick jet-black hair flowing over as a shawl—was impossible to determine. Nighttime came, departed. Sun rose and set. Clouds gathered. Shower fell. Pavement became wet. Wheels of cars cried-out traditional slippery, anxious voice. Heavens cleared. Further time elapsed. All was dry.

Whatever the length of time, Pascale wanted only sleep. Deep blank, unconsciousness or diverting dreams brought liberation. Occasionally opening eyes, she momentarily thought the entire trip was imagined. All a nightmare passed, she in fact never left her warm, shielding, nurturing, consoling home. Father was still nearby as her all-knowing, all-powerful, never-failing guide. Then, an instant later realizing the horrible truth, daughter closed eyes again to recapture tender, welcoming forgetfulness.

I

"Time to get-up, Sweetheart" instructed Marie-Sabine-Véronique Castellane, the fetching, cherry-blonde hotel proprietress, age in early-thirty thirties. "You must've been sleeping two days. The trays I brought always remained outside the door untouched. First, I thought you were away temporarily. But when noticing your front door key never removed downstairs, I became worried. I thought you might be ill. Luckily, it doesn't appear to be the case. You simply needed extra rest. All the same, you can't spend your whole lifetime in-bed. Besides, that clinched, worried expression you've been making recently as you dream isn't good for your pretty face."

Sitting on the side of Pascale's bed, Véronique parted the thick jet-black mane covering dispirited-girl's face. Next, placing adult right hand upon troubled teenage forehead, she pondered decision. Soon, coming to favorable conclusion, she smiled at patient, assuring worried youngster now possessed a trusted, intimate friend, protector.

"Good! No temperature" announced Véronique, refastening the buttons of Pascale's blouse; next, brushing girl's long hair. The serious, concerned expression on adult face, rhythm of breath and movement of adult upper torso, all exuded maternal obligation. "I thought I was done with responsibilities caring for children" she volunteered. "It appears not!" Rather than representing anger or annoyance, her words denoted pleasant surprise. This child, hotel proprietress already concluded, was no ordinary guest.

Pascale reached-out, hugging securely, never wishing to let-go. Wishing she be absorbed into another's wiser, more, clever, understanding body.

"I fully understands how you feel" consoled Véronique, gently removing Pascale's clinging arms. Next, kissing her softly on forehead and smoothing-out diminutive girl's massive tangled hair. "I know what happened. All so sudden and unexpected! You weren't at all prepared. No one thought to ask your opinion. Just a little girl to whom politics and world affairs are a total mystery! Swept along in a crisis not of your own making! Caught-up in someone else's struggle! Someone else's argument! Terrible, I know! It's so unfair!"

Pascale, sniffling meekly nodded, tried to speak but instead once more burst into tears. She reached, out again.

"I'm sorry, too, Sweetheart" consoled new friend, taking Pascale to bust firmly, applying second loving kiss on mournful adolescent's forehead. "The world's often a nasty cruel place. Innocent people are accused of things, punished for crimes they aren't responsible—never even knew occurred. Still, that doesn't mean they can't later pick themselves up and go on—even, find a better, happier, more fulfilling life in a different land! One day you may be saying so to another unhappy little girl!"

Véronique inspected her new ward up-and-down.

"Go take a bath, Dear! You've been in those same clothes two days. Don't be frightened. Take all the time you wish. I'm not going away."

Pascale returned after twenty minutes, her ocean of newly-washed jet-black hair wrapped in a thick, large white towel; the rest of her enveloped in a patterned bathrobe meant for someone much taller. Refreshed in four-foot-ten-inch body if still weak in soul, she nevertheless dared to believe the worst might now just possibly be over.

"Here I am Mme. Castellane!"

"Good. See! I told I wouldn't go away!"

"Yes, so you did, Mme. Castellane"

"I was looking through your folders over by the window" illuminated Véronique, deeply impressed by what she just surveyed. "I see you quite enjoy drawing pictures—portraits, landscapes, city views, other

49

drawings which are purely abstract. Some you've done in color, others in chalk, others in charcoal, a few, in pencil. Excellent! All of them! I'm no authority on the subject but your drawings each certainly look very well done to me! Very original too! They aren't attempts to copy someone else. No, no. They've a style all their own!

"You really like them, Mme. Castellane?"

"Indeed, I do."

Adult received another passionate adolescent embrace.

"It appears you're a real artist!" declared Véronique. "I'm not saying this simply to be polite! While I'm no official authority on the subject, over my years on the stage I've met, conversed, become well-acquainted with enough distinguished gentlemen who *are official* authorities. One or two of these gentlemen you've likely even heard of yourself! I also go regularly to enough museums and galleries to definitely know what great art looks like! Therefore, I can guarantee with some measure of indisputable confidence that I've just been pictures drawn by a young lady possessed of real God-given talent!"

"Thank-you, Mme. Castellane" answered Pascale, modestly.

"So as an artist, you've certainly landed in the right location!"

"Thank-you, Mme. Castellane."

Véronique's conscientious pretty face grew searching, pensive.

Her scrupulous brown eyes fixed themselves meditatively beyond the window.

Responsible, attentive red painted lips moved in silent debate.

"But first, I need doing something about your current precarious situation. I must put you in a warm, quiet, out-of-the-way place for safe-keeping. Child's in no condition yet facing-the-world, making important decisions! Let alone even try. I don't want others *taking-advantage-of-you, leading-you-astray."*

"And unfortunately" she confided, *"being-taken-advantage-of, being-led-astray* is precisely your fate if not immediately placed under my strict-supervision. Henceforth, I must keep close watch on you, be sure you mind-your-manners, say your prayers. Child must promptly receive a good spanking whenever disobeying or wandering-off without permission. A sweet, simple, trusting, creature like you, is just the sort for whom pimps are forever out-on-the-prowl! Easily lured-into the pimps' power by their fine words, charming trinkets, lovely promises, you'll be trapped in a brothel before even understanding what's happened!"

"Still, there's no reason fearing **White Slavery**" pledged Véronique. "Your virginity is safe. From now on your principal fear isn't confronting pimps. Rather, it's when next your little girl-mischief lands you across Madame's knee!"

"Yes, Mme. Castellane. From now on my fear isn't confronting pimps. Rather, it's when next my little girl-mischief lands me across your knee!"

Pascale pressed her face against the loving-disciplinarian's large, firm, welcoming bust. She hugged ever so tight. At this saddest, weakest, most vulnerable moment in her life, receiving an adult's stern warning was exactly the emotional reassurance the girl needed most. Rather than frightening, it confirmed Pascale's hope she now under the authority of an all-powerful, unchallengeable guardian.

"I've got to get some documents for you to fill-out" elaborated Véronique. "That should be the easy part. I saw your passport is in-order. You didn't come under false-pretenses and fully planned going home on the appointed-date. None of the foolishness happening in the last few days is your fault! No one with a pinch of respect will make you leave immediately."

She debated next step, perfected plan-of-action.

"And if I get you reputable employment, you can settle in France. In time, I'll find you a good husband. You'll produce a set of fine children to cherish. You'll acquire your own lovely little house to keep, garden with flowers and vegetables to tend. People you pass on the street will make sure always addressing you respectfully as—*Madame*. Honored by all your friends and neighbors! A pillar of the community! You'll be asked by the priest to manage the charity bazaar, say a few words at the local fair, help teach *Catechism*!"

"And most of all, Marie" prophesied Véronique, "you'll finally be recognized as the brilliant artist I already know you to be! People from across Europe will seek the privilege of meeting you! What do the

51

Americans call it? Marie will be a young ladies' *Role Model,* be, their female *example* to follow!"

"The time will come, too" she concluded, "when Marie becomes a French citizen. You wouldn't mind calling yourself French one day, would you? Of course not!"

Véronique at last lifted Pascale gently from her bust. One steady grownup hand took each troubled adolescent cheek. Wise adult looked tenderly into teenager's reddened-eyes, guaranteeing guidance. Girl eagerly awaited her elder's wisdom.

"Whatever you think is best for me, Mme. Castellane."

"It won't precisely be employment for an *artist* at the beginning" explained Véronique. Unwrapping the white towel around Pascale's head, she took-up a large pink-handled brush to put in proper order the girl's newly cleaned thick, independent-minded jet-black hair. "But I wield considerable influence in this neighborhood. I can promise a post both respectable and with good salary. I'll also find an employer I can safely entrust you. It'll be a post a young lady of your traditional, conservative upbringing won't find slightest fault. A job leading you to precisely the life you well deserve and your parents intended for you!"

JOB-HUNTING

....

$\mathcal{M}$lle. Kedari never obtained the money wired to her family's bank account in Paris. Once more, events far beyond a teenager's control intervened. If, she long kept uninformed about politics, *Chere Petite* was now swiftly, rudely introduced.

Pascale's birthplace, once a central feature of the vast French colonial empire, regained independence only following a savage, pitiless, eight-year guerrilla war. A struggle often illustrated by terrorism, betrayal, assassination, acts of blood-curdling revenge committed on both sides. A protracted conflict witnessing the liberal use of napalm, torture and poison gas, displaying the worst in the human soul, it took over two million lives the great majority of them, innocent noncombatants.

That fifty years following independence, the country continued reliant on Paris for economic aid, its government still francophone, Roman-Catholic, French-oriented in culture, was a source of deep resentment to the Muslim, Arabic-speaking majority population. One, harboring deep bitterness against its former European overlord. When the nationalists seized power claiming to prevent imminent reassertion of French colonial domination, they received massive public support.

The nationalists promptly confiscated all French business and financial assets, abrogated all commercial treaties with France, expelled the French ambassador and demanded swift return of all their culture's priceless art works held in French museums. Paris immediately responded in kind—freezing all business and financial assets held on its territory by citizens of Pascale's country, severing all economic development aid, expelling her country's ambassador, refusing to surrender any museum objects.

Both to avoid a situation similar to the *1979-1981 U.S Tehran Hostage Crisis* and to make a dramatic demonstration of which side continued exercising a decisive position in the world, Paris dispatched the nuclear-fueled aircraft carrier *De Gaulle* along with a regiment of muscular, armed-to-the-teeth paratroopers to escort westerners home. Throughout *Operation Paramountcy*, French fighter jets flew low, often and loudly above the former colony's capital. Their near-interminable roar caused windows on buildings underneath to violently rattle and crowds of pedestrians to desperately scramble in search of cover.

The dispute then shifted to the World Court at The Hague where it's still dragging-on hyperbolic today with no hint of settlement. As a fine means of stirring aggrieved, victimized, nationalist-fervor at election time, an effective devise for distracting voters' attention away from the short-comings of domestic policy, neither government sees any advantage resolving controversy.

The freezing of all bank accounts in France held by citizens of Pascale's country included those of high-ranking members of the former regime. Were Father present or his fate known, it would be different. Unfortunately, he wasn't present and all reliable news about events back home was cut-off. His daughter being a legal minor instantly raised the question whether she needed a court-appointed trustee or step-family. Absurd as was the request posed by uncooperative officials, Pascale had no documented-means of disproving Father, if still alive, wasn't now a member of the revolutionary junta!

Over several months, twice weekly, Véronique escorted her protégée to every government office she imagined might possess the authority to unfreeze the Kedaris' Paris bank account. The two ladies became near-fixtures in the waiting room of the Ministries of: Foreign Affairs, Defense, of Finance; those of: Justice, Interior, Housing, National Education, Commerce, Health; Housing, Youth, Tourism, Overseas Territories, Immigration, Culture.

Sadly, the effort was to no avail.

At appointment after appointment, interview following interview, a similar: double-chinned paper-pusher with receding gray hair informed Pascale in annoyed, monarchical voice that her case was taking-up his own valuable time. Her "little matter," "minor oversight" needed settling in s still different ministry. That *different* ministry, next announcing itself unable to investigate until first provided a series of complicated, multistage forms filled-out in triplicate (both by hand and typewritten, then delivered personally, by regular mail and *FAX*). Should, one means of delivery accidentally arrive at the office before the other, or just one piece of paperwork be filled-out slightly amiss on its many, elaborate narrow lines—all the complicated, multiple page forms required to be filled-out in triplicate (both by hand and typewritten, delivered both by hand, regular mail and *FAX*) must be resubmitted. Eventually, as was tactic of bureaucracy all along, the two ladies gave up. Mme. Castellane owned a hotel she must manage daily and Pascale at least obtained political asylum.

Initially, Véronique's efforts obtaining employment for her protégée were disappointing. As a *pillar* of the Roman Catholic community, highly attractive, engaging; renowned for her non-bigoted piety, sense of selfless charity; she once one of history's greatest prima ballerinas— Mme. Castellane exercised immense: subtle, cultural, social and political influence over the families, merchants, police and civil servants in her circle of Paris. In contrast, Pascale appeared to be just another refugee "from one of those *istan*-countries."

If a supremely-gifted artist possessing the intelligence of genius, Pascale, until her arrival in France had no acquaintance with the coarser aspects of life. If easily-recognized as brilliant, she lacked any formal education or vocational training. Nothing, or so it appeared, enabled the girl to find a meaningful career in the rough-and-tumble capitalist environment she was so abruptly cast. In addition, many employers didn't trust Pascale to remain long at a manual job so clearly far below her personal abilities. Others, feared hiring her would cause resentment among the current staff who could reasonably expect new positions opening in the company belonged to members of their own families.

Have you–*experience*?" Pascale was asked by first job interviewer. "We do like hiring new workers who come to us with—*experience*."

"No, Monsieur" girl naïve but truthfully admitted, "but I'll have *experience* after someone hires me."

She wasn't invited back.

"What motivates you joining our terrific team?" queried second job interviewer. "We're a team here, all members inspired by common spirit. It's devotion to the team, common spirit which, guarantees lasting success."

"I can't really say what motivates me, Madame," replied Pascale. "However I promise to quickly learn what motivates me. I promise to quickly acquire the common spirit, make myself part of your terrific team."

She wasn't invited back.

"So, why, Dear" asked next merchant, "do you–*want*–a job?"

"To support myself" applicant answered all too honestly.

"Don't call us back Dear" replied merchant. "We'll call you."

"So what can Mademoiselle *do*?" interrogated fourth business owner.

"I'm fluent in six foreign languages, Monsieur!" instantly informed Pascale, hoping she had at last found a position. "Besides French, I'm also fluent in English, German, Italian, Arabic, Russian and Japanese! I engrave! I make woodcuts and lithographs! I paint and draw! I'll be ever-so pleased if you wish seeing examples of my work! The former Regent of my country purchased two of my pictures!"

"Yes, yes, but what can you–*do*?"

Another applicant was selected for the position.

"We don't have Mohammedan holidays or permit veils or head-scarfs," informed fifth merchant, surprised observing Pascale wearing miniskirt, makeup and heels rather than covered head-to-toe as ion television. "You also must work on Fridays."

"I'm Roman Catholic, Monsieur" explained girl, pretending not noticing the bigoted insinuation.

"Oh! I thought all your *kind* are Mohammedans?"

"No."

"Since, when?"

"Since always, Monsieur"

"But I thought your country was always Mohammedan?"

"No, Monsieur" enlightened Pascale. "Christianity is six hundred years-older than Islam. In fact, people in my country have been Christians longer than people in France."

"Never mind. That part of the world's already too hard to fathom!"

"It's not as hard to 'fathom' if simply given the close attention and consideration it deserves!" Pascale responded with uncharacteristic anger. "After all, my part of the world created human civilization! While my ancestors were inventing writing, inventing poetry, mathematics, accurately tracking the movement of the heavenly bodies, your ancestors were –running around naked!"

"You're ever-so talented, Precious" commented sixth employer, effusive. "I wish I was as intelligent and as talented as you, Sweetheart!"

"Awesome! Thank-you very much, Madame!" replied Pascale graciously, again hoping she at last found a job; one, under an employer not merely understanding but perhaps even a soul-mate.

"Clearly, you'll make a very essential, most valuable worker, Dear."

"Awesome! Thank-you, Madame ever so-so-so-so much! I'll do any task you wish me to perform! I'll never cause trouble! I'll be loyal! I'll do my absolute utmost to be as energetic and efficient and hardworking as I ever-so-so-so possibly can! I'm ready to start tomorrow morning! What time should I arrive?"

"Unfortunately" answered the businesswoman, embarrassed at arousing false hopes, "we're looking for someone with—*experience*."

"How can I ever get *experience*" muttered Pascale, "if no one hires me!"

I

"Once more, the answer was–*no*" sighed Véronique in frustration, escorting Pascale back to the hotel following latest unsuccessful-job interview. "It's been far more difficult finding you a suitable position than I ever expected. Perhaps it's because you're so unique, so special, that ordinary people can't appreciate you? It's almost as if in this godless, *so-where's-the-profit-in-it-for-me*, bourgeois society you're too smart, too gifted for your own good."

"I speak in jest of course, Marie!" she, hastily adding.

"Yes I know you speak in jest, Mme. Castellane," comforted Pascale. "Good!"

"Yes, Mme. Castellane, it's clear to me."

"That's a tremendous relief!"

"Don't fear, Mme. Castellane."

"You were promised a secure place though, Sweetheart and a promise is a promise! The Bible says we must not bear false-witness."

"As you say, Mme. Castellane."

"You certainly deserve a secure place after all you've undergone, Cherie! For the time being, I am now for-all-intents-and-purposes your *Mama*." The hotel proprietress paused. "And if for-all-intents-and-purposes I'm now your Mama, you've got the full right to expect her performing a Mama's duty"

"Thank-you for all your concern, Mme. Castellane" answered Pascale, deferential. Her words if deeply poignant, fondly moving, were also stimulated by an increasing sense of personal-guilt. "Isn't it shameful" she thought, "permitting myself to become such a burden on this nice, Christian, lady!–Such an awful deadweight I've allowed myself to become on her pious shoulders–Mme. Castellane never expected still having her hands-filled-with-me when she first found me balling-away like a *Scatterbrained Female*!–I should do better than this to prove I'm not just another *Witless Woman*. –I must find some way to repay!"

That late-afternoon, as a brilliant tangerine sun retreated majestically behind distant brown battlements, Pascale wore a short pattern dress, white gloves, heels and white socks. Her mane of jet-black hair was tied together behind in a big satin red bow. A large, antique, pure sterling silver crucifix hung from her neck. It was a present she received last week as birthday present.

Under a gray apron she just tied-on, Véronique wore a short, pattern dress, an unbuttoned pink cardigan and regular-tone pantyhose. At the hotel, where she frequently sped the stairs, raced corridors, cooked all the meals, often handled boxes and packages, she found it much more convenient setting aside white, black, green, red or blue high heels to wear brown flats. Her long, cherry-blonde hair was tied back. As always, a large antique, pure sterling silver crucifix hung at the end of chain necklace. With left genteel hand set rigid behind erect back at waist, right, poised at chin, she carefully weighed next strategic ladylike-move.

"Where am I finding you a permanent home?" Véronique debated. "Where's Sweetheart at last to be placed? Child can't stay at the hotel forever –people will start developing unsavory ideas."

Standing at attention just beside, *Good Little Soldier* gazed up silent, dutiful, prepared. She loyally awaiting *Better's* decision on subordinate's fate.

"I recall when you first appeared, Marie" confided Véronique, stroking her protégée's jet-black mane. "It instantly touched my heart. That trunk you brought was bigger than yourself! Your socks drooped. On your pretty, yearning face was detected uneasiness at being forced learning the terrible truths about the world your sheltered-upbringing left you little if at all able to survive. 'A tender, idealistic virgin like her'—I thought—'belongs in a convent!'"

And that" the prima ballerina elaborated, "was before I learned of your splendid gift for art! This dimwit, back-stabbing world doesn't deserve you, Child. It's unworthy of my Little Marie! No wonder it fails seeing your fine qualities!"

Again, she paused.

"Yet as much as I think you belong in a convent, I acknowledge too, that like Michelangelo, Leonardo and Rembrandt, my Sweetheart was chosen to illuminate the entire world. But how's it all to be engineered? How precisely am I to make you and your blessed message known?"

As earlier Matilda Eisenberg was drawn irresistibly within the diameter of Pascale Kedari's captivating, mysterious, otherworldly aura, so, too now, was Véronique Castellane. However, if the left-wing, agnostic professor believed she taken into the orbit of an extraordinary human being, the politically-conservative, deeply-devout proprietress of *La Nouvelle Heloise* was no less convinced she encountering a saint.

59

NEWCOMER

....

$\mathcal{I}$f unable finding the girl outside-employment, Véronique easily integrated her sidekick into the local religious community. For Pascale, life beyond *La Nouvelle Heloise* soon revolved around a beautiful nine-hundred-and-fifty-year-old *Romanesque-Gothic* church. Once every Sunday and twice on all major religious holidays, wearing: a pretty dress, white gloves, bobbysocks and heels, huge red satin bow in hair– Pascale accompanied her benefactress to Mass. Daily, the devout pair read aloud from the Bible together, recited the *Rosary*. Each evening, following completion of hotel chores, they spent time in silent prayer. Whenever the silver and brass ornaments on the altar needed re-shining, or the church's *Nave* required vacuuming—both operations guaranteed to occupy many hours—Mme. Castellane and Pascale were the first to eagerly volunteer.

This historic church in the 5th Arrondissement was situated on the opposite bank of the Seine from the hotel. Except during rain or snow, Véronique a healthy-living and exercise enthusiast, insisted the two ladies always walk to destination. The serpentine, medieval cobblestone streets surrounding the basilica were also no simple length of space to cross for travelers wearing heels. Many other houses of worship were far closer to the hotel but Mme. Castellane insisted attending this more distant one. The priest was her beloved brother. She was fond of describing him as "the ideal fusion of an intellectual and a caring-soul."

Graduating first in his class from France's most distinguished medical school, possessing a surgical license as well as religious Vocation, Father Richard Castellane originally wanted to spend his life serving in the Third World as a member of *Medecins Sans Frontieres*. Unfortunately, epilepsy and a weak heart compelled him to remain in France. Until health collapsed, he operated a free clinic in the roughest industrial suburb north of Paris. A clinic at which he was often called upon to operate on patients with gunshot and stab wounds, treat others with drug overdoses, to shelter battered wives, stitch-up the wounds of prostitutes assaulted by their pimps for not collecting enough johns.

A highly-acclaimed United States television documentary was made about the clinic. It provided Richard brief worldwide fame. The documentary brought him an avalanche of self-serving praise from politicians and celebrities but most vital, much dearly needed financial assistance, precious new medical supplies and other valuable equipment. Hollywood even seriously considered making a movie or television miniseries (venue shifted from Paris to Los Angeles; Richard now Southern Baptist, having an affair with a bisexual, *Crack*-addicted, illegal alien gang leader's half-black daughter).

The General Public with a short attention span, twelve months later, few of even the priest's most effusive supporters still remembered he and his clinic ever existed. The reliable flow of financial contributions and new medical equipment donations proved as fleeting as glory. Once more, the clinic in the roughest outlying industrial neighborhood of the capital just managed staying open underfunded, understaffed, its survival essentially dependent on the enthusiasm and dedication of its leader. Questioned once by Pascale about his earlier experience, Richard replied fondly "At least I got to meet Bob Dylan! At least I know Bob Dylan still supports me!"

Richard ran-away from home as a child, leaving a message behind for his mother: "*I want to be like Heinrich Schliemann.*" The little boy was finally found at the Cherbourg harbor docks looking for a ship to stow-away on heading for Istanbul. He was captivated with ancient myth and archeology. At age seven, he learned in school how Heinrich Schliemann astounded the world in 1871 when he announced finding fabled-Troy where once lived Hector, noblest of men and Helen, whose beauty forever defies words. If long dismissed as mere legend, Heinrich Schliemann was nevertheless convinced this particular city upon a hill really existed, that Homer's saga was based on fact. He was correct. Discovering, Troy's actual buried location through interpreting verses of the *Iliad*. From age seven, Richard dreamed of he too one day unearthing the ruins of a lost civilization through interpreting ancient poems and ballads.

Prevented active field-work, he sought his goal through academic research. Visitor request records at both the Bibliotéchque Nationale and Archives Nationales indicate a number of particularly rare books and documents have over nearly two hundred years been investigated only by Father Castellane. Besides speaking Latin, Greek and Hebrew, he also read Cuneiform and Sanskrit.

Richard annually published at least three major articles in Europe's most respected academic journals. His latest piece, was a path-breaking analysis of the founding of agriculture and birth of village community on the upper Indus River valley during the Eighth Millennia BC. Both the University of Heidelberg in Germany and of Louvain in Belgium, sought hiring him as a tenured professor of ancient Middle Eastern studies. He declined, explaining his first duty was to his church and clinic. As Mme. Castellane, who'd strongly advised her brother accept one of these prestigious teaching positions mused: "Richard's goodness often gets-in-the-way of his career. Alas there aren't more such starry-eyed individuals! We've gone through a century of unsentimental pragmatists and look where it's gotten humanity!"

Not every member of St. G parish was so favorable. The old crones grumbled endlessly. These biddies serving in the church office as receptionist, typist, housekeeper, kept a close self-righteous eye on their unusual priest's activities.

Richard's private study, confided Mme. Rameau to her gossipy allies, contained more books, manuscripts and documents relating to Greek and Hindu epics, Sumerian culture and archeological expeditions than works of traditional liturgy, lives of the saints, or volumes of Roman Catholic theology. "He subscribes to the most ungodly, leftist,

Israelite-periodicals!" The pure fact Mme. Rameau couldn't understand the highbrow, "*Israelite*-subject" of these learned journals convincing her they "must be dreadfully immoral!"

The last time Mme. Clermont was reading her employer's mail, she was horrified noticing above his writing desk not a portrait of the Virgin but a photograph of Heinrich Schliemann.

Mme. Lambert was grievously insulted Richard preferred obtaining ancient Cycladic statuary over her own taste for collecting antique rural French crucifixes. "He worships idols!"

All, firmly agreed their priest's homilies "too intellectual," "leftist," "too over-our-heads." His words "lacked dogmatic correctness," were too ecumenical. "They don't call us to lead a Christian life" declared Mme. Joubert, rifling through employer's file box. "They're not *proper* for a *proper* priest in a *proper* church."

The crones wondered if Richard "is a Communist."

Mme. Rameau often asserted she uncovering reliable evidence to prove "He's really an Israelite!"

Later, following his untimely death, Richard's personal art collection and first edition library became a small but highly renowned museum and research center. These same malicious biddies would then squabble over which of them was "the young holy man's, precious saint's earliest and most selfless admirer."

Véronique was immensely proud of her learned-sibling. Although she was the younger of duo, viewers upon first introduced to the pair understandably reached the opposite conclusion. If six-years older, Richard was two-inches shorter. Of fragile build, less than one-hundred-and-twenty-pounds in weight, plagued by constant cough and soar-throat, Richard at forty still possessed the face of an undergraduate college student. Few imagined how much mental-zip, intellectual-zap, existed within such a small body.

Whenever she appeared, Richard instantly deferred to Véronique. Each time his sister visited, her brother's green eyes lit-up with joy as he hurriedly set his many searching thoughts in order to deliver a brief account of his activities since last time the affectionate pair crossed-paths. It was a brief account not merely of his newest scholarly research but of the latest operation he performed free-of-charge at the clinic.

Childless, Véronique felt a personal responsibility for the frail polymath. As Pascale recently became her surrogate-daughter, so Richard fulfilled Véronique's desire for a son. It was "a sacred obligation," she believed. One, not merely to guard Richard's poor health, encourage his medical career and scholarly pursuits but also make sure he understood that despite the frequent criticism leveled against him by busybody-matrons and their henpecked-husbands, the vast majority of his flock considered their priest an extraordinary human being.

"Excellent! Excellent, Richard-dear!" his sibling proclaimed in protective voice at conclusion of her brother's latest account. "You never fail making your mother—I mean *sister*—proud."

"I'm always so grateful receiving your approval, Véronique."

"Did you take your medicine as Dr. Gambetta ordered, Richard?" questioned his sister, she worried by the sound of her brother's nasty-cough. "I'll be most upset hearing otherwise! How can I expect to continue listening to your splendid achievements if you don't take care of yourself? You don't want to make a *Witless Woman* like me lose her *Scatterbrains*-head with worry and take-to-her-bed?"

"Yes, I take my medicine just Dr. Gambetta prescribed. I take all the medicines I'm ordered. It's simply that these medieval churches, lovely as they so are, also contain terrible draughts."

"That's further reason it's your mother's—*sister's*—duty looking after you. Draughts aren't selective in whom they trouble, genius and fools alike."

Such praise made her brother embarrassed.

"This is my faithful, trusted protégée" announced Véronique, motioning to her four-foot-ten-inch companion standing timidly beside. Pascale wore a short pattern dress; white socks; white heels. A huge red satin bow was in her voluminous jet-black hair. "Come, come Little Marie, don't be shy, Richard wont bite!"

Pascale cringed.

She looked into the Kindly Lady's eyes pleading.

Véronique set her ward at ease with a loving, knowing-glance. "Don't worry, I understand"—affectionate brown eyes, red painted-lips promised.

Reassured, cale stepped haltingly toward the priest, motherly hands remaining secured on her shoulders.

"I've spoken of Little Marie frequently before, Richard. She's an artist. You're a scholar. Here's the first chance you two savants can meet. As I've also told you, Little Marie comes from the same section of the world whose ancient cultures you find fascinating. I'm sure you two gifted dears will find much to talk about. Not simply now but on many future occasions."

"I'm so happy we at least meet" welcomed this singular priest. "I've indeed heard much about your gift for art." The Kindly Lady advised him with gesture of face that the girl disliked being touched by men. "I've waited a long time to speak with you, Marie."

"Yes indeed!" encouraged Véronique. "Go-off and chat with Richard. Only just make sure Richard takes his next dose of medication. It's scheduled for five o'clock."

"At five o'clock, Mme. Castellane" responded Pascale.

"Now run-along you two brainy dears, concern yourselves with uplifting things!"

The hotel proprietress was correct—both in her guess the two *brainy dears* would become friends, and in her confidence their relationship would be *uplifting*. Pascale and Richard soon were dedicated friends. Her unique gift for art, his own singular aptitude, combined with mutual deep religious faith, assured a bond not just lasting but for both partners: intellectually productive.

As expected, the old crones gossiped.

Mme. Rameau—unable reading her employer's mail with Pascale often in the parish office—became convinced the teenager was Richard's illegitimate-daughter.

In contrast, Mme. Clermont was no less sure that Pascale was a prostitute.

"She's such a shameless tart!" seconded Mme. Lambert.

Not to be denied voicing her own scurrilous opinion, Mme. Marchand announced that while eavesdropping, she frequently heard "the most obscene, erotic groans" emanating from Richard's office whenever he and Pascale were inside alone. "It's not at all Christian behavior! It's not at all *proper* in a *proper* church!"

"We all agree, they're probably both Israelites!"

Were these malignant-biddies to discover the truth, they'd be gravely disappointed. Pascale and Richard often attended lectures and visited museums, together. Following Sunday morning Mass, they engaged in discussions about art and history, alone. The pair were a regular feature at evening church events. These special friends shared precious confidences. Pascale frequently volunteered at the clinic. But that was as far as intimacy went. Theirs was a purely intellectual, spiritual camaraderie.

"Ultimately, a scholar only interprets the accomplishments of others," confided Richard, one afternoon. "An archeologist can't find lost civilizations unless those *lost* civilizations are already waiting to be discovered—the lives and deeds, hopes and fears of their long ago inhabitants already waiting for future historians to record. You by contrast Little Marie, are an artist! I don't want to hinder you from creating timeless masterpieces I can only comment upon!"

The priest too, now felt himself drawn irresistibly inside the diameter of another's powerful, mysterious, unseen aura. It was an entrancing, beckoning, transcendent light made even more compelling through fact the girl from whom illumination shown appeared unaware she either possessed or emitted it.

At first, Pascale often went to *Confession*. She spoke of her sense of guilt at consuming so much of Mme. Castellane's time and attention, sense of guilt at failing to repay that same time and attention in the manner she thought right. Pascale repeatedly mentioned the shame she experienced at forgetting to ask about Pierrette, Francoise and Agnes during that last telephone call with home.

Richard listened sympathetically. Understanding, he was being confided in not merely as priest but as personal friend. He perceived correctly he was the first to hear these troubled thoughts and wished his friend keep her feelings in perspective. It wasn't long before he told

Pascale not to return to *Confession* until after committing sins truly requiring only a benevolent higher power to provide absolution.

"Considering all the shameless murder and mayhem, blatant persecution and destruction freely occurring across the globe, Little Marie," instructed Richard in a voice as impressed with Pascale as protective, "your passing misdeeds—*occasional missteps* is a more accurate term–sins of *omission* not *commission*–don't amount to much! You've no worry being brought before the criminal dock at Nuremberg or finding an international arrest warrant issued for you."

"That's not to say you should blithely-ignore those occasional *missteps!*" he stressed. "You must forever seek becoming a better person–always atone for your sins. And as flawed mortals, we all commit them, even you! Even the saints were sinners. On the other hand, put those adolescent wrongs of yours in perspective! God wants you to love Him, follow His word, not become so self-absorbed, self-obsessed you start thinking you're the single deserving inhabitant of the universe! Why in fact, believing your teenage-missteps comparable to the bloody crimes committed by adults who clearly know-better, is Narcissism! God has far more than enough contending with as it is in these hectic times. So long as you realize your sins, sincerely regret them, honestly seek amending them, attempt not repeat them, God is satisfied."

"From this day forth, Little Marie" said Richard, "unless a drastic change occurs in your life and worldview—a drastic change I'm not expecting—instead of coming to frequent Confession, try following the words of M**icah**: *Do justice, love mercy, and walk humbly with thy God.* As, Hillel, observed of all further Biblical teaching—'the rest is commentary.' If you accept and honor the spirit of those words with all sincerity, with all sincerity and honor seek to follow the words *of* **Micah**, even if at times falling short—as sometimes you indeed shall—I, and more important, God, will be fully confident with your soul's development."

Pascale never forgot the advice.

"Nor" Richard added, "will I ever forget receiving the immense honor providing you counsel! Now go forth, create! Give abundant witness to God's loving glory"

THE SISTERHOOD

....

$\mathcal{B}$esides her brother, Véronique also introduced Pascale to the nuns operating the nursery school. This pretty, energetic duo, each in her mid-twenties, were inseparable girlish-friends, indivisible, graciously-feminine buddies. Always seen at church wearing a similar long black habit and white wimple, *Crucifix* and *Rosary* beads at slender waist, many thought them to be identical twins. Even their melodic voices, refined physical comportment were alike. Since the two were first assigned to the parish eighteen months ago, most people instinctively described these distinct individuals as if a single unit like: Ferdinand and Isabella, Lewis and Clark, Sacco and Vanzetti, the Rosenbergs. Already intimate before they taking Vows together, each nun, occasionally set aside best friend's adopted religious name to call her by the one she born. Sister Claire—christened Mary Preston, was British. Sister Genevieve—Leopoldine Fauré—French, came from Rouen.

The former, was the *intellectual* of pair. The latter, eagerly deferred to—"Sister Claire's better judgment;" "Sister Claire's always so insightful explanations;" or, on, occasion, to—"Mary's closer-understanding of the world and how it works." Sister Genevieve immensely loved watching friend expound on an entire series of complex, weighty matters. Each time people praised Sister Claire for choosing to dedicate all her worldly talents to the service of God, more reticent comrade instantly smiled with deep rightful pride, heartfelt just sense of personal accomplishment. In a large scrapbook, Sister Genevieve meticulously collected all the articles and photographs chronicling Sister Claire's exploits not infrequently appearing in major European newspapers, magazines, journals. Shy, retiring, Sister Genevieve to any casual acquaintance, sought nothing else in life than playing unobtrusive *Second Fiddle.*

After closer examination, however, upon noticing—Sister Claire immediately clutch Sister Genevieve's arm tight whenever her companion remarked well of Brit's learned erudition, latest perceptive analysis of critical events; Sister Claire often rub her needy *intellectual*-head against loyal ally's protective, ever-sympathetic shoulder; she, gaze long and humbly into Sister Genevieve's eyes like a child believing no greater honor exists than receiving a grownup's approval—it became apparent meek sidekick was in fact unquestionably the dominant member of this close, unique and mutually-fruitful personal relationship.

"My teacher is so-so wise!" pledged Sister Claire. "She's so-so-wise! I'd be lost without her help! Without Leopoldine, I wouldn't have the remotest conception of what to do with myself! Anything of significance I'll ever achieve I owe entirely to the guidance of Leopoldine—I mean *Sister Genevieve.*"

"I simply suggest the path to follow" insisted her comrade, modestly.

If only a decade older, Véronique still possessed for the sisters a maternal affection. She took every opportunity to hold them close, shower each with kisses, provide each with encouraging, well-meant if unsolicited "grownup's advice." Sister Claire and Sister Genevieve were to Véronique: *My Girls, My Sweeties,* or *My Dears.* Rather than offended at what might easily be misinterpreted as condescension, the nuns understood their friend was motivated by love and pretended not noticing the goodhearted-eccentricity.

"My Girls are quite exceptional kids" proudly explained Véronique to Pascale. "Like Richard, they're social activists." Gesturing toward the church office biddies down the way, she continued: "Some Old Farts—pardon, my unladylike language—Mature Females–don't approve of My *Dears.* They believe nuns should only pray, rattle-off liturgy, choke on incense, or, talk a confessor's ear-off about once chewing bubblegum during Retreat or getting their hands on an issue of *Vogue.*"

"Personally" she added, "I'm most impressed with of my two noble *Dears*. At least once a month you'll see both their names printed in the newspapers, each shown on television, discussed on the radio. Not simply by *AFP* but also *AP, BBC, Reuters*! The Sweeties joined a religious Order permitting them to *Give Witness* to their deep devotion to Christ. The form of *Witness* they seek can only be achieved through embracing this fallen, troubled but God-created world. Not through fleeing it! When you've become my two Dears' mascot, as I've no doubt their mascot you soon will become Marie, you'll discover Sister Claire, Sister Genevieve aren't at all unlike yourself!"

Just as the proprietress *of La Nouvelle Heloise* fervently hoped, her two noble *Dears* soon acquired a deep affection for this unusual exile from the Middle East; they also speedily gained a keen appreciation for the orphan's artistic gift.

"Listen my girls!" Véronique instructed Sister Claire and Sister Genevieve motherly, after mutual protégée was beyond hearing-range. "Our Little Marie possesses an even more remarkable quality! Not only is she on the path to becoming a splendid artist, she's also capable of becoming a great artist for our faith! I therefore urge you to do all humanly-possible assisting me providing our *Timid Mouse* emotional support and spiritual encouragement. We Christian ladies must do all we can to nourish this second, even more admirable quality in the child. If she's given the right degree of navigation, treated with the proper loving-firmness, Cherie will become another Giotto! She'll become another Giotto celebrated down the ages! Just like Giotto, she'll become a great artist for our faith!"

Each of the two nuns was easily mistaken as Pascale's sibling. So often were the girls fondly-united, the neighborhood assumed the trio were closely-related. Pascale, others thought, was the youngest of a devout, colonial family's three daughters, she soon following her older siblings' *Vocation*. The friends wasted no time adopting the roles believed of them. Sister Claire, Sister Genevieve—shielding, protective, ever-conscious they invested with responsibility for baby-of-the-family's welfare, guidance. Pascale—loyal, trusting, she intrinsically offering her wise guardians immense deference. Strong mutual-affection, shared-faith, a firm sense of common purpose, characterized the trio's relations--+-hip throughout.

I

Every-so-often, persons from small provincial towns, rural farming communities curtseyed to Sister Claire, addressing her as *Madame La Duchesse.* One elderly woman, falling to knees, kissed the young religious' hand. If she acknowledging each demonstration of sincere, humble respect with incomparable grace, their receipt also made the former-Mary Preston uncomfortable.

As her unaffected, graceful comportment might indicate, this young lady really was a duchess. Although British, she spoke French as if it her first language. Roman Catholicism didn't vanish from England with the *Reformation.* Nor did its surviving adherents consist solely of unmarried gentlemen-of-leisure, neoconservatives, erstwhile *Flower-Children,* or *High Church* Anglican converts. Several centuries of sometimes bitter legal, political and social discrimination rather than weaken, served only to strengthen this minority's spiritual beliefs, sense of common identity.

Mary Preston was a questing soul long before the fiery-redhead took holy Orders in a foreign land. As far back as memory served, she could like Wordsworth distinctly "hear the still sad music of humanity." During course of her life, she was to experience ever-increasing mental and physical pain resulting from both what she considered her insufficient effort to relieve the world's misery and nagging sense she was herself in part responsible.

It wasn't enough regretting one's sins, Mary believed. It was necessary atoning for them, experiencing some of the same sorrow one's personal misdeeds created for the lives of others. Being told she wasn't required judging her conduct by moral, spiritual or intellectual standards far beyond ability to achieve, didn't dissuade her conviction. Just as weakness is no excuse for sin, the girl insisted, neither is it one for neglecting to make at least an honest attempt to atone for those wrongs.

The redhead was prepared to suffer, even eager. Eager making recompense for all the harm she brought the world, either directly or indirectly. She wasn't frightened, possessed no second thoughts, no secret misgivings. None! She realized that while a terrible sinner, she was definitely no "shameless coward."

Mary Alice Frances Caroline Preston became—*Her Grace, the 23rd Duchess of Airandel* at age just four when her parents and brother were killed in a plane crash. Of them, she retained just the vaguest, most fragmentary recollections. As the previous-Duke of Airandel's only surviving offspring, Mary was the first female reigning-holder of the title since *The Wars of the Roses.*

Aware she was only an *accidental*-duchess, Mary knew too her vast wealth, sprawling real estate holdings, social influence and enjoyment of class privilege, were hers simply because random chance found her born into the aristocracy not the poor. Just through blind luck, was she clothed, fed and grandly sheltered while billions of other souls were naked, hungry and homeless, or she loved while they, scorned. Mary did nothing to earn her better luck. She was intrinsically no better a human being, she was sure, than billions of others on the planet. Many of whom, she was convinced, were far her moral and intellectual superiors and conducting struggling lives infinitely more worthwhile than the Duchess's idle, pampered own.

Mary felt increasingly the aristocracy was no more than a political, social and economic parasite. Once, performing invaluable service to creating the very best of English history, art, literature, science and culture, its positive role was exhausted with Churchill. Today, intellectually and morally-enfeebled if no less self-interested and grasping, the aristocracy continued in existence only as an obstacle to establishing a more just, benevolent and egalitarian Britain.

Despite harsh criticism of the aristocracy, Mary understood that as Duchess of Airandel, she was also the wealthiest representative of this privileged, exclusive milieu. From an early age she couldn't but feel a degree personally responsible for much of the same social inequality she condemned. Few casual acquaintances in Paris like Véronique ever imagined the apparently sweet, pious, ever-upbeat young nun from England harbored such brooding thoughts, troubled unfulfilled longings.

So how was Mary to atone for her sins, make recompense for the wrongs she brought the world? She'd been looking for the answer since still sucking her thumb.

At age six, she renounced sugar on being told it unavailable to conscripted peasant troops under fire, renounced knee-socks thinking poor girls owned none.

At seven, the girl ran-away from home seeking martyrdom in a glorious cause.

At eight, she became a labor union organizer and advocate for just wages, shorter working hours and safety in the workplace.

At nine, lifted atop wooden barrel to be visible above the rostrum, Mary earnestly addressed a bemused but encouraging crowd of striking Welsh coal miners. "The moment is arriving, comrades, perhaps sooner than we dare imagine—*For the day of the Lord will come like a thief in the night*" piped the miniature champion of the people, long fiery-red hair in braids tied with big ribbons, she wearing a silk blouse, tartan skirt, white bobby-socks and red buckled flat shoes. "*When the first shall be last and the last shall be first*! The unregulated-derivatives moneychangers shall be cast from the modern temple! People will learn not to put their trust in billionaire princes! When once more Pharaoh's Wall Street and City of London chariots will be consumed in the sea! Caesar and all his Offshore Bank, non-unionized, pharmaceutical industry, gouging health insurance legions will be wiped away! *Love of money is the root of all evil*! *The meek*, well, maybe not exactly the meek *will inherit the earth*. Remember: *For though the Lord is high He regards the lowly but the haughty He knows from afar*!"

"The age of righteous is at-hand!" she further chirped, hair in face. "Our cause is a Pillar of Fire! Our cause isn't merely the burning bush! It is *the bush that burned but was not consumed*! The voice from atop Sinai! The cause manifesting, the voice trumpeting the truth since before all time began! Our holy cause, that holy word is—*Socialism*!"

"I am a socialist!" many in Mary's rarefied, Eton-Harrow circle were aghast she declaring on front page of next morning's Tory newspaper.

"I'm a socialist because Christ is a socialist! He says Love your Neighbor. Socialism tells us to love our neighbor, to feed the hungry, clothe the naked, comfort the lonely, shelter the dispossessed! Sound familiar my, comrades? So, it should! It's no coincidence! It's easier for a camel to pass through the eye of a needle than for a rich man to enter the kingdom of Heaven—you cannot love both God and mammon! Our Lord died for the salvation of the working class! For your salvation, my comrades! Wasn't he a carpenter! Christ died for His comrades, the workers! Christ suffered at the hands of the capitalist and landowner and militarist and collaborator and bureaucratic oppressors!—Yet just as He rose on the third day into eternal glory, so too through His Socialism, the workers shall find salvation, cast off their chains and achieve eternal glory! *Be not afraid*! We're not like John: but a voice crying in the wilderness. The workers are not alone! Christ is with them! Remember what He says: *Wherever two or three are gathered in my name so there am I—yea until the end of the age!*"

"Christianity and Socialism are one!" another Tory newspaper recorded the revolutionary in jumper, pigtails, frilly blouse and mary-janes informing her stodgy, adult colleagues in the House of Lords. "It's the duty of Christians to go forth and spread *The Good News* to all the kingdoms and principalities of the earth! Be not afraid! Spread *The Good News*! So that it's learned, spoken, praised in every tongue and voice in every culture, on every hill and in valley, seashore and landlocked province! Proclaim that we are all brothers and sisters in Christ and thus all brothers and sisters in Socialism! Christ calls us t0o create a fair, just and equitable society under His name! Under the name of Christ is under the name of Socialism! Under the name of Socialism is under the name of Christ! *Know the Truth and the Truth will set you free!*"

Often, the prophetess of *True Socialism* tried joining Roman Catholic missionary organizations, only to be repeatedly, if politely, rejected. "The Duchess of Airandel possesses far more than enough faith in Christ, devotion to our common cause, physical energy and undoubted love for her fellow man to work for this foundation," she was informed on one of successive instances. "Unfortunately, Her Grace's personal interpretation of the Gospel and of sacred doctrine are currently at too decided variance with that of official Vatican policy for her application to be accepted. Has Her Grace considered charity work?"

No, she didn't *grow-out-of-it*. Quite, the reverse! Passage of time, adult experience, provided nuance to her original message. Still, the words Mary piped at age nine were an unpolished description of convictions motivating an entire lifetime. Puberty—as her family hoped and generally assumed, failed diverting the girl's attention. The few self-absorbed, unintellectual, affected upper class-dandies crossing her teenage path offered no evidence boys worth serious investigation. As occurs for the great majority of cerebral adolescent females, Mary wasn't popular.

"Girls aren't smart or assertive"—proclaims timeless perceived-wisdom. Yet any boy striking-up acquaintance with the little Duchess of Airandel invariably discovered she was brighter, she, always the partner setting the subject of conversation, she, making all the pair's decisions. Rather than satisfied just holding hands or kissing, Mary also wanted to discuss J.S. Mill's essay *On Liberty,* Marx and Engels' *Communist Manifesto, The Secret Diary of Harold Ickes,* or, traveling on The Sealed Train to the Finland Station. She owned a tom and she-cat named Tristan and Iseult. Her favorite novels were *Tess of the d'Urbervilles, Buddenbrooks* and *The Brothers Karamazov;* favorite movies: *Andrei Rublev, The Sorrow and the Pity, The Grand Illusion.*

Some boys found this brainy, assertive Redhead positively frightening, scampering from the room or hall as soon as she made poised, delicate, intimidating entry. In their eyes, Mary was member of an entirely different animal species: a ferocious, insatiably-hungry dragoness consuming in single, swift gulp all males foolish enough to approach.

"Imagine being married to one of those weaklings!" she confided to Sister Genevieve. "A lifetime of yammering mindless chit-chat at garden parties, constantly *Playing Dumb* so as not embarrass my ignoramus husband! Me, forced to listen to his endless stories about Cricket, foxhunting, 'the club.' Humiliated in all the right-wing tabloids when 'Lord Bildgewater' gets his midlife-crisis and abandons me and my children for some cheap, dark-roots gold-digger less than half his age! No thanks! If I ever submit to the authority of a man, he must be one greater than myself." Such a figure, Mary discovered, wasn't to be found in this world.

Taking the advice of missionary organizations, Mary involved herself in charity work. Civil rights; labor unions; political prisoners; feminism; orphans; arms control; famine relief; refugees; floods; the blind, handicapped; Apartheid; drug rehabilitation; Tibet; free press; human trafficking; homelessness; illiteracy; autism; global warming; *Holocaust* memorials; reforestation; vocational schools; fair housing; clean air, clean water; libraries; museums; child abuse; healthcare; battered-wives—numbered among the issues adolescent Duchess of Airandel either championed or campaigned against with the same evangelical fervor voiced at age nine. Success in each endeavor represented a further victory for *True Socialism*. "All the fever of the world" she remembered from Wordsworth's *Tintern Abbey*, "has hung upon the beatings of my heart."

The generous donations Mary provided might be far more effectively spent, argued some, if concentrated on a few causes rather than spread so wide. But there was never a single noble, non-blatantly-partisan cause she felt in good conscience might be denied her largesse. Wealth, she acquired not by hard work but mere accident of birth.

If never abandoning a happy, girlish outward demeanor, Mary was in fact burdened with an ever-mounting sense of guilt. Try as might, she could never give but a fraction of the donations she wished. Each time after delivering a rousing speech on a strike picket-line, at a union rally, a left-wing civic organization, antiwar protest or charity dinner and soon hearing the delighted crowd reward her with loud cheers, the little Duchess couldn't but feel the approval undeserved. She couldn't avoid on occasion secretly suspecting herself a fraud, a charlatan. She knew she never personally suffered poverty or injustice or discrimination.

For centuries, most members of the English landholding aristocracy considered occupying money-making professions or engaging directly in finance, commerce, beneath their collective dignity. "*Real* gentlemen, *real* ladies," so, it was long argued, "don't work, or soil their hands with trade." Personal wealth, if not inherited or acquired through marriage, peers and peeresses largely accumulated from collecting rent from tenants and charging market fees on their sprawling, sometimes over one-hundred-and-twenty-thousand acre private country estates. By the mid-Twentieth Century, however, ignoring economic progress left nearly all these titled families of leisure in tremendous debt. Some totally bankrupt, their former princely homes and sprawling estates either managed by *The National Trust* or sold to *Pop* Singers, Sports Stars, nouveau-riche businessmen. A few more enterprising lords and ladies survived through industrial farming, opening family domains to paying tourists; renting palaces, castles to movie and television film-makers.

The Dukes of Airandel in contrast, never experienced the slightest class-engendered aversion to active participation in business. Consisting of—*Wall Street, City of London,* Frankfurt and Tokyo stock investments; banking shares; South African diamonds; petroleum; electronics, computers; television and radio stations; commercial real estate; shipping; pharmaceuticals; cosmetics—*Preston Holding Company Ltd.* if deemed "gauche," "common," by aristocrats born in homes now owned by Donald Trump, Madonna, or Boy George, was doing "bloody fine today, thank-you very much!" Tight legal restrictions on how this steadily-growing fortune could be disposed prevented Mary ever giving sway more than fraction. For a *True Socialist,* it was a terrible moral dilemma.

What was she to do? Renounce title? That wasn't a solution. The same strict legal restrictions imposed on her authority over the Preston fortune would apply equally to whichever relative succeeded as leader of family. Renouncing title, the Duchess suspected in her idealistic, young, troubled heart-of-hearts, was also an act of grave cowardice. If she truly wished to atone, she must embrace not flee responsibility. Unable returning all the money and land the Duchess believed her family stole from the working class, she might yet attain forgiveness through sharing the workers' own difficult, underprivileged and often very painful daily existence. By freely abandoning an easy, pampered life on vast rural estates and in massive London *t*ownhouses to live instead among the poor, she could finally give legitimacy to all her frequent *Milady* speeches, show her charitable donations were not simply self-promotion.

Transferring daily-management of all business and legal affairs to her two most trusted, beloved relatives: Uncle and Auntie who raised, cherished their niece as if own child following her parents' death, Mary of the Airandels ventured out into the world. Not as a famous aristocrat this time, but as just another member of the faceless, unhappy multitude.

It proved a far more arduous journey than *Miss Evans* imagined. *To the Manor Born*—from infancy she addressed as *Milady;* each cap instantly doffed, head deferentially bowed, all knees swift bent whenever little mistress approached; a host of servants employed to assure Her Grace need never even contemplate physical exertion; exceptionally intelligent, well read but never formally educated—she found the expedition trying from start. No degree of amateur book-reading, unrestrained girlish-enthusiasm, unadulterated-goodwill and selfless sense-of-purpose—could make up for insufficient strength, ill-preparedness, lack of personal familiarity with task at hand.

Miss Evans first tried being a farmhand. Only soon: to slip in the pigsty and sink in two feet of mud; be chased-off by roosters; allow the rabbits escape; drive tractor into tree.

Joining a fishing trawler, *Miss Evans:* got seasick; entangled in a huge net; fell overboard and nearly drowned; proved too squeamish gutting the catch.

Unionized miners and dock-workers currently out on strike, she didn't intend exchanging her role as Duchess for that of *Scab.*

On a construction sight, she couldn't learn to operate a forklift and was neither strong nor big enough to use a jackhammer.

Selling tickets on a city bus, the girl often got the change confused and was several times groped.

The assembly-line job she imagined taking after reading *Factory Journal* by Simone Weil, was now replaced by robot.

As waitress in a fast-food joint, *Miss Evans* was often too slow; dropped trays; mixed-up orders.

Next, the girl was fired from a cannery after reporting to the foreman seeing a human finger packed with sardines.

She couldn't type fast enough to be a secretary.

After turning down two admittedly-flattering offers to be a gentleman's *escort,* she at last obtained steady employment as salesgirl at a department store in the cosmetics section.

Whether in city or countryside, *Miss Evans* insisted sleeping in a small, poorly-lit single room without central heating. Against her strenuous insistence it come out of own meager income, the rent was always paid by Uncle and Auntie. Her guardians also frequently delivered their surrogate-child extra supplies of food and warm clothing. Auntie, an Iranian, visited week lyto cook her step-daughter Persian delicacies "and make sure my *Noble Sweetheart* is wearing a proper dress, isn't turning yellow from jaundice or being eaten by rats."

Frequently the real identity of *Miss Evans* was discovered,. This, followed by her receipt of repeated bows, deep curtseys and heartfelt-apologies. "Don't let her carry that box, she's a Duchess!" "Open the door for her, she's a Duchess!" "Help her with her coat, she's a Duchess!" "Get out of that chair at once for your *Better*!" Having embarked on a pilgrimage to humbly, contritely repay the great debts she believed she owed them, Mary found British workers more class-conscious than the aristocracy. Instead of obtaining the workers' forgiveness, they all too often pleaded to receive hers. "We're so thankful for all you try to do for us, Milady. We should show Milady far more respect."

Then, seeming by pure chance in London one afternoon while resting atop tree-shaded wooden bench in *Regent's Park,* discouraged-*Miss Evans* struck-up a conversation with a French girl own age. Equally pretty and nicely proportioned in delicate feminine body, Leopoldine Fauré was the daughter of a working class family in Rouen. Currently, she was employed in England as a nanny. Like *Miss Evans,* her new acquaintance was the "bookish," "scholarly," "brainy," "too-smart-for-us" kind of girl who regularly frightens-off boys. The pair of gifted teenagers shared too a deep love for *Nineteenth Century* literature, history and philosophy. In addition, both were devout Roman Catholics. Each, wishing she give witness to her faith through a life of social activism. When *Miss Evans* described herself as a *True Socialist*, her friend was immediately intrigued.

"Yes, that's what I am too Mary, a, *True Socialist!*" exclaimed Mlle. Fauré, grateful to at last be provided a proper description of her own as yet unnamed religious-political worldview. "Perhaps it's not by accident we've met!"

"Perhaps not, Leopoldine!"

These chance acquaintances were soon inseparable confidantes. If the two virgins often physically-divided because of Leopoldine's heavy responsibilities as a nanny, the pair, in a far deeper, truer sense, were never parted. On Leopoldine's free Saturdays, she and Mary spent all day together. These faithful, unmeddled-with comrades spending each treasured occasion, morning till night, passionately debating not merely all the major problems besetting the world but also seeking to devise practical solutions.

When at last *Miss Evans* confided her true identity, Mlle. Fauré wasn't surprised.

"Yes, Mary. You're the 'radical' Duchess of Airandel. I knew all along."

"You did Leopoldine?"

"Indeed, Mary, I knew it all along."

"And you pretended not?"

"I understood you wished keeping it hidden for a time."

"You did, Leopoldine?"

"Yes, Mary. I understood you've always wanted to live and struggle as Christ did among the workers. However, you weren't completely sure if the workers would freely, willingly, accept you among them. If the time arrived when you sensed receiving our acceptance though, you'd reveal us your true name. I realized all along but didn't wish embarrassing or making you feel small or weak."

"Of course, Mary" added Leopoldine. "I've never once considered my unusual friend to be either *small* or *weak!*"

"Bless you!" cried the incognito-Duchess, touched. "Bless you!"

The girls pecked cheeks, pressed hands.

"Bless you, Leopoldine!" repeated the former-*Miss Evans*, no less touched; thankful tears racing. "You're someone special, someone awesome, Leopoldine!"

"I'm only trying to be a good, loyal friend, Mary."

"Well, you're my *good, good, loyal, loyal* —*my* wisest, dearest-friend forever and forever more! —And them some, too!"

A few weeks later, Leopoldine announced she was returning to France to enter a religious community. "It's not one of those anti-Semitic, rattle-off prayers, feel guilty, talk a Confessor's ear-off about silly foibles–kind of women's Orders, Mary" Leopoldine explained. "No. The Benedictines allowed one of their members, a girl not much older than we are named Sister Jeanne Navarro, to spread their reformist message beyond the convent. Sister Jeanne wants to establish a group enabling socially-conscious girls like us can employ our faith to truly leave a deep, lasting and positive mark on the wider, secular world."

"Fascinating, Leopoldine. I'm sure it's an Order just right for a person like you."

After several days intense thought, Mary decided asking if it was at all possible she might come along. While the "Red Virgin" was easily-recognized in the *UK*–she a frequent subject of unkind jokes; her "Victorian eccentric," "bluestocking," "pious do-gooder" activities often parodied on late night television–the duchess was still relatively-unknown on the Continent. Here at last was the chance she long sought. Unable returning all the money and land Mary believed her family stole, she could at least seek forgiveness through sharing the workers' sad, humble lives, experience the same injustices and prejudice she felt her wealthy upper class inflicted for centuries. And to give such atonement without fearing intervention by the privileges she obtained only through accident of birth.

"Would you like accompanying me, Mary?" inquired Leopoldine enthusiastically even before her friend asked permission. "Would you like coming with me? It'll be awesome if we can give our lives to Christ together!"

"Yes, awesome! I'll be most honored to come with you Leopoldine! That sounds *really* awesome! We'll give our lives to Christ *together!*"

"I'll lead you, Mary."

"Yes, you lead me."

So, it was to this controversial, recently established sisterhood rather than an old, historic one with name familiar to most readers, that Pascale's two new friends devoted their collective, engaged lives.

EXILE

....

$\mathcal{R}$equired no urging, Pascale volunteered her immense teenage-enthusiasm to redecorating the nine-hundred-and-fifty-year-old Romanesque/Gothic church on the Seine's Left Bank. The opportunity provided a wide and essentially independent chance to demonstrate her great artistic talent.

Besides the creatrix of engravings rivaling any by Durer, Daumier, Goya and Hogarth—her workshop with all its tools reconstituted in the hotel basement by Véronique and Richard—the siblings' new ward possessed an even more remarkable ability. That, for painting murals on wet plaster—fresco.

These activities too, offered much-needed mental diversion. In spite of the passage of months and the winning of cherished new intimacies, Pascale could never forget how she found herself a resident of Paris. The experience of being abruptly marooned so far from home led her to suffer periods of the deepest sorrow and the blackest, almost physically-painful depression. Activities, at the parish proved essential to reviving her youthful spirits.

These artistic projects were also more than a small degree critical to saving Pascale's life. A life, the world would be greatly deprived without.

Twice, during these first months of exile, she tried committing suicide.

Mournful thoughts of home compounded with survivor-guilt and sense of shame at being so long passively ignorant of the larger world, grew so strong Pascale again developed a nervous twitch in left cheek. Her speech impediment returned. It became impossible to converse effectively with strangers on the telephone, give geographical directions to strangers on the street. She was plagued by headaches which pain relievers did nothing to alleviate. Worst of all, was insomnia. Often, she only fell asleep near dawn through sheer exhaustion.

Yet when blessed unconsciousness arrived, it often brought little rest. For most of the following day, Pascale staggered about the hotel, drowsy. Too many times when illusive, fitful sleep came at last, it brought a familiar recurring nightmare as if in punishment for rest being momentarily captured at all.

No sooner was Pascale at last liberated from her daytime worries than she frequently dreamed vividly—sometimes the images in color—of being on the debarkation ramp for the cattle cars at Auschwitz-Birkenau. At least twice each grim succeeding week, she saw herself amidst the gray fog created by the smoke belching twenty-four hours a day from the crematoria. She saw the residue of burnt human flesh come down upon the heads of both murderers and next set of victims like gentle snowflakes.

"Come with me, you mangy kike, dirty little Jew-bitch *WOG*! I'm taking you straight to the showers where all chopped-cock, Christ-killer vermin belong!" demanded in each all-too-real-nightmare the same sweaty, pockmark-faced, pederast *SS* officer in jodhpurs and cavalry boots. Cracking his whip, he shouted to be heard over the fierce, snarling Alsatian, its fangs biting Pascale's leg. Wide grin invariably on tormentor's ugly face, the *SS* officer would take Pascale by neck, shaking her fiercely. Making a sadistic laugh he would then drag her off screaming helplessly to the gas chamber, ferocious Alsatian still biting girl's leg. "Come with me devious, grasping, unsanitary *Yid*! it's time for your *Final Solution.* I'm taking you straight to the showers! I know you'll make me a fine lampshade! You'll make me excellent false teeth, wallpaper, dog food! Now make it snappy devious-Yid! Little dirty Jew-bitch WOG! You don't want to keep the gas chamber waiting! I'm getting you and all your money-grubbing kind exterminated! *Heil Hitler!*"

Following each similar nightmare, Pascale awoke terrified, screaming.

Primal fear raced from head to toes, seizing mind, heart and intestines.

Her entire body was drenched in cold sweat.

She soon reverted to sucking her thumb.

Like all European structures built without central heating, *La Nouvelle Heloise* was in winter, extremely cold. The violent shaking of Pascale's limbs ripped-off all the sheets and blankets, hurling them half-way across the substantially-sized bedroom. On these dreadful recurrent nights, the Persian cats "Scheherazade" and "Esther," always fondly nestled up against their mistress when she went to bed, shrieked in all feline terror and scampered, off. Their hasty flight also usually left painful claw marks on Pascale's soft skin. So loud were her cries she often woke many of the pension's guests who promptly trundled downstairs in bathrobes to see if a bloody crime was committed. Mme. Castellane, barefoot, wrapped in long kimono, baby lotion on face, would need to assure them it was only her emotional-protégée's recurring nightmare.

When suffering unpleasant dreams back home and desperate for adult reassurance, Pascale could only return to sleep after climbing into bed with Father. Now in Paris, she required similar intimate, physical comfort. She needed to climb into another adult's divan. Father now gone, Pascale clutched a warm, soft, maternal body tight, losing her fears listening to Mme. Castellane's gentle, soothing, protective words. Finally she drifted again into peaceful unconsciousness when feeling the steady, confident, ever-present motion of the Kindly Lady's lungs and heart. The next night Scheherazade and Esther remained fondly nestled up against their mistress's side on her own bed until the morning.

Unfortunately, this was always only a temporary reprieve. Just a few nights later, the human residue belching from the Auschwitz crematoria once more covered Pascale like gentle snowflakes. The same sweaty, pederast-*SS* officer with whip and snarling Alsatian would reappear to drag "the dirty little Jew-bitch WOG" off to the gas chamber so she could become a lampshade, false teeth, wallpaper or dog-food.

Only one logical means appeared existing, to be free of such ever-increasing mental, physical pain. A burden, anguish often felt both day and night.

And what of God, once so critical, so immediate a factor in Pascale's life? Where now for her was, God? Offering as much tangible aid and comfort as provided others with infinitely greater need of His intervention.

Since earliest childhood she delivering fervent daily prayers to God, as long as memory served she trusting unquestioningly in God's protection and guidance, Pascale came sincerely to believe the pair established a warm, personal relationship. On occasion, dare it be said, the two were even lovers. Now, just at the time Pascale required the benefit of this unique, intimacy, special companionship most, God abruptly turned away. Capriciously abandoned His loyal, adoring partner. Now, like a spoiled child or a Louis XIV demanding of constant attention, effusive adulation, God seemed resentful of any suggestion He might possess responsibility to offer affection, tenderness, in return.

Pascale, frantic, looked and looked for her lover.

Desperately, she searched and searched.

But nowhere was her lover to be seen.

Pascale felt personally deceived.

"You betrayed me, God!" she shouted. "You deserted me!"

Not at all the tender, shepherding, paternal Being written of in the 23rd Psalm and New Testament, celebrated in the music of Bach and Handel, or depicted on the *Sistine Chapel* and in Italian Medieval *Primitives,* God, so Pascale concluded, was in fact quite the reverse. Instead of closely involved in the world, often desirous of direct engagement in the affairs of all His struggling creatures, God was for even devoted believers, forever, infinitely, beyond remotest contact.

Aloof, detached, God, concluded Pascale, loves His faithful no more than hates them. God no more wishes relieving the suffering of good people than preventing the crimes of scoundrels. *He*—was in fact just literary convention. A better designation of this cold, unreachable deity encountered only as a law of Physics is—*It.*

85

As for immortality, Pascale never believed in this. "One existence is quite enough for me!" she often said. "If permitted living it to the full, I'm quite satisfied with just one! 'Life after Death' is only something for Mamas to tell children when they're scared going to sleep at night. 'Life after Death' is only something to make people become suicide-bombers. I'm not scared of dying. What I *am* scared of is being forgotten! What I *am* cared of is not doing something important."

"God doesn't give-a-shit what happens to me!" commented Pascale angrily, upon opening bottle of sleeping pills, she previously swallowed an entire *fifth* of vodka. "God didn't give-a-damn about Auschwitz and Treblinka and Sobibor and the Warsaw ghetto and Babi Yar! God didn't give-a-damn what happened to six million Jews in the *Holocaust*!"

"God didn't give-a-shit when *SS* guards at Auschwitz yanked babies out of mamas' arms and smashed their babies' heads against the wall!" she cried. "Hitler was permitted coming closer to achieving his ambitions than those he murdered! God didn't give a shit for all the people who prayed to Him in the gas chamber!"

"God cares for the Jews no more than He condemns the Nazis! If God doesn't give-a-*god*damn what happened to a great person like Anne Frank, sees, no difference between Anne Frank and Dr. Mengele, then God clearly doesn't give a *god*damn, care a *god*damn about little me! If that son-of-a-bitch God doesn't want to assist human beings when they love Him, need Him most, He's got no-fucking-business judging the actions human beings take to make up for fucking-God's snotty lack of help! Nor can fucking-God escape bearing the responsibility for what happens when He abandons us! Fuck-you God!"

"God, you're one real, uncaring, conceited son-of-a-bitch!" cursed Pascale after gulping down the whole one-hundred-pill bottle of sleeping pills. "I hate this world you've created and I'm going to work to be free from it and you as fast as I can! *Arbeit Macht Frei*!"

The sleeping pills and vodka only made Pascale lose consciousness, vomit, suffer a violent seizure and be rushed to the hospital. In the emergency room, her stomach was pumped, she received a blood transfusion and stitches to close the nasty gash in her scalp made by hitting her head against pipes during seizure.

Véronique was unable to accompany in the ambulance. Thinking devoted protégée was dead, she became hysterical, believing herself entirely to blame. Only the stronger male guests could prevent the proprietress of *La Nouvelle Heloise* hurting herself with a butcher knife. Swiftly summoned from his church in capacity as physician, Richard at last calmed his sister by injecting her with strong sedative.

When she at last returning from the hospital, Pascale immediately received a spanking over Véronique's knee and was locked in a dark, damp basement closet for a day. Drug cabinet henceforth locked, the girl was never again permitted independent access to the medicine supply.

On her second, near-fatal suicide attempt a month later, Pascale leaped from the Pont Neuf into the murky Seine. "God, I hate you!" she screamed from atop the stone balustrade. "I want no more of your damned, awful, stupid, damn world!"

"God!" she called-out, jumping, "I hate you six-million-times-over!"

Were, it not for chance appearance of a speedboat and its quick-thinking passengers' ability to fish the girl out of the water, she would certainly have drowned.

"Leave me alone! Leave me alone!" shouted Pascale angrily on being unwillingly pulled aboard the speedboat. "I want to die! I don't want to be in this world anymore! I want out of it!"

All identification papers lost in the grimy drink, she kicking-and-screaming, uncooperative with both rescuers on river and doctors at *Hotel de Dieu* hospital—Pascale was assumed a deranged homeless person. From the girl's complexion, sudden inability speaking French, police and emigration officials judged her an illegal alien. They guessed Pascale was either a Gypsy, Cypriot, a Kurd or Iranian. She was confined to the *Hotel de Dieu* psycho ward while the Ministry of Interior prepared her deportation to parts as yet not precisely known. Heavily doped-up with medication, her memory of these events was vague at best. One incident of confinement Pascale did clearly recollect. It was of meeting the director of the psycho ward. With his martinet gestures and beady eyes behind wire spectacles, she mistook the doctor for Heinrich Himmler.

"Help, help, it's the *SS,* the *SS!*" the girl shrieked. "They're taking me to the gas chamber! I'm going to turned into a lampshade!"

An entire fortnight lapsed before Richard managed discovering Pascale's whereabouts. Yet the saga wasn't over. An additional two weeks passed with she doped-up in the *Hotel de Dieu* psycho ward among real crazies. Only after the Castellanes initiated a highly-publicized law suit against the government and Cardinal Casimir Blanchard, Archbishop of Paris, advocated Pascale's case in a homily given at Notre Dame did, the Ministry of the Interior at last relent. She was released into Richard and his sister's custody. On condition, however, the Castellanes first accept full legal responsibility for the girl, keep her for a period under strict watch, schedule their charge weekly sessions with a hospital-affiliated psychiatrist.

I

SMACK

SMACK

SMACK

SMACK

SMACK

SMACK–on small teenage fanny.

Véronique was confident she possessed a far-speedier, infinitely less-expensive means of keeping Pascale's head on straight than any renowned *Dr. So-and-So*-psychiatrist. First, she delivered her worrisome potégée the severest spanking yet. Next, surrogate mother locked addled *Chere Petite* alone in the child's bedroom for three days deprived of both lunch and supper. All cords, coat-hangers and sharp objects in the chamber were previously either removed or secured out of mischievous occupant's four-foot-ten-inch reach. The sole reading material pesky inmate permitted was the autobiography of St. Therese of Lisieux. Each morning, for the rest of week, promptly at 6 AM, Pascale was given a bath in spine-cringing, teeth-chattering cold water.

Splish, splash, slosh, splash

"I know how making Child finally see the light!" reprimanded Véronique, she once more dunking wayward Pascale's head deep beneath icy, freezing water, scrubbing-down rebellious little ward until thick bar of soap completely dissolved. "You don't need a *shrink*! You don't need yammering-away for hours self-indulgently on a narcissistic couch! No! What you need is a short leash!—To be treated with discipline, resolve!—Be given a simple, distinct, uncompromising set of rules to obey—Instantly, without fail, you receiving firm smacks on little girl-fanny whenever daring to challenge those desiring nothing else in all God's creation than to love, protect and cherish you!"

Splish, splash, slosh, splash

"That father of yours spoiled-you-rotten!" insisted Véronique, again dunking confused, frightened Pascale gasping desperately for air, beneath freezing cold, soapy water. "It's now my responsibility getting Child into shape—**mind** as well as body!"

Splish, splash, slosh, splash

"Now down my brilliant, precious but so disobedient baby's hot-head, goes deservedly again under *cold* water!"

Splish, splash, slosh, splash

Just as Véronique expected, Pascale never attempted suicide again.

II

The troubled-girl soon discovered a less violent, more productive means of easing her sorrow. One, she could employ to provide Father, Pierrette, Francoise and Agnes a far nobler, lasting monument than any achieved through swallowing bottles of sleeping pills or leaping from bridges. Yet her anger at God, sense of God's personal betrayal, remained. Among the indications of her exceptional creative talent is the fact none of the paintings the artist produced on biblical subjects display any conflict with religion.

Pascale's sorrow was above all the sorrow of exile. The French capital was hardly a cultural wasteland, its inhabitants speakers of a strange, unintelligible, gibberish. Or, naked savages desirous of collecting the girl's shrunken head and eating her for lunch. Nor was *La Nouvelle Heloise a* prison and its affectionate, ladylike owner the cruel warden. All the, same, as magnificent as her new surroundings might be, Pascale didn't fully consider them home. *Home*—in, that unquestioned sense of personal-belonging, possessing all those irreplaceable endearing qualities—spiritual and material, the word H*ome* uniquely, similarly evokes in each individual human heart. Even so, the day when the life of this artist and the city of Paris were linked forever in both history and popular imagination, fast approached.

Pascale never ceased spiritually viewing *Home* as the land of her birth. Yet the unquestioning-affection, absolute-loyalty mere mention of its name once instantly summoned in mind and heart, was now fading. As time passed, if she continuing to regard her birthplace as the *Home* of her childhood, family, own ethnic group, ancient culture–Pascale increasingly looked to France as the *Home* of her expanding intellectual horizons, the *Home* of her greatest personal accomplishments, most rewarding friendships. Until death, she continued suffering (if in steadily-diminishing frequency) the same nightmare and near-physically painful grief only attention to art proved a viable means of relieving. Yet in future, Pascale's was a sadness of emotional loss, disabused religious faith, not one representing a desire to forsake life. The experience of abandonment and disabused religious faith, she realized, might even prove the inspiration for great art.

III

The nationalist junta seizing control of Pascale's homeland made available an entire archive of written material relating to the harsh domestic policies of the former regime. That these new leaders were themselves hardly guiltless of human rights abuse was no justification for even more authoritarian conduct in the past. Over a period of two weeks, many archival documents appeared verbatim in the French newspapers. Véronique subscribed to the Roman Catholic national daily *La Croix.* Her protégée followed the revelations closely; sometimes reading the same articles in the newspaper three, even four times a day. While fascinating study, it was also unsettling.

"Lord! Father certainly kept a lot from me, Mme. Castellane!" exclaimed *Chere Petite* one evening, upon reading today's edition of *La Croix*. Three of her latest magnificent engravings, newly framed, hung on the papered wall to left. The girl squirmed nervously in chair; crossed her bare legs opposite, then opposite again. Her pretty face exhibiting deep concern over what she'd just learned in the newspaper's foreign affairs section. It was a deep concern formed in no small measure by a sense of guilt, a feeling of personal shame at not becoming aware of the facts recounted in the article, long ago. "It's amazing how naïve I was before coming to France, Mme. Castellane."

"*Uninformed!*" swiftly, guardian corrected. "It's not *naïve* possessing certain rosy assumptions about the world if never shown evidence certain rosy assumptions are merely—rosy assumptions. Sweetheart wasn't naïve! Only—*uniformed*! There's a clear difference."

"If you say so, Mme. Castellane"

"Yes, I *say so!*"

"All these nasty things were going on in my own country, Mme. Castellane!" elaborated protégée, appalled by revelations read in *La Croix* about the authoritarian domestic policy long implemented by her native land's former government. One, which, like-it-or-not, as daughter of the Minister of Defense, engaged to the Premier, she too, was an ancillary member. "I didn't know any of this was happening! And right under my nose too! Well if I wasn't naïve, I was awesome, *really* awesome—uninformed!"

"You must read *this* Mme. Castellane!" urged Pascale, setting newspaper turned to the relevant page on benefactress's lap. Her right forefinger tapped urgently on the germane column.

"Yes, Sweetheart, I promise reading the article in a moment," assured Véronique. "First, sit-still like the good, obedient little creature I know you are and let me retie the splendid ribbon she selected for your marvelous long hair." The Kindly Lady retied the enormous red satin bow crowning her ward's jet-black mane. "*There!* It's magnificent!

91

Brilliant! That big red bow makes Child appear the perfect *Little Darling*!—Wait, stay there! I must record this for all ages to come!"

She stood up, left the room, soon returning with camera.

"Don't move Little Marie. Give me one of your precious smiles!"

Véronique enthusiastically took a dozen pictures with complicated Japanese camera. Taken indoors, they required flashbulbs.

"That giant red bow in my hair makes me look so terribly old-fashion!" mused Pascale, her eyes still adjusting to the recent glare of flashbulbs. "That giant bow makes me look like a doll. But if Mme. Castellane is so fond of making me look like a doll and means so well in doing so, I must get used to looking like a doll."

"Don't you so-enjoy that big bow, Little Marie? Aren't you so happy I decided you must wear that big red bow in your mane?"

"Oh yes indeed, Mme. Castellane!" replied protégée dutifully, forcing a wide grin. "I'm so happy and grateful you decided I must wear a big red bow in my hair! It's precisely what I always dreamed of!"

"Just as your guardian suspected."

"Indeed, Mme. Castellane. You always know what's best for me."

Unlike in your homeland" informed Véronique, "in France, ladies are permitted to vote. You'll be allowed too, when reaching age eighteen. Here, in France, when ladies learn of issues they find particularly troubling, ladies can do more than get upset. Ladies in France can do something practical about the issues troubling them!"

"You too" she guaranteed, kissing her protégée's right cheek. "One day Little Marie will demonstrate her sublime, heartfelt, personal convictions in a far larger theater of operation than this hotel. And when that day comes—maybe sooner than we know—Little Marie can depend on receiving her protector's support to-the-hilt!"

"Indeed, Mme. Castellane. When that day comes, maybe sooner than we think, I'll demonstrate my artistic talent in a larger theater of operation than *La Nouvelle Heloise*. And I can depend on receiving your support to the hilt!" Soon providing dutiful nuance: "As long of course, Mme. Castellane, as I don't stop attending Mass or become a Socialist."

"Yes Little Marie, unless you stop attending Mass, or, become a Socialist— although, even if that occurs, I'll daily pray you realize the error-of-your-ways and come back to God. As I've no doubt, Cherie soon will."

Véronique poured them *Russian Caravan* tea in Limoges cups.

"I promise, Mme. Castellane" assured surrogate-daughter "that if I become an activist of some kind, and it appears you're confident I'm going to become one, I'll still always attend Mass and I'll never become a Socialist!"

"No fear, Little Marie! You'll never stop attending Mass or become a Socialist."

"But please read this article in the newspaper I've shown you," reiterated Pascale. "It's about my birthplace and it's most disturbing, Mme. Castellane."

"Let me see it."

"Mme. Castellane?" queried Pascale uneasily after benefactress completed reading the *La Croix* article with keen interest. "I've got something I need to ask."

"Yes, Sweetheart"

"And please answer me truthfully, Mme. Castellane."

"I promise."

It was clear Véronique already knew the question to come.

"Mme. Castellane, you understand that my—"

"Yes, Cherie, I understand. Don't be frightened."

Véronique offered a warm, encouraging smile.

"You know, Mme. Castellane" resumed Pascale, reassured but still anxious, "my family supported the former regime. In fact, my family did more than simply support that former regime. Father, *my* father, was a field marshal. He was the chief of staff of my country's army and one of my Regent's—my *former* Regent's—top ministers. I was originally going to return home from Paris after ten days in order to marry my country's former Premier."

"Yes, I'm aware."

Véronique gently stroked much-desired child's jet-black mane adorned with huge satin red bow. Adult's large, empathetic brown eyes explained girl had nothing to fear. "I already know everything you wish to say. If it's painful to mention, there's no reason that unfortunate

93

matter be ever raised. Still, if Sweetheart feels she must speak of it, I'm listening."

"Mme. Castellane" said Pascale, "even if Father was basically a good man—"

"I've absolutely no doubt Father was *a good man.*"

"Father, I've come to realize Mme. Castellane, was deeply involved in maintaining an authoritarian political regime. I don't know the details. I don't want to know the details of what Father did to maintain that authoritarian government. Of course, I'm sure Father believed he was doing it all for the right reasons. Anyway, whether I knew it or not, by being Father's daughter, I benefited from that undemocratic regime. Others from my country, who're artists like me, maybe even more talented than me, were never able to achieve the recognition they deserved because they or their families opposed the regime, I, like it or not, was a member. I by contrast, received all these advantages only by accident of birth. I feel I've wronged these other people. The very fact it took me so long to understand–"

"No more!" intervened Véronique. "First of all, no other child is as talented an engraver, as you. No other child makes as fine woodcuts. Certainly, no other Sweetheart paints as sublime frescoes! As for events happening in your country during years passed, Cherie possesses no personal responsibility. If accident of birth forces some experience injustice, accident of birth forces others to be unfairly numbered with those applying injustice."

Véronique paused.

"However, I'm terribly proud you've developed such worries. I'm terribly proud you've revealed these troubling thoughts. That confession alone, proves Cherie is a superior individual."

"I love you, Mme. Castellane!" cried Pascale, holding protector tight.

"And she loves you, *too!*"

"This district of *Paris* historically contained a large Jewish population" resumed Véronique. "Today the Jews are all gone. There's not a trace they lived here for more than a thousand years! I once suggested raising a memorial but I was told that would only cause bitter-recrimination and not achieve the objective it was built. During the *Occupation,* half of our neighbors collaborated with the Nazis. More than a few 'pillars of our community' with whom we regularly cross-paths, eagerly rushed to denounce the Jews, happily hustled the Jews on the trains to Auschwitz. *French* trains they were in fact, driven by *French* engineers."

She continued: "They'll tell you today: 'Oh but we thought it was **Resettlement in the East**. Nonsense! They knew exactly what they were doing. They knew exactly where the Jews were going and the fate soon befalling them! In fact, the French rounded-up the Jews of their own country, the French put the Jews of their own country on *French* trains even before Himmler and Eichmann planned! The railroad route to Auschwitz was temporarily clogged to a halt because the French wanted sending so many Jews to the gas chamber immediately. The Nazi railroad system to the death camps wasn't yet prepared handling so many victims at once! Today, those very same 'upstanding,' 'God-fearing *Christian* souls' or members of their devout, patriotic, 'Christian families' will instantly bring a libel suit, if you ever mention their crimes."

"There are true scoundrels you and I meet each day at the market, in the square, on the bus, each Sunday morning at Mass," explained Véronique. "Yet while these true scoundrels are in addition the most shameless of cowards, you Cherie, a victim too in your own particular way, feel compelled accepting responsibility for things of which you're truly innocent!"

She held Pascale close.

"I'm so proud of my Little Marie. You're indeed a special soul. Have no fear. While it's so touching you feel part of the guilt for those crimes mentioned in the newspaper, you're actually innocent."

THE LETTER

....

Matilda-Gisela Eisenberg
Department of Political Science, Department of History
University of Paris I (Panthéon-Sorbonne)
Office: no... Rue Saint Jacques Tel:– Fax –

My dearest Marie,

Forgive this message arriving so much time after we last spoke. If my long silence gave you emotional distress and left the impression I forgot about you, I am terribly, terribly sorry and offer my deepest, most heartfelt apology. Be assured though, Cherie, I didn't forget you. Not for an instant!

No one with the slightest sense of honor or slightest element of self-worth would ever forget a brilliant, magnificent, uniquely gifted child like you. For my entire life I will savor our conversation on the airplane traveling from Frankfurt to Paris. Whatever problem prevented our meeting as soon as we planned, I take full responsibility. Please understand too that I was required to travel abroad for several months to do research for a book. One, dedicated to you, Cherie!

Only yesterday did I at last uncover your present whereabouts. Hope all is going grandly for you in Paris. As soon as I learned your whereabouts I immediately penned this message. We must meet soon and talk ever so much about what has transpired during the intervening months. I've no doubt however you've been up to far more exciting things than me. As soon as you are free and willing please, write to me at the address shown on my letterhead or better yet, please call me at any time of day or night at my cellphone number .... I'll arrange it all. You can't imagine how excited I am! I'll take you to my favorite eating place where we girls can chatter away to our heart's content!

Remember how upset I was on being told about your lack of formal schooling. No precious child like you should be wasted! Yet don't upset your sweet, gifted head, Cherie! During the intervening months I learned how you can still take your Baccalaureate examination. I will personally give you all the coaching and tutoring needed first. When you do win your Baccalaureate and there is absolutely no doubt you will pass the examination grandly, there is no limit to what you can obtain in this world! I'll also be proud of obtaining a footnote of my own in your heroic, noble story.

Talk about the name-dropping I can do at turgid evening parties. "Guess what? I'm friends with Mariette!" Won't that ever instantly silence the room, instantly, grab everyone else's rapt attention?

Now look at my phraseology! All those years of being a cynic and pessimist were instantly wiped away as soon as I was granted the opportunity meeting a child like you! Looking forward to seeing and hearing from you soon Cherie,

Love, Mme. Matilda

Sister Claire collected the morning post arriving at the parish office's walnut front desk. Swift inspection of new letters, packages and boxes demonstrated she'd for once managed getting hold of them before the old crones. Those scheming biddies remained convinced Sister Claire and Father Richard were engaged in a "sordid" love affair. They regularly snooped at the young people's mail searching for "incriminating evidence" to bring to the attention of Cardinal Blanchard. Continued failure discovering such "damning proof" served just to strengthen the gossipy, bad-tempered, *Soap Opera*-devotees' belief "that Israelite-priest" and "*MI6* agent" long ago "threw their sacred vows to-the-winds!"

"I've learned" Mme. Rameau asserted, "Father Richard belongs to MOSSAD!"

"I've been told they're both Israelites!" added Mme. Marchand.

As one old biddy appeared, her wrinkled, pudgy face exhibited embarrassment at being caught-in-the-act. Sister Claire delivered the crone a happy, girlish show of her tongue. "Got here first this time you dirty, filthy, poisonous snake!" she giggled. "Seems you're starting to get slow! Simple, too! Granny ought to seriously consider if shrew's developing *Alzheimer's Disease!*"

One piece of new mail, return address showing it sent from nearby Sorbonne, immediately caught the eye.

To: Mademoiselle Marie Castellane, Saint G Church, Arrondissement V, Paris.

"Aha! I'll give *this* to Sweetheart myself" said the young nun, warm, protective smile on charming face. "It appears my child's remarkable gift for art is finally being recognized!"

Picking-up the newly arrived letter unopened in one hand, a large manila folder already in her other, Sister Claire exited the parish office. Advancing at ginger, merry step, singing Bob Dylan's *Mister Tambourine Man,* she crossed the public square leading to the east portico of the *Romanesque-Gothic* basilica. Its majestic steeple rose high above the undulating tiled roofs and narrow, serpentine, cobblestone medieval streets of the *Latin Quarter.* "My child's remarkable gift is finally being recognized!"

Today, Sister Claire didn't wear a habit. Instead, she wore a light-gray ladies' *power-suit*—a wide lapel jacket with padded-shoulders; hem of skirt above knees; frilly white blouse with ribbon at collar; neutral shade pantyhose; black high heels. Save for a silver crucifix around the nun's slender neck and wedding-ring symbolizing her eternal marriage to Christ, this lovely, mid-twenties religious could easily be mistaken for a professor, an attorney, a physician, a business executive, or any other dynamic young career woman. Like her buddy Sister Genevieve, Sister Claire also required no makeup being attractive. Even were she not in heels, her lower limbs would still capture men's swift, eager, fond, prolonged attention. The workers currently atop a restoration facade along the basilica's east portico delivering amorous whistles, bold kisses each time one of the intriguing duo passed—compliments swiftly rewarded with an explosion of giggles and flirtatious flutters of feminine eyes—represented the tiniest fraction of the two nuns' legion of male admirers.

As Sister Genevieve, her best friend saw no logical reason why possessing a pretty face, graceful figure and splendid legs should impair a woman's ability fulfilling a religious vocation. "It's sinful not taking advantage of the blessings God chose providing Leopoldine and me" observed Sister Claire, slyly. "In the process we can demonstrate our immense gratitude to Him through returning men to Mass!"

I

Swish; tap; swish; tap, scrape; scrape; tap, scrape; swish, tap, swish

The diligent melody of Pascale at work on her latest project within the nine-hundred-and-fifty-year-old Romanesque-Gothic edifice, reverberated far and wide. Its echo swiftly encompassed the entire *Nave* from *Narthex* to *Chancel*. Jumping effortless atop leaping *Vault*, the memorable song without words traveled queenly the wide *Transept*.

"In painting these pictures" mused the artist, "I'll win more than enduring personal glory and fame. I'll also make sure Father, Pierrette, Francoise and Agnes are never forgotten. In addition, I'll guarantee all those who love and befriended me here in France are never forgotten, either!" And as for that false-comrade, summer soldier, sunshine patriot, God? "Well, if God chose to so blithely abandoned me, chose to so swiftly desert me when I needed Him most, so be it! *Chere Petite* is going to demonstrate she can survive perfectly well without Him!"

"I'll show you, God! Just watch me, God!" cried Pascale before sticking out her tongue, shaking her fist at the sky beyond *Vault* ceiling. "Just watch me, God! I'm not going to be as Mme. Castellane says—a

Scatterbrained Female. I won't drop from the scene so you can quickly forget how badly you hurt me, God! How badly you hurt me even though I loved you so-so-so much! I'm going to become a great artist without your help! I'm going to show I can become a great artist without your help God and you'll just have to live with it!"

Then, hinting the unique couple's special bond wasn't unalterably broken, the girl added: "God, I'll make you so regretful losing me, you'll beg to take me back!"

Accepting her future now lay in France, initiated paperwork for naturalization as citizen, Pascale's creativity began to fully-bloom. She demonstrated herself not only an engraver equal to Durer, Daumier and Hogarth, but also a muralist as remarkable as Giotto, Fra Angelico, Mantegna, Rivera, Orozco and Siqueiros. She knew it too. Understanding proper young ladies are—modest, demure—*Chere Petite* judged it inappropriate "tooting-my-own-horn."

Romanesque-Gothic in design, a church once attended by Abelard and Heloise, Eleanor of Aquitaine, Blanche of Castile—its small Marian Chapel just to Pascale's left was added in the Seventeenth Century. Unlike the architecture of the High *Middle Ages* rendered so glorious in its matchless, unrivaled simple beauty, the *Baroque* chapel exhibited all that later style's preference for busy gold, silver decoration, gruesome frescoes of Christ crucified, Bernini-spin-off erotic female statues. In comparison to the older sections of the church, this later addition was nowhere near as fine a piece of art or welcoming harbor for contemplative, questing souls.

Luckily, whoever constructed the gaudy annex was tasteful enough not removing a splendid Fourteenth Century stained-glass image of the Virgin located above the altar. Unlike most *Gothic* stained-glass placed at least twenty-feet above the floor, this particular window, even Pascale could touch by standing on her tiptoes. Not that she'd ever be boorish enough to try! How on earth his priceless piece of art escaped being smashed during the 1789 Revolution, no one, many famous historians included, could explain. Fortunately it did escape. Every day at 12:02 PM, when not raining or overcast, as if by long prearranged schedule, this stained glass window received a direct sunbeam. Even in winter.

For an instance, the Virgin appeared in primary colors so magnificent, she defied all human description.

Standing atop three meter-high wooden scaffolding running a section of the Nave's east wall, Pascale was hard at work for the last month painting narrative fresco recording a New Testament story. Then abruptly she was not alone.

Click, click, click, click—sure, confident, click of lady in heels reverberated.

"Marie, dear!" cried lady in heels, "Marie, something in the mail just arrived for you this morning!"

"Sister Claire!" cried Pascale, delighted at her friend's unexpected appearance. "Sister Claire! Come closer! Come and see my latest addition to my picture! I think you'll like what I decided to add on to the picture!"

"Here, I come! Here I come, Sweetheart, to see the latest addition to your picture!"

"*See*" advised Pascale from atop scaffolding, directing attention to her latest figure created in fresco. "See what I just added over *here*, Sister Claire!"

"Oh, yes, Sweetheart. It looks magnificent even from the *Narthex*! Let me come and get a better look!"

Redhead sped across granite floored *Nave* as quick as high heels and ladylike comportment allowed.

Turning away so pious Sister Claire didn't observe, Pascale again thumbed nose defiantly at sky. "So *there* God!" she whispered at the deity, with all idealistic schoolgirl enthusiasm. "So *there*, God! See what I just painted without any belated assistance from your department, thank-you very much!"

"You're so talented Cherie!"

"Thank-you, Sister Claire. I hope my work continues to please you."

"No fear!" promised Redhead with mounting emotion. "There's no doubt your art will always please me—impress me, keep me in awe of the ease with which you produce it! Your art work will always provide me a unique, special—impossible-to-ever-describe-in-words soft, warm, gentle, precious sensation in both my mind and heart! It's a unique, special—impossible-to-ever-describe-in-words soft, warm, gent sensation in both my mind and heart only your art and your art alone evokes! I'm not just talking, either! You've known me long enough to understand I never pander to others whims. I speak only the truth. Likely, I'd have achieved far more in my life if I did pander to people's whims, tell them only what they wish to hear."

"Yes, Sister Claire, you don't pander to people's transitory whims. You, only speak the eternal truth!"

"I'm grateful for your confidence in me, Marie, my so gifted child. I hope I'll always possess the strength of character to remain worthy of your praise. I don't want to ever disappoint you."

"I know you'll never disappoint me, Sister Claire."

Like Matilda Eisenberg and Véronique Castellane, so too now the Brit perceived a captivating, otherworldly light emanating from her young friend. An aura, glow, as beautiful as it was indescribable, as clear, as it was invisible. This luminance, made grander still through the fact Pascale was unaware she possessed it. Like Matilda and Véronique, Sister Claire Preston also witnessed the brightness first surrounding Pascale alone, steadily expand in diameter until encompassing the viewer's own body as well.

Tears raced the nun's cheeks.

"Is anything wrong, Sister Claire?" inquired the young source of this compelling light. "Is anything wrong? Are you ill, Sister Claire?"

"No, no!" replied the nun, wiping here cheeks with a handkerchief. "I'm fine." She returned her attention to the three-fourths completed, life-size fresco emerging along the east *Nave* wall three meters above the floor. "Goodness, gracious!" she cried, emotion making her unconsciously break into *BBC*-English. "Goodness, gracious Marie!"

"You like my picture?" queried multilingual-Pascale, also in English.

"Goodness, gracious Marie, I do indeed! It's your best fresco yet!"

Painter looked away, bashful.

Sister Claire Preston—prophetess of *True Socialism* experienced an immensely exciting, arresting, above all transcendent sensation running throughout mind, soul and body. Gazing up at the image with rapt brown eyes, she understood in some uncanny but quite clear way that mere sight of this fresco made its viewer at one with the entire universe, at one with all ages passed and still to come. She knew sight of this fresco transformed its onlooker into a part of the *Grand Design*, of the *Natural Order of Things*. An infinitely small and trivial part of the *Grand Design*, the *Natural Order of Things*, yet part of it all the same! Chains being no stronger than their weakest link, each viewer was absolutely essential, critical to the continued existence, proper functioning, of all God's creation.

"Goodness, gracious Marie!"

Sister Claire began elaborating but soon abandoned attempt. Like the Fourteenth Century strained glass window touched by daily sunbeam, truly accurate words for the fresco's beauty and the unique spirituality it provides onlookers, don't exist. *Goodness, gracious Marie*—is as fitting a statement of appreciation as any. Her dynamite legs planted firmly to granite floor, her arms akimbo above woman's power suit's jacket, Sister Claire gazed up at the picture for several minutes reflectively. In time, happy tears again raced her soft cheeks.

"What did Saint Therese write?" sniffled the genteel Brit, still speaking in *BBC* English, her eyes remaining linked to fresco. "What did Saint Therese once write? Ah yes, 'There are things the heart feels but which the tongue and even the mind cannot express.'"

"I love you, Sister Claire!"

"I hope I'm at least a fraction worthy of your affection, my priceless child!"

Gazing up at the fresco tearfully, her voice choked, Sister Claire carried in her right hand not only the letter arrived from Matilda Eisenberg but also a large manila folder. The folder contained her latest extensive, single-spaced typed report on the nursery school she and Sister Genevieve operated.

The nursery school was located in the same immigrant, working class neighborhood on the industrial-outskirts of Paris as Richard's free clinic. More than half the children attending were delivered by him. Sister Claire described the current teaching methods and curricula, their successes and difficulties; she gave suggestions for the future. She detailed the students' alertness, educational progress, physical and emotional health. Besides the tots as a whole, she composed an in-depth monthly analysis of the progress of each individual boy and girl. In addition, Redhead presented a monthly budget, staff evaluation and inventory, on occasion requesting further funds for supplies or field trips. When judging them critical or specifically relevant to her superior, Sister Claire recounted current parent-teacher relations, supplied her personal interpretation of political and social developments which might have bearing on management of the school.

Richard remained director of the *Castellane School*. At the unanimous request of neighborhood, the institution was given the cleric's name. Both the teachers and maintenance staff were ultimately answerable to his supervision, alone. In turn, through serving the children *in loco parentis*, Richard was legally responsible for any mistreatment of the tots. This last issue, was of particular sensitivity after the outbreak in Europe and America of the priest child-molestation scandal with its heavy, long lasting moral, criminal and financial consequences to the Roman Catholic Church. Trusting his chief assistants implicitly, however, Richard granted the two young nuns effective authority over the nursery school. He frequently assured Sister Claire she needn't feel obliged writing him such very extensive and detailed monthly reports.

Sister Claire continued anyway. Copies of all her reports were saved in a file box to serve as the basis for a still ill-defined project in the undetermined future. Over time, in fits-and-starts, halts-and-renewals, that vague, amorphous scheme emerged into clearer subject and shape, gradually coalescing as a book. This piece of literature would prove infinitely more valuable to the world than its author dared imagine herself capable. At painfully slow pace, Sister Claire completed a brilliant, unforgettable memoir. One, about a socially-engaged Roman Catholic religious committed to making her faith relevant to the current age. The work recorded not just the battles waged in advancing public causes but also the conflicts her position as a woman forced she often fight against outmoded tradition and entrenched male hierarchy.

Much moved by the tale, greatly impressed with the manuscript's fine literary quality–Mme. Castellane, Richard, Sister Genevieve and Professor Eisenberg, all, urged it be published. Sister Claire declined, dubious as to possessing any true talent. She asserting creative-writing was merely a "hobby," a "diversion." Hopefully, one day she can be persuaded changing her mind.

Setting-down her tools, next, shimmying-out of far too-large painter's smock, Pascale then, descended the wooden scaffolding to greet her wise, elder sibling with a warm hug. "You know how I so-respect and so-hope receiving your good opinion of my work, Sister Claire!"

Artist received a warm hug in return.

"Marie precious, you needn't keep addressing either me or Genevieve as—*Sister*. You've long ago earned the privilege being regarded as a member of our family. Besides, the vast majority in our parish already believe we three girls are–*blood*-sisters."

"Yes, Sister Claire. I understand I needn't keep addressing you, so. You and Sister Genevieve regard me as a member of your family. I also know the vast majority in our parish already believe we three girls are—*blood*-sisters."

"Well if it really makes you feel better addressing me as you do, continue. But please don't ever think you must! Perhaps in return, Genevieve and I should start addressing you as—*Sister*."

"Mme. Castellane prays I really do become *Sister Marie*!"

"Who can know what the future bears."

"Yes, Sister Claire, who knows what the future bears."

Continuing to treat both her older friends with immense deference, studiously addressing each with a religious honorific, brought this Trio's youngest member great comfort, personal security. As witnessed in Pascale's attachment to Véronique, it wasn't equality in a loving relationship she sought, but rather guidance, protection.

"Come here at once, Little Marie!" instructed Sister Claire, the youngster swift complying. "Come here at once! I so adore that big red satin bow in your mane. It's absolutely ideal! It's unquestionably what you're meant to have. No one with even a fraction of brains can ever dispute you're always meant to wear a big, red, satin bow in your mane! Such Precious Little Darling! I see it's come a bit loose during your work up on the scaffolding. I must make it tighter. Now hold still!"

Finished, Redhead stepped back to survey her repair job. "Wonderful! Glorious! Fantastic! Now aren't you so happy it's fixed, Little Marie?"

"Oh yes, Sister Claire I'm so awesomely happy it's fixed!" was loyal response.

"I'm going to make sure you always look so cute!"

"Yes Sister Claire, you want to make sure I always look cute."

"You're exceptionally talented, Sweetheart!" reiterated Redhead, further contemplating the beautiful image developing on far wall.

The fresco was crafted primarily in dark, deep, expressive, even melancholy shades of color like: cobalt blue; burgundy; forest green; marigold, russet. Created by the teenager alone, she needed over a month of intense work completing it. Mme. Castellane having forbidden her sidekick to travel the *Metro* alone after dark without permission, Richard, Sister Claire and Sister Genevieve volunteered to drive Pascale back to *La Nouvelle Heloise* on alternate nights.

As expected, the parish office crones gossiped.

"Guess what those infernal characters are up to now?"

"What's their latest flouting of the Christian faith?"

"They've lured that poor refugee girl into *White Slavery*."

The subject of Pascale's new ten-by-four-meter fresco is a traditional one—*The Nativity*. This time however, she provides this familiar tale a singular, modern interpretation. In this updated-rendering, the Virgin possesses the same skin complexion and jet-black mane as the artist. Is she an Arab? Or is she a Roma, a Turk or Armenian? Perhaps even a Kurd, Afghan or an Iranian? That's hard to tell. One, thing is certain, Mary and her remarkable mixed-race child definitely aren't Europeans.

Instead of looking vacant as customary in her images, this new Madonna is an extremely smart, reflective teenage unwed-mother. She's more than just a fertile womb. The Virgin in Pascale's fresco also strikes onlookers as someone they might encounter on the street. Or maybe, even as someone each viewer is already well acquainted. She's the Madonna who understands infinitely better than any viewer humanity's pain and loneliness.

"Pray to this particular sacred Lady" observed Mme. Castellane after the fresco's completion, "and you'll perceive this Mother of God truly intervenes to provide us tender, unquestioning maternal love. She offers the sympathy of a most trusted comrade. No worry here of just mumbling into oblivion. When tortured souls speak to this Virgin, she's actually listening!"

From the pensive expression on her pretty face with Middle Eastern complexion, the Madonna in Pascale's fresco no doubt comprehends she's now been placed in a position allowing her no alternative to forever exercising tremendous responsibility for the welfare of all others. Many of whom, she knows, will never honor or demonstrate the slightest show of thanks or acknowledgment for receiving her freely given aid.

If she confident all the same of succeeding in the imposing role, this Madonna secretly still chides herself at the schoolgirl-impulsiveness with which she leaped to take the part so unexpectedly offered. She is less than overjoyed she took no time to first consider all the personal consequences of accepting the historic mission.

"Well, it's too late trying to get out of it now anyway, Joe" concedes the Madonna, *"so many are now depending on me! Besides, if I quit there'll never be anyone else up to taking my place!"*

Don't ask me supplying any words of wisdom, honey! I'm as new to all this Kind-of-thing as you!" begs-off Joseph, *an Asian of similar age, as he changes their crying, out-of-wedlock baby on a bench.*

Despite Joseph's conviction he's an open-minded, left-of-center, socially-enlightened male, he exhibits no more enthusiasm than any other father when asked to change his offspring's soiled pampers. The three's long uncomfortable bus trip has also left Joseph quite bleary-eyed.

"Have I got it right Mary, honey?"

"No you don't Joe! Give the baby back and I'll fasten them correctly."

Both Mary and Joseph are somewhat out of their element. Personal responsibility, parental obligation, need to make own decisions, are new and less than fully desired intruders upon these kids' previously regimented adolescent lives. Like the artist-in-bobby-socks herself, Mary and Joseph look as if they could well benefit from spending time under Mme. Castellane's firm authority, receiving occasional smacks by her wise hand on their own immature rears.

Clothed in—raggedy blue-jeans, baseball cap, old sneakers and sweatshirt—depicted not in a manger amongst cute, cuddly farm animals but instead bus terminal populated by dope-fiends, pimps, whores, transvestites, juvenile delinquents and other unsavory characters, not angels and Magi—unsympathetic emigration police officers fast approaching—Jesus, Mary and Joseph appear far closer to hunted, poverty-stricken, Middle East refugee illegal aliens than the classic, ethereal, bloodless, Holy Family. These troubled kids are infinitely more realistic and appealing too!

Christ was born into a self-absorbed, often tawdry, back-stabbing world. He learned of and experienced all its worst aspects from the very start.

Crafted in matchless artistic style, the fresco is compelling to any viewer, agnostic and believer alike. Naturally, written words cannot do it justice. Like all visual art, this picture can only be fully appreciated with the eye. As unfortunately is the case with all the great works Pascale created before she achieving national, later tragically, international fame, *The Nativity* is little seen by the General Public.

"You're a genius!" exclaimed Sister Claire, "a genius! You're the finest painter it's been my immense honor to meet! And considering where I was born, grew-up, I've been given the opportunity meeting, seeing the work of a good many artists!"

"I do my best, Sister Claire" answered Pascale modestly.

"I think the Virgin in your picture looks like Sister Genevieve."

"Yes, Sister Claire. I persuaded Sister Genevieve to model as the Virgin."

That's so very nice! Leopoldine–I mean *Sister Genevieve* too is eager to advance our Little Marie's career."

"Sister Genevieve is always most encouraging, Sister Claire."

"Your art is so moving, Sweetheart! The pictures you create also show viewers the message of Christ isn't one bound to just one specific time and place! You show viewers the message of Christ isn't the sole property of any one people, or restricted to just one interpretation, applicable to just single historical or cultural tradition!" Arms akimbo, she walked closer to the picture in order to better see a certain detail catching her special fancy.

"Don't let paint get on your pretty skirt, Sister Claire!" warned artist.

I'll be careful."

"Good! I don't want you getting paint on your pretty skirt, Sister Claire."

"You show Jesus is no less relevant today than in Roman times."

"I don't want being disingenuous" explained Pascale, she too, arms akimbo surveying latest work, now two-thirds finished. "I don't want leaving you with a false impression. I'm nowhere near as devout as you! I'm sure you've been told how I twice tried committing suicide."

"Yes" answered Sister Claire, reassuring. "Both Mme. Castellane and Father Richard told me how you tried hurting yourself. I'm sure it was a sad and painful time, Little Marie. You were suddenly cast-up on a strange shore and—"

She cut herself short.

"But no need continuing to speak on such a sad subject–Today, you're with us, today, you're protected, loved, understood. No one will ever let you be lost again. Now you'll be a brilliant artist. And like every brilliant artist you can use unfortunate things from the past as inspiration for eternal beauty."

She pecked teenager on forehead.

Pascale clutched Sister Claire's right arm tight in appreciation.

"As for your spirituality, darling," explained the nun, once more pecking youngster's forehead, maternally, "I never acquired any false impressions. I've developed my views on your relationship with that issue from watching at a distance—watching you over the months without you noticing."

"Ooh!" exclaimed Pascale embarrassed. "I hope I didn't ever make you angry? I hope I didn't ever offend you, Sister Claire?"

Redhead emitted a comforting refined laugh.

She brought Pascale close.

"No, no, Little Marie darling! Quite the opposite! For someone claiming not to be concerned with God anymore, you certainly maintain a steady conversation with Him! You're closer to God than anyone else! You're precisely the artist to paint this picture. God isn't for you a vague intellectual theory. God is an everyday companion! If you and He are supposedly on bad terms at the moment, how many others are so close to God they ca get into *Lovers' tiffs*!"

"Oops! Oh *goodness, gracious*!" exclaimed the nun, sudden recalling original reason she came but observation of Pascale's developing fresco created so much emotion she totally forgot. "Before arriving, I l collected the mail at the parish office front desk. I discovered a letter for you, Sweetheart. Naturally I left it unopened. From the outside though, it looks quite important. it's from the Sorbonne."

BRENDEL'S DAUGHTER

Tuesday sunset arrived in a Paris enjoying an extended, soft and gentle autumn. Leaves yet to change color thoroughly covered wide-branched chestnut, oak and plain trees in famous parks, broad public squares and along grand avenues. *Continental Style* flowerbeds still bloomed in the Place Vendome and Luxemburg Gardens. The once-a-week outdoor flower market on the Ile de Cité between leaping Notre Dame and the massive Conciergerie remained filled with customers, merchants doing excellent business. Horse racing season, usually ending last month, continued this year at Longchamps. Lovely, fashionably-dressed girls on the Rue Rivoli and Champs Elysée, in the Place de Concorde, Auteuil and Bois de Boulogne took furtive inspection of one another in short skirt. Each fetching beauty, concluding hers were the better legs.

Cafés along the winding, cobblestone streets of Montmartre, the Marais and on the Left Bank filled with philosophizing-*regulars* harboring no intention abandoning debate soon. On the Boulevard St. Michel, from its opening at the Left embankment to the Panthéon—university students in blue-jeans or short skirts flirted or discussed grand principles. More than a few eagerly involved themselves in both enterprises. Heroic figures in *neoclassical* fountains jetted plumes of foam, high. Abutting the Louvre, in the Tuilleries Gardens, romantic couples, strolled gravel paths hand–in–hand as children, mamas or nannies in hot pursuit, scampered.

Atop the white steps running down from Sacré Coeur in Montmartre, sat men and women dressed in summer attire admiring the breath-taking view. At the foot of the celebrated staircase, a *La Belle Époque* styled-carousel remained both in-operation and well-patronized. Ice cream stands as well as book stalls lined the embankment. Outside vaulting *Gothic* St. Eustache Church, a man continued selling refreshments from inside a booth shaped like an orange. Contemplating the magnificent vista available to the eye from the Trocadero, people discovered the Champ de Mars, the Eiffel Tower at its center and the vibrant, lusciously green massive lawn approaching the Invalides. Beneath the streets of this Paris enjoying an *Indian Summer,* attractive, thirty-two-year-old Professor Eisenberg traveled the *Métro.*

Matilda unquestionably earned that triumphant smile on her moist, red painted lips. She, more than deserved adopting that confident, queenly comportment of her fetching, well-dressed figure. Born out-of-wedlock in a declining industrial town with low job prospects and high teenage pregnancy rate, father killed in a factory accident, mother frequently ill—chance, money, culture, social environment all seemed coalesced to form an immovable obstacle to this girl ever demonstrating her exceptional intellectual gifts. She rose nonetheless (with no small assistance from Mama) to international academic fame, honor and accomplishment. The remarkable young lady presented a rigidly-traditionalist, stodgy, uncooperative and above all since the Middle Ages entirely-masculine university faculty, no choice but to grudgingly acknowledge her own immense female abilities.

Capturing academic scholarship after academic scholarship in both France and Germany (Brendel Eisenberg born in Upper Silesia allowing her offspring to apply for prizes in both countries), winning essay contest after essay contest both in France and Germany, setting still-unmatched scores on national tests in both countries—Mama's remarkable child was the youngest person hired in either nation as a full-professor. Last year in France, she was asked to become director of her department of research at the University of Paris. At the same moment, two no less great German universities were eagerly working to lure the distinguished savante back permanently to their own side of the Rhine. To both the French and German public, even among those members without interest in academics, *Matilda-Gisela Eisenberg* became a popular, frequently-used adjective to describe:—*Triumph against the odds*—the living proof—*Girls, especially poor girls, can too, make a lasting, worthwhile mark!*

"Mama" reflected Brendel's Daughter in German proudly, traveling the Paris *Métro*, "Mama insisted I'd one day thank her for all those smacks she regularly gave me on my fanny. Mama promised I'd one day thank her for being so strict with me. She pledged I'd one day appreciate her scolding me so often, sending me to bed without supper, not allowing me to ever stay outside after dark! I certainly didn't imagine it then, but it's true, absolutely true! All I've ever accomplished is Mama's doing. Mama deserves all the credit!"

Prodigy reflected fondly upon her yet latest triumph, this one achieved just three days ago, in, Germany. Those of Matilda's supporters with a liking for melodrama, described the event as: *The Battle of Heidelberg*. With its graduates going on to win fifty-six Nobel Prizes, other distinguished alumni including Robert Schumann, Georg Wilhelm Hegel and Max Weber, Germany's most prestigious seat of higher learning was founded in 1338. "If only Mama were present to see it!" Heidelberg's latest celebrated-graduate mused. "Mama would be so proud of me!"

Through the darkened passageway, the *Métro* trundled on.

"A new era is at hand!" pledged Brendel's Daughter. This evening back in Paris, she was traveling from her office in the *Latin Quarter* to eat dinner elsewhere in the city with a very special, no less remarkable friend. The neighborhood in which she lectured acquired its famous name, during the, Middle Ages, when both faculty and students at the University of Paris were prohibited conversing in any language save Latin. "A new era is at hand! A new era Matilda's going to lead!"

From earliest recollection, Matilda described memorable personal experiences in *Third Person*. Brendel vehemently disapproved. She sternly lectured that this affectation made her gifted-offspring appear "odd," "eccentric," a *"poseur."* However, years of spankings and banishment to bed without supper failed breaking the child's "atrocious habit." So reflexive did it become, Matilda today spoke in this manner without even noticing. As for Brendel, she in time came to find her daughter's "singular prattle" endearing.

Bump, jostle, groan roar—the *Métro* trundled along dark subterranean path.

So engaging were the charming professor's thoughts at present she no longer felt encased in a stuffy, cramped sardine can, over-stuffed human pickle jar.

So what glory occurred at Heidelberg?

Every two years, the directors of Matilda's autonomous institute within the university, or–as she derisively called them: "The Eunuchs"—took a week-long, self-gratifying retreat. Amidst inspiring *Gothic* vaults and pensive *Romanesque* quadrangles, the all-male hierarchy leisurely reviewed the progress of its field of study since last convening. These intellectual Pharisees evaluated the results and significance of their underlings' original research projects over the last twenty-four months. The aristocrats cast what was considered ultimate judgment on the value of the scholarly articles published by the institute's plebeians. The elite assessed its topic's current and future significance in both lecture hall and larger world, boasted of the politicians, public opinion-makers and national leaders they'd won over to their side. Suggestions were offered on how faults best might be corrected and successes further enhanced. Inevitably, there arose the issue of fund-raising.

This year, the president of the Institute, or in Matilda's phraseology: "The Supreme Eunuch," reached the lose of a second, decade-length term of office. He, unable serving a third, the latest retreat would also be used to elect a replacement.

"A new era has begun!" whispered its pretty creatrix, "the era of Matilda!" Wearing light-gray lady's *power suit:* hem of skirt above knee, splendid legs in regular-shade hose and red high heels, delicate ribbon around collar of frilly-white blouse, gold brooch on jacket; dabs of fragrance; left hand carrying her *Coach* handbag, white chapeau atop long brown hair tied loosely behind erect back, she was quite a fetching-innovator.

The *Métro* halted at a station for a few minutes, then no less crowded, trundled on. If Matilda was aboard physically, she was in spirit, elsewhere.

During normal times, the identity of the next president of the institute was predictable. The *smart money* was bet on the out-going chief's longtime-dauphin, second in command. Like the College of Cardinals or Soviet Politburo, governing elites consisting of individuals each wielding significant autonomous power and anxious retaining it, tend picking a new titular captain from among their well-healed, like-minded own kind. They prefer *One of the guys*—a *Good Ole Boy*. He's trusted not to let management of the overall show interfere with what he readily concedes to be his colleagues' personal fiefdoms, private spheres of influence. Forever indebted to the kingmakers leveraging him into office, the new official leader is a first among equals not an independent operator. These, however were not normal times.

Whether motivated by flight-of-fancy or last-minute eagerness to be a reformer, the outgoing-president as his last major act in office expanded the institution's suffrage. Now, election of his successor instead of being restricted to *"The Eunuchs,"* would come about through a secret ballot cast by all doctorate-achieved, license-holding, dues-paying members of the scholarly profession.

Seeing her chance, the dainty insurgent wasted no time seizing it. Matilda, never forgot the many times back in grubby St. Clothide when Mama counseled: "Remember *she* who hesitates is lost! History is made by he, I mean *she* who dares!"

Mama—who even with just a grammar school education was often far wiser, far more perceptive than all the *experts,* advised crucially: "Don't flinch, Child! Reach out, grab destiny by the throat and bend it to your own will! Like Simone Weil, Eleanor of Aquitaine, Marie Curie, Mrs. Roosevelt, Anna Akhmatova, Colette, Marina Tsetaeva. Don't wait to develop second thoughts. Remember also, Child, most of your male opponents will assume you're just a *Scatterbrained Female, Witless Women*. Their defenses will be down when you strike."

"Also never forget" warned Brendel, *7541803* tattooed above left wrist, "in this masculine-dominated society, one of that governing tribe frequently gets away winning the cup even though he's made just a mediocre performance. I've seen it occur too many times to count. The judges—members of his own kind will already be prejudiced in their compatriot's favor. They'll be prepared to overlook some of their fellow's not too visible mistakes. A girl, though, since she's expected to fail, since the judges are always prejudiced against her, needs to perform her very best when she strikes. She needs to be three times as good as the best man! That's a tough objective to fulfill but Mama knows you can easily do it if you summon up the courage, keep, all your talent fast and bubbling."

Save for her eccentric speech pattern, Matilda-Gisela Eisenberg was an obedient child. She learned from experience—Mother *does* know best. "I'd have accomplished nothing without Mama! I owe all my success to Mama."

The *Métro* stopped, its doors opening. If disgorging a large number of current passengers, the train promptly swallowed a seeming-equal number of newcomers. The precious open space briefly created by those exiting, permitting those still aboard to adopt more comfortable postures, capture a treasured seat, or adjust crumpled clothing, was soon refilled with a similar profusion of anxious, hurried, bodies.

The young professor wasn't superstitious or believed in hocus-pocus. Still, the coincidence of this great encounter with destiny occurring at her beloved Alma Mater provided an otherwise skeptical mind a vague sense that higher forces might be at work. Should cosmic powers indeed actually exist, she perceived uncannily, these deities smiled upon her endeavor. "Mattie blesses you, Heidelberg!' she cried "blesses you, Heidelberg! Mattie promises she'll always make cherished-Heidelberg proud!"

During the weeks immediately leading up to the vote, this fetching university faculty member discovered she possessed an unexploited-talent for extemporaneous oratory and face-to-face politicking. This was the one-on-one style of campaigning which in small, relatively-homogenous constituencies, is essential to achieving victory. Mattie was as fluent in German as Mary Preston in French. Not limited to its classical form, both knew their second language in all its euphemisms, slang, even obscenities. Brendel from Upper Silesia, her daughter was also a dual-national. Residing in Germany for fifteen years, Mattie was as well-versed as any native in that country's: latest entertainment fad, newest female fashion craze, its *you-positively-can't-live-without* piece of merchandise, most juicy scandal. She could easily alter the conversation from high-brow academic debate to speculation on gender-challenged *Rock* stars and adulterous government ministers.

Mattie quickly found *personally*-advocating her candidacy, personally-explaining her message, going from office-to-office and dinner-to-dinner canvassing for support tremendous, ever-so exhilarating fun.

Ladylike; physically attractive; nice to smell; local girl who-made-good without forgetting roots; as warm, empathetic as she was accomplished, brilliant; author of award-winning research books any layman found an entertaining read—Mattie spread her message as champion of reform. She slapped backs, told off-color jokes; discussed sports, hose, television shows, perfume, and pulp novels. When shaking hands, she was meticulous taking her acquaintance's paw firm. If speaking, did so looking straight into the listener's eyes. She even kissed babies!

Knowing instinctively the proper words for the proper times, at the appropriate places and to be used for the correct malleable individuals, Mattie understood the right moment to exploit her refined femininity, when best restrain it. Understood by instinct when the public prefers a woman soft and gentle, when it's most impressed, most nicely surprised at finding a woman bold and strong.

"Maybe Gisela's been in the wrong line-of-work these passed years?" commented one bystander, fondly.

"Gisela would certainly contribute an immense and long badly-required intellectual boost to the Bundestag" observed a second.

"Were the cutie born in another time and place," mused third, "who knows! She might today have her pretty face on our currency notes."

"Mattie certainly has great legs, terrific cleavage!"

Riding skillfully the wave of massive discontent among the institute's rank-and-file caused by their decades' denial of any voice in policy-making, she often telling own inspiring life story, promising only what could actually be delivered, Mattie won the presidency by a landslide. "Landslide" was putting it modestly. At Heidelberg's *Karl Jaspers Hall* on victory night, using famous quote, she instructed the self-absorbed, unproductive, doddering male elite: "Out! Out I say! In God's name you have sat too long!"

Promptly, if in a more ladylike manner than Oliver Cromwell dealt with the *Long Parliament*—Matilda too, sent the full-of-themselves, careerist, intellectually-exhausted, totally male elite packing.

Admittedly, *The Battle of Heidelberg* raged largely unobserved by the vast majority of the world's population. Still, the liberal, expansive, farsighted reforms Professor Eisenberg engineered were to prove as decisive in molding the future course of her particular field of academic research, as for a larger world was the outcome of The Battle of Hastings.

As the *Métro* trundled-on through dark subterranean passageway, at least one passenger was consumed in thought about places far-away. She beamed like a schoolgirl, bubbled with teenage hope. "You've done it, you've done it Mattie! Mama will be so proud! Mattie did just as Mama instructed!"

"But all that can wait for later," soon added the dainty-scholar in melodic voice. "All that can wait for later! This evening you've got far more important matters to deal with. It's time for dinner with that precious creature fate privileged you meeting on the airplane from Frankfurt. Meeting, the precious creature was awesome, no, *really* awesome!"

Dear Professor Eisenberg,

It's so AWESOME you still remember me!!!!! I'll never forgot our wonderful conversation on the flight from Frankfurt. I'll be so delighted having dinner with you tomorrow evening at 8 PM at the restaurant you want. Please, please know if we failed meeting again earlier as you instructed me on the airplane that was entirely my own fault. I really wanted to see you again soon but

I foolishly lost your business card and other unexpected things occurred preventing our meeting I also became very ill. Don't worry. Mme. Castellane, Sister Claire, Sister Genevieve and Father Richard, the kind people who took me in nursed me back to health. Maybe I can introduce you to them one day. Madame Castellane, Sister Claire (who handed me your letter), Sister Genevieve and Father Richard are all such kind, good, loving people. I know you will feel exactly the same when getting to see them. I'm so delighted we can finally get together again. I take full responsibility for the failure it didn't take place long ago. Once more, it's so awesome you still remember me!!!! I certainly remember you!!!! See you tomorrow evening at the restaurant you wish at 8 PM.

Your obedient servant,

Mlle. Kedari

P.S. With Mme. Castellane's help, I'm applying for French citizenship. The process is taking time since I never formally fled and sought asylum from my country. What happened to me took place all of sudden without me ever expecting it. Still, I'm coming to believe it's the unexpected things that make life worthwhile living.

Reader placed the letter back in her *Coach* handbag. "Bless you, Mattie's incomparable little Tosca, pint-sized Tess of the d'Urbervilles! Mattie found you again at last! And this time, she won't lose you!"

Since arriving yesterday at the professor's office on Rue Saint Jacques, this message written in elegant feminine script employing deferential *Vous* on pink stationary inside pink envelop, hardly left rits eceiver's sight, often even body. She read it over-and-over and yet further times over again. Each time doing so, tears of satisfaction ran from deep, watery green eyes. At last, Mattie concluded it best leaving the message in its envelope lest too much handling damage the priceless object. Some of her tears might wet the turquoise blue ink. She placed the envelope in the left breast pocket of her jacket, securely close to her fast-beating heart. "Mattie's own Tosca, own miniature Tess!"

After months of searching, the professor at last located her former acquaintance. She finally tracked-down the whereabouts of the uncannily-magic teenager whose chance encounter made such a profound and lasting intellectual, emotional, spiritual impression.

What was it? From moment the pair first sat down side-by-side on *Row 10* in a plane still attached to the terminal of the Frankfurt airport, Mattie unquestionably detected something special about her chance traveling companion. Yes, this child was an adorable Little Thing, the most adorable *Little Thing* encountered before or sense! So cute, so friendly, well-behaved the young lady was and when entering into conversation, she also proving so exceptionally intelligent, talented, compelling. The child was the *most* a*dorable* kind of adorable little thing, adult admirer imagined ever possible. Even then, Mattie reflected, the quality making Pascale truly special, was her wondrous, fetching, personal magnetism.

"Truly a Divine Child, my *Little Thing* is!" declared Brendel's Daughter, never one of those *New Age* pseudo-sophisticates unable deciding whether in former *life* she'd been Cleopatra, Hildegard of Bingen, Nellie Bly or Amelia Earhart. "My darling is truly a Divine Child." This uncharacteristic spiritual comment recalled memory of pious Mama back in St. Clothide. Mama years-ago throwing up her hands in despair for daughter's faith. Yes, this chance-flight companion was "The Divine Child." One, exuding a brilliant and comforting glow, a luscious radiance, marvelous sparkle—Mattie (or so, she believed) was alone privileged observing. Pascale's, was a light as *uniquely*-fine, *singularly*-beautiful, *exceptionally*-grand as the precious, transcendent, otherworldly joy its view brought to Mattie's skeptical heart and soul.

Was there a more accurate description? Mattie never allowed her students to be so vague on term papers. No. The words needed don't exist. As Americans would say: *You just had to have been there.* That The

Divine Child was thoroughly unaware of her aura, radiance, made its attraction all the more irresistible.

"It must've been just like this when people met Napoleon!"

The *Métro* rambled on its course.

So how was Pascale Kedari or increasingly—*Little Marie*—relocated? As purely through chance as when she and Mattie first crossed-paths! All these months, it was discovered, the two were never far separate. Who knows? The scholar and painter might on occasion have been just steps apart on the same jammed street or busy public square without noticing!

Richard Castellane's *Romanesque/Gothic* church is located within the 5th Arrondissement. An area, encompassing much of the *Latin Quarter* and the *University of Paris*. All those months, while an exiled-teenager honed her artistic gifts within one of the basilica's chapels, a professor in early-thirties was delivering lectures less than a ten minute walk distant. Given the *Latin Quarter's* narrow, irregular, serpentine cobblestone streets, the two friends were all this time often just a few thousands meters apart!

Pascale remembered Mattie taught at the University of Paris. However, the idea of *Chere Petite* without a single day of formal education snooping inside the confines of a campus attended by so many great scientists, philosophers, writers and theologians made her more than a bit too intimidated.

As for Brendel's Daughter, she often passed Father Richard's domain twice daily but never entered, often when just inside, Pascale *was* busy on a fresco. Then one afternoon, by pure accident, the professor overheard two of the church office crones outside to take a smoke, discussing the latest political event organized by Jeanne Navarro and her Sisters of the World. "That troublemaker, anarchist, terrorist, radical feminist-who should be wearing a habit" lamented Mme. Rameau to Mme. Marchand, "now has designs on that sweet, Middle Eastern girl, Sister Claire's little protégée."

That sweet, Middle Eastern girl, Sister Claire's little protégée

"Could this be the same child I encountered on the flight from Frankfurt?" conjectured Mattie, filled with delight. A stranger's chance overheard-words resounding in own ears like Heifetz playing the *Violin Concerto in E-minor* by Mendelssohn.

"He, *she* who hesitates is lost" advised Mama back in St. Clothide. "History is made by those who dare! Seize the world by the throat and make her your own!" Gifted offspring wasted no time in making further inquiries.

Exiting the *Métro*, coming above ground, Mattie crossed the wide Place Hotel de Ville. Currently, a huge television screen was erected at the center so crowds might watch the deciding match of football's *World Cup*.

On attaining the Rue Rivoli and provided a temporary lull in traffic congestion, Professor Eisenberg scurried across as swift as high heels, large chapeau kept in place by single frail hatpin and short skirt in confrontation with gust of wind, permitted.

"Eek!"

Latest frantic scamper achieved with slightly less than usual sartorial mishap, dainty traveler next made a left; a right; a second left. Thinking it now safe releasing hem, she advanced directly forward up Rue des Archives. Four and five story pre-1789 residential buildings running uninterrupted on both sides of these serpentine cobblestone streets gave feeling of traversing a narrow canyon, of journeying back in time several centuries.

On finally reaching her objective, Mattie glanced at a delicate watch on delicate wrist. "Ooh! I'm early." Dinner with newly-recovered Pascale was arranged for 8 PM. "It's now just 7:40."

As frequently when pensive, Mattie looked above. Peering intently at the narrow slice of nighttime sky pre-1789, serpentine cobblestone streets granted, she found at last an ivory-colored star. It was the first she'd seen in ever-so long while living in metropolitan Paris. Normally, reflection of great city lights blocked-out all celestial bodies. "*There*" she cried excitedly in German. "*There* I see one! My star! That's awesome, no *really* awesome! What should I call my star? I'll call you Marie after my own Marie!"

Each year when between age eight and eighteen, Brendel sent her daughter to Roman Catholic Youth summer camp in rural Bavaria. If now long ago abandoned faith, Mattie still intended sending her own daughter (if she had one) from age eight to eighteen to Roman Catholic Youth summer camp in rural Bavaria. She send the child to the very same Church-sponsored summer camp. That facility was now expanded since Fraulein Eisenberg was last a happy-camper.

"Is that a two-faced, hypocritical decision?" she mused, still speaking in German, deep, watery green eyes still fixed upon star its discoverer named *Marie*. No, quite the opposite. "*The truth will triumph in the free market of ideas*" Mattie observed, quoting John Stuart Mill. Sweep of her left arm providing emphasis.

Forbidding daughter (if she had one) contact with religion, intentionally preventing daughter (if she had one) reaching independent judgment on the issue was behaving just as fanatical, as prejudiced, closed-minded, as the worst *Jihadist* suicide-bomber or Appalachian snake-handler!

"No" reflected Fraulein Eisenberg, still gazing at Paris sky. "No, there isn't anything two-faced, hypocritical about sending Little Marie to Roman Catholic Youth summer camp in Bavaria. If Little Marie is religious, her Mama won't interfere. Hopefully, the child is just going through a *phase* common to a great many Roman Catholic adolescent girls. A *phase* breaking-out exactly at the moment teenagers desperately seek and require their elders' intellectual admiration, their elders' respect for them as autonomous individuals. Heavy-handed adult interference leads only to juvenile intransigence. Heavy-handed adult interference will only cause Little Marie to hold on to the mumbo-jumbo even longer!"

"Above all" her prospective-mother decided, "my Little Marie must go to Roman Catholic Youth summer camp in Bavaria! There, she too must know the priceless innocent joy, un-meddled-with inspiration I discovered when attending."

The nighttime sky visible in pastoral Germany was quite different from that seen in metropolitan Paris.

Capricorn, Aquarius, Cetus, Big Dipper, Hercules, Great Bear, Sagittarius, Orion, Sculptor, Pleiades, Pegasus, Cassiopeia, Taurus, Gemini, Perseus, Lynx, Hydra, Draco, Cepheus, Centaur, Libra, Bootes

Save if overcast or raining, all these Northern Hemisphere constellations looked fondly down upon their inquisitive earthbound admirer on summer nights in Bavaria. Mattie looked back with innocent, impressionable, un-meddled-with green eyes. Her virgin's mind and virgin's heart were incomparably moved by her friends in the starry dome; she with them and they with her, seeming in eager communication. That original, pure joy brought through personal encounter, direct, mutual-communication with Nature still reverberated in tonight's worldly-wise, disabused, thirty-two-year-old soul.

"Precisely as you'll appear in books" giggled Mattie on those Bavaria nights, dressed in cut-away denim shorts; sweatshirt and tennis shoes. Her hair then in pigtails kept together at the end with ribbons.

Mattie would address *Capricorn, Aquarius, Cetus* and the rest of them as if they and she were closest friends. "You're just as you appear in planetariums and movies, only here, you're the real thing!"

She waved at her friends excitedly on those blessed rural summer nights.

Big Dipper, Hercules, Great Bear, and all the others in would twinkle back with deep love and protective affection.

"We're so delighted seeing you again, Mattie?" *Sagittarius, Orion, Sculptor* and all their celestial sisters and brothers for a decade beckoned flirtatiously to the future distinguished academic. "We're always here for you Mattie love, Mattie our love!"

"I love my constellations too!" would later gleefully pipe, further schoolgirl-wave the victor of *The Battle of Heidelberg.* "I always belong to my constellations and my constellations always belong to me. Fraulein Mattie loves you!"

Truly, it was a magnificent sight. One, grander than all the *Gothic* cathedrals combined. And unlike *Gothic* cathedrals, these celestial friends replied when spoken to. From age eight, Professor Eisenberg possessed a strong interest in astronomy. All the letters she wrote Mama from Bavaria were filled with information on the heavenly bodies. On the few occasions permitted telephoning home, she filled Mama's ear with further information about the heavenly bodies. Each year from age eight to eighteen from the day summer ended and daughter returned to France, Mama learned yet additional facts about the galaxies, stars, planets and comets. Only when Brendel fell asleep at last from exhaustion did her exceptional child's account of the night sky, come to conclusion.

Interest in astronomy didn't cease with Roman Catholic Youth camp. During Matilda's university years—first, as undergraduate at Gottingen, later while earning doctorate at Heidelberg—she monthly drove into the Baden-Wurttemberg or Saxon countryside to enjoy gazing into an unobstructed night sky similar to that of pastoral Bavaria.

After setting-up her elaborate, sophisticated scientific apparatus, Mattie tracked the German heavens from sundown into the following dawn. The *Astronomy Fraulein*—she became among the local farmers. If not the best means for keeping an urbanized-male companion, Mattie's boyfriendless-nights alone in the fields peering through telescope were more than abundantly compensated by chances to see impressive, thought-provoking nebulae, star and planet shifts, meteor showers. Twice, she closely recorded paths of comets. The second, last passing earth in the time of Julius Caesar, offered Mattie looking through lens, a union with history. Letters home to Mama in St. Clothide were, like those earlier from Bavaria, filled with details on daughter's nighttime observations.

"No matter!" she pronounced tonight in Paris, "your constellations aren't vanishing. Other things right now demand your attention. Mama, I'm sure would also like to read about more than just astronomy."

Mattie glanced again at delicate watch on delicate wrist.

7:55 PM—almost time for the grand encounter.

La Petite Madeleine—the restaurant selected for occasion, was found just a few serpentine cobblestone streets from the fortified Renaissance complex known as the Hotel de Guise, once home of Mary Queen of Scots. Also located in this colorful neighborhood were the residences of Catherine de Medici, Diane de Poitiers, Gabrielle d'Estrée, Sarah Bernhardt, Casanova, Richelieu, Victor Hugo, the birthplace of Mme. de Stael. Not to mention, the Carnavelet Museum where during the Seventeenth Century the great wit and beauty Marguerite de Sévigné penned famous letters to her daughter. In no less comfortable walking distance, was the building where once lived Mimi and Rodolfo of *La Boheme*.

Situated in the historic, pleasantly secluded Marais district once stomping ground for Cyrano de Bergerac, traffic congestion and camera-snapping tourists distant, tonight's chosen eatery inside *Baroque* townhouse was an ideal venue for an academic Mama reuniting with her artistic, romantically-minded long-lost child. They fondly reminiscing, catching up on latest personal events, discussing the future. Establishment serving fine cuisine at reasonable prices, located off-the-beaten-track, there was no fear disappointing the magical Sweetheart. Nor, for the two ladies be quickly shooed to make room for impatient new arrivals.

Often dining here alone, Mattie developed a close bond with the restaurant's owner. Her married name *Roussillon,* Magda Schwarzenberg too possessed a degree from Gottingen. Mention of the coincidence rising by happenstance when first Mattie chose dining here, immediately launched the two women into a long chat from which they arose over an hour later as the closest of feminine friends.

Were Mattie devout, she'd select Mme. Roussillon as confessor. In the event, the restaurant owner carried out much that same role in secular fashion. Mattie confided all her private emotional concerns, career botherations, personal hopes and dreams. Subjects, she'd usually reveal to no one but her mother. Increasingly-deaf after a protracted illness, however, Brendel was difficult to communicate with on the telephone. She, not yet being on the *Internet,* Brendel and her daughter corresponded primarily through traditional post. While loving, illuminating, delightful reading as those letters invariably were, mail delivery between Paris and St. Clothide took time.

Most in Mme. Roussillon's position, would find receipt of so many unsolicited intimacies tedious if not downright irritating. Most, would plainly inform the giver of all these unrequested confidences that her listener hadn't volunteered to become a *Wise, Protective Big Sister* or serve as *Unpaid Shrink*. Perhaps, even demand Professor Eisenberg henceforth dine elsewhere. Instead, Mme. Roussillon, a deeply empathetic, affectionate character to begin with, readily accepted both unofficial if clearly exercised roles.

The ladies were unbreakable confidantes—addressing, one another in German and by first name. Professor Eisenberg, in spite of all her academic, scholarly accomplishments was quite content to be the sheltered junior partner. As the first to be told of Pascale's existence following the encounter on airplane and she heard so much about the girl since, Mme. Roussillon was eager this evening's encounter be a grand success. She guaranteed protégée could dine for as long and as late with her surrogate child as Professor Eisenberg wished.

"I know the child must be a sweet, well-behaved, charming little creature, Matilda" promised Mme. Roussillon, withdrawing into the interior, motioning to the waiter that he take excellent care of the special guests. "I look forward to hearing all the details about your evening with her tomorrow."

"Bless you, Magda" answered Mattie. "You're so kind."

On warm evenings like the present, the restaurant's polished mahogany French windows were opened; allowing small cloth-covered cherry wood tables and wicker chairs extend to sidewalk edge.

I

8 PM.

Pascale appeared on other side of serpentine cobblestone street.

Mattie waved in recognition, threw a maternal kiss.

"Little Marie! Little Marie!"

"Mme. Matilda! Mme. Matilda!"

Pascale approached as swiftly as high heels allowed. She wore: an open pink cardigan over short sleeveless white dress; white socks and white heels. A very valuable, artistic antique sterling silver crucifix, the gift of Mme. Castellane for her recent sixteenth birthday was around slender neck. "Mme. Matilda!"

"Little Marie, Sweetheart!"

Pascale neared. The huge, emblematic, red satin bow Véronique, Sister Claire, Sister Genevieve brooked no opposition be placed daily in protégée's voluminous black hair, she now swiftly untied. Her mane now descended freely below her narrow waist. Decision she remove headgear was a statement of independence as much as a declaration of style preference.

"Little Marie you look so lovely this evening, a perfect lady!"

"Thank-you so much Mme. Matilda" answered Pascale anxiously in formal *Vous*. A form of address the speaker employs not merely conversing with non-intimates but social superiors. She carefully folded the huge, emblematic, red satin bow, then placed, it in her *Coach* handbag. Without doubt Mme. Castellane, Sister Claire and Sister Genevieve all expected the bow again crowning *Precious Little Thing's* head on her return home. "I'm so, so sorry I'm late, please forgive my tardiness."

"No trouble, Sweetheart" assured Brendel's Daughter in intimate *Tu,* giving her child a peck on right cheek.

"I see you made a very good choice for place to eat, and amidst all this history, Mme. Matilda!"

'Thank-you, Sweetheart, I thought you would enjoy it."

Pascale allowed the chair to be pulled-out for her before sitting down gracefully, crossing legs. Hem of short dress receding.

Mattie sat down, crossing her pretty legs, hem of own short dress receding.

"Remember the famous novel we discussed while on the airplane?"

"Yes, I do, Mme. Matilda."

"The one you insisted I reread, having I done so originally under pressure in school and not taken time to make a full assessment of its quality."

"Yes I do, Mme. Matilda."

"Well, I reread it just recently. As you predicted, I discovered it's indeed a piece of truly superb, immortal literature. I owe my rediscovery of the book completely to your fine artistic judgment."

Pascale looked away modestly, crossed her legs opposite.

"*See.* Just as I promised you would find it, Mme. Matilda."

A waiter presented menus.

"I'll let you order for me," insisted Pascale.

The idea of the girl asking the meal be selected for her, she trusting in a certain adult's better judgment, produced in Mattie a warm, endearing sensation. "If you so wish, Cherie."

Just as on the pair's flight together from Frankfurt, Pascale emitted a matchless aura. As on previous occasion, the marvelous uncanny radiance expanded outward until bringing viewer within its own glittering diameter. Just as before, the gleam and the experience of being privileged spectator were too beautiful, exhilarating to put into words. As an American would say—*you just had to have been there.*

Mattie opened the ornate, *La Belle Époque*-style menu to investigate what Mme. Roussillon was offering tonight. As on every occasion patronizing *La Petite Madeleine* both the food and the choices offered, were, to say at the very least, excellent. After telling the waiter her choices, she turned gaze intently, though furtive upon the four-foot-ten-inch artist. A tear came to right longing, adult green eye. "The child I never had," Mattie thought.

Slowly, fondly, her deep, watery green eyes protective and approvingly surveyed the "Divine Child," *Mattie's* "Divine Child," from head to foot. She inspected her *Little Tosca's* clothes. Watched the manner Pascale crossed her pretty legs, how she sat daintily in chair, placed sculpted hands in lap. Mattie inspected even the steady rhythm of *Miniature Tess's* breathing. It produced by fine, healthy lungs beneath well-developing teenage breasts. Finally, she contemplated loving on the girl's so cute face applied it given just the proper touch of makeup and no more.

"The most splendid little lady imaginable!" thought Mattie. "She's grace itself! Her clothing, personal comportment, manner of respectful address, way in which she sits in a chair, places her hands. Even the smile, she, makes! Perfect! What's more and this is the true sign of her being a lady, Marie conducts herself as she does instinctively! She doesn't *try* to be a lady, she is a lady reflexively! Marie is a *lady* to her very soul! She couldn't stop being a lady even if she tried!"

"The child's body is developing most admirably" judged the adult with a delight similar to any mother in same situation. "So sweet a face, she has! She's developing fine curves and fine proportions! I see she's developed considerably since we first met her on the plane and that was less than a year ago. Fine legs and bust. Two more years are still necessary for her physical development to complete but then she'll be a truly striking piece of femininity!"

The food arrived.

"*Mmm*!" declared Pascale with big smile, indicating great enjoyment of the meal and deep appreciation for the one deciding on meal courses. "*Mmm*! You're a real gourmande, Mme. Matilda!"

"Thank-you, Cherie. I'm so delighted to receive your approval."

Mattie crossed her legs opposite.

Pascale crossed hers opposite, same.

Dr. Eisenberg poured them each white wine in narrow necked glasses. "So tell me what's happened to you since we last crossed-paths, Marie? Tell me all the details. I'm dying to hear every last teeniest, tiniest, teensiest awesome one." She listened with rapt attention.

Pascale recounted events since the two friends separated at *Charles de Gaulle Airport*. Beginning with a description of those wonderful first six carefree days while imaging come to Paris only as a tourist, she next, described the series of unexpected and ever-more suspicious telephone calls from Father. Then, she spoke of the horrible nightmare turned all too real life the sheltered girl experienced on finding herself marooned forever far from home.

The fetching victor of the *Battle of Heidelberg* made an expression of deep concern. She pressed her friend's hand tight in a sign of immense sympathy. "How dreadful, positively dreadful! If only I'd been there to protect you!"

"So kind of you Mme. Matilda" replied Pascale, "but these were international events out of any of our control. I understand today those events were long in the making, long in the brewing. I guess I should actually feel fortunate I was in Paris when they broke out. Father knew it too but didn't tell me. That's why after so long refusing to allow me traveling alone, he one day suddenly announced I could. I see now he wanted me out of the country before the crisis occurred."

"So you came from *that* country?"

"Yes Mme. Matilda, I came from *that* country."

"Well you're safe today. So good indeed you were away when the nasty business all erupted."

"I'd not be such a helpless-baby now on finding myself on my own" insisted Pascale. "I'm not quite as stupid as I used to be, Mme. Matilda. I've come to understand a lot more about the world. At least I'm certainly trying, making every possible effort. It's slow for me I confess since this learning, understanding, came to me a bit late. Father, as wonderful and loving and caring of me as he was, also deliberately kept me ignorant about the greater world. Ignorant, until I was forced to learn about it all of a sudden. It's a greater world before coming to Paris, I'd little considered, or had any reason to. It's because of the way I was raised."

"Don't be angry with Father, Mme. Matilda!" pleaded *Chere Petite.* "Father is a wonderful, loving, caring man who thought he was protecting me. Protecting me from things back in my own country, at least back in my own country in the past, I'd never, as a *girl* need to know."

"Don't worry" injected Brendel's Daughter, expression of deep concern on pretty face. "Don't worry, I'll never think ill, of *Father.* He was raising you as he believed was best I in his society."

"Though of course the last time he and I spoke" Pascale said, "Father for all his effort keeping me sheltered too long from the world assure me—and I certainly didn't think so then—assured me I would succeed in that world."

"Life can be ironic."

"Yes, Mme. Matilda, life can be ironic."

"But please, please, Cherie, tell your special friend more! Tell her all the thrilling, stirring, inspiring details!"

Pascale recounted Mme. Castellane's blessed intervention which in turn led to precious new friendships, irreplaceable emotional bonds never thought possible back home. "Even now, after all these months, though" she confessed, "even with all these new friends I've made here, it's difficult to fully think of Paris as *home*. Home—in the way only *home* is ever *home*.'

"I'm sorry, Cherie."

Adult stroked lovingly Teenager's multitudinous jet-black hair.

"I'm sorry, Cherie"

"Still, Mme. Matilda," assured Pascale, "I'm making progress 'in that department'—as Mme. Castellane would say. I've completely accepted the old home I came from, the old home where I was born, old society in which I was born and grew up in, no longer exists. It can't be found even if I actually went back. It's gone. 'You can't go home again.' Especially to to one that no longer exists! Paris is my current life, Paris is my future. As I mentioned in my note, Mme. Castellane is helping me with the process of becoming a French citizen. Paperwork takes time."

Mattie held her companion's hand in show of warm personal sympathy.

"I also know for certain" promised the Divine Child, "the day on which Paris will be my home, be my home in the way only my *home* is my *home,* isn't far away."

"Good, good!"

"And I know the *Stupid Kid* first coming to Paris" added Pascale, referring to herself, "no longer exists! Or, praise God, ever-so soon wont exist anymore."

"Don't denigrate yourself, Darling. Remember, I met you before all these nasty events transpired! I met you when you claim to have been a *Stupid Kid* and that's clearly not the impression I got of you!"

"That's so kind, Mme. Matilda. I hope I can live-up to your expectations."

"*Mme. Matilda"* she admonished, "doesn't want hearing any more foolishness! Now describe more about your adventures."

Pascale concluded her colorful account with a description of Richard Castellane.

"Fascinating, exciting!" declared listener, enraptured. "Amazing! Terrific! Glorious! I pray now that we've linked-up again, I can perform a bit larger part in your thrilling saga!" If not given to hyperbole, on this particular evening, terms like: *fascinating, exciting, amazing, terrific, glorious* struck Mattie as quite appropriate. This unique teenager's tale was nothing less than a *saga*.

Pascale didn't supply every *tiniest, teeniest* detail. She from refrained mentioning her two suicide attempts, scrupulously avoided telling the silly way er friend's professional card with address and phone number was lost. "No matter what Professor Eisenberg thinks" reflected young artist silent, "I was a stupid baby to let that accident happen!"

Mattie crossed her legs in sheer hose opposite.

Pascale crossed own bare legs opposite, same.

"As memory recalls Dear, you were originally to be in Paris ten days.'"

"So I assumed, Mme. Matilda."

"Then, you were going directly back to your parents?"

"Yes, Mme. Matilda."

"Your family wanted you back?"

"Before the crisis in my country broke-out and Father sent me abroad for safety, it was arranged for me to to be married the following month. I originally looked upon the trip to Paris as a last chance being independent. I was going to become the wife of Father's political and military ally, Field Marshal Chamoun."

"Good Lord!" exclaimed Brendel's Daughter, wincing. "Married at your age? Obscene! In France that's illegal! You're a child! You've the sacred right to remain a child for a few more years! Married? *Good Lord*!" She recalled Field Marshal Chamoun photographed in a recent issue of *Der Spiegel*. Today the ousted-military strongman was living in comfortable, well-healed exile in Rome. From photograph in the most popular leading German magazine he appeared in his fifties. "Good Lord!"

"It wasn't my choice, Mme. Matilda."

"Of course not, Sweetheart."

Mattie visualized this unworldly, four-foot-ten-inch adolescent lying naked, prone as a hairy, sweaty, lusting middle-aged male descended proprietary from above. The very idea caused her to wince. "How revolting" she thought, unspoken words breaking henceforth into *First*

Person, "how, unimaginably revolting! It ought to be a crime! That virgin, *my* virgin forced under the power of some dirty man who should be with someone his own age! Not if I have anything to do with it! If he dares come from Rome after my child I'll go to court! I'll speak to the government! I'll speak to the newspapers, television! I'll never allow that dictator anywhere near my innocent daughter!"

"It wasn't my choice, Mme. Matilda," explained Pascale. "I don't want a husband or wish to get pregnant. World culture claims women constantly yearn for a man and possess a natural *Mother Urge.* It asserts women can be awarded a *Nobel Prize,* paint a *Sistine Chapel,* compose a *Ninth Symphony,* sculpt a David, write *Hamlet,* forever alter the course of human events yet still feel total failures if they never get a man or have a baby. Who decides these crazy things? Certainly not members of our sex! I'm a woman too but never believed I'll be a failure without a man or baby."

"I positively adore, treasure children, though," she added. "Briefly, I contemplated becoming a nanny. I'd rather like to one day own a few children myself. Maybe one day I'll adopt some. I think I could be a good Mama."

"How wonderful that's to hear. I know you'll be an excellent Mama."

"But I've never wanted to be pregnant" reiterated Pascale. "And since I don't want to be pregnant, never want to produce children, I'll be the wrong one selected for that assignment. If Field Marshal Chamoun wants a wife to bear him children—and Field Marshal Chamoun's actually a very good, loving, sweet, well-meaning man if terribly clumsy expressing his feelings—there are many other fertile girls who do possess a supposed-*Mother Urge* and are infinitely better-qualified for the assignment, better suited to give what Marshal Chamoun wants from a wife. I hope those last sentences didn't come off as vulgar, Mme. Matilda."

"Not-at-all, Darling. I perfectly understand. You described it quite delicately."

"Good." Pascale made no mention of her unconquerable terror, physical as well as mental loathing of being touched by any male except Father. Being touched by any male except Father gave her the *Creeps.* It was a *The Creeps,* made only creepier because she couldn't explain the reason. The prospect of being naked, prone beneath Marshal Chamoun's body she too found *unimaginably revolting* but not for the same reasons.

"No, Sweetheart, it wasn't your choice."

"But that's the way weddings are done in the society I *came* from Mme. Matilda" explained Pascale momentarily assuming role of protective, older partner. "At least in the section of the society I came from. Arranged Marriage, has been our tradition since the days of *the Old Testament.*"

"I see"

"Every husband and wife I ever met, were brought together in this fashion. In fact, they expected it to be so. Doing it independently would seem as strange back home as Arranged Marriage is to you."

"I see"

"I'm not personally opposed to Arranged Marriage. It's the practice I'm accustomed to, Mme. Matilda. Arranged Marriage where I was born is nothing as you assume from movies or pulp-fiction. I've seen a great many, a very large number of Arranged Marriages prove quite successful—my father and mother, all my aunts and uncles, cousins, neighbors, my three best friends' parents. An experienced matchmaker is hired by a family to find one of its members a husband or bride. A matchmaker can be as skilled in her career as I'm sure you are as a university professor. Considering too, how fifty-percent of the 'love-matches' in the 'more enlightened" West end in divorce, my country's 'old-fashion' matchmakers, appear infinitely better able to determine which couples best fit together than do boys and girls in Europe and America trying on their, own!"

"That's an interesting point you make."

"Cultures are different in different countries."

"Well you live in France now Sweetheart" injected Brendel's Daughter, she taking Pascale's right hand reassuringly with own adult left. "You don't need to be penetrated by a man until you want to, or if you wish, never at all. Queen Elizabeth I, Simone Weil, Emily Dickinson and Jane Austen each created a lasting mark on history though never once penetrated by a man! They didn't need lying with a man to leave a permanent and positive influence on civilization and history! Don't be pressured into consenting to something you truly don't want to do. Don't consent to something which will only make you unhappy, unable to live your life, exercise your talents as you know best! Sex is hopefully the product of mutual love and devotion. Not force and another's domination."

"If you ever feel troubled about how to confront this issue" she promised, "you can always depend on me protecting you, offering encouragement and advice."

"That's ever-so kind of you, Mme. Matilda" answered Pascale, touched. "I'll always turn to you. I'm so happy, grateful you want me as your friend!" Lifting her narrow-necked wine glass, she proposed a toast. "To: friends!"

"*To friends!*" endorsed older friend, "*to friends!*"

"We're friends beyond the end of time, Mme. Matilda!"

"*We're friends beyond all time and space,* Sweetheart!"

They downed one serving of wine, then a second.

"But no more toasts for tonight" then directed Dr. Eisenberg. "Marie's unaccustomed to liquor. Mme. Matilda doesn't want you tipsy!" She poured them coffee. "Now let's talk about some lighter topics, my friend 'to the end of time and beyond.' I want this occasion to be a celebration, a glorious reunion. You can't imagine how I so wished finding you again!"

Pascale smiled humbly, gratefully. "You can't imagine how I've yearned seeing you too, Mme. Matilda!"

"Two contented, easy-to-please ladies we are it seems!"

"So we are, Mme. Matilda."

Setting worrisome matters aside, the pair eagerly embarked on relaxing, mutually-enjoyable *Chit-Chat*. Or what was for them *Chit-Chat*—piping about Thomas Mann, Goethe, Colette, The French Revolution, *Return of the Native, Tess of the d'Urbervilles, Jude the Obscure,* Wordsworth.

This being only second encounter with her magical little friend, Mattie was yet to learn of Pascale's greatest, truest and most unique talent—painting.

The narrow, cobblestone streets of the Marais were hushed. Streetlights on shepherd crook-shaped lanterns provided an intimate glow. Above front door of several old houses was an historical plaque. The hectic, unfriendly, self-consumed modern age was far away. If Colbert, Racine, Ronsard, Talleyrand or Balzac were to wave from a horse-drawn carriage, even climb out to say some kind words to the two ladies, it wouldn't be a total shock. Far from it! This particular treasured evening, Pascale and Mattie were "friends beyond time." If the other patrons of *La Petite Madeleine* departed, Mme. Roussillon signaled permission the remaining two stay as long as they wished.

Pascale fastened a button of cardigan.

Each lady crossed legs opposite, same.

Mattie placed napkin to mouth, soon, set it down again on lap.

"Oh, see the time!" exclaimed Pascale, looking at own delicate watch on delicate wrist. "Having dinner with you this evening has been positively *awesome* Mme. Matilda. I look forward to us enjoying many dinners together if that's not too bold of me."

"Oh it's not being 'too bold' at all Cherie" answered Brendel's Daughter, happily. "I look forward to us enjoying many, many, many evenings together, if that's not too bold of me!"

The two giggled with mutual schoolgirl excitement. For the older of friends-beyond-time, this reunion was more successful than she dared dream. For yet a third time she witnessed Pascale's aura gleam at its full indescribable brilliance, the sensation Mattie received at being witness too was just as uncannily remarkable. "My child" she said Mattie under her breath, "*my* Divine Child."

"You've graciously let me run-along not permitting you a chance-getting-a—word-in-edgewise, Mme. Matilda," apologized her special friend. "I so-apologize for my-unladylike behavior. Normally, Mme. Castellane doesn't permit me outside this late. She must be very worried. Luckily, since we had dinner she can't send me to bed without supper. Mme. Castellane is old fashion about raising daughters. Of course it's in no small part because she's *old fashion* that I've survived to meet you again, Mme. Matilda. I must leave now but we've got to meet again soon—*very* soon. Tonight was Awesome! I promise next time I won't dominate the conversation."

The ladies rose to go.

"And when we do meet next" advised Mattie in responsible voice, leaving on table a big tip, "we must discuss your future prospects. I feel so ashamed-of-myself not bringing the matter up earlier. I've been terribly remiss in not mentioning this when first we met."

"Yes, Mme. Matilda?"

"You're truly exceptional. You're a soul who comes along just once in centuries."

Miniature Artist turned away embarrassed.

"Listen to me! It's absolutely true!" declared Mattie, taking hold of Pascale by shoulders. Her own adult voice making it unmistakable she'd tolerate no further teenage opposition. "It's my responsibility. You're a soul who comes along just once in several centuries. And you're a woman, too! You've a sacred duty to yourself and an equally sacred duty to every woman! They all depend on you! Success for you is a success for all our sex! Hear me?"

Pascale turned away embarrassed.

Dr. Eisenberg instantly applied her special friend a resolute shake before looking her directly in eyes. "Listen to me Child! Listen carefully to my every word! Carefully do and perform all I instruct!"

"Ironic, is it not" mused the professor. "This is just how Mama spoke to me–squeezed my shoulders–left me in no doubt who was in-charge–what was expected of me and the consequences if I disobeyed–This is how Mama made me a success. '*Win the first prize Child!*' Mama said. '*Get the highest score on the test or your fanny will really regret it!*' Now I'm doing the same with my own offspring. Little Marie wasn't poor, illegitimate, or from a rough town, like me. Yet ultimately our two situations aren't all that different. In a different way, we're just the same and with the same obstacles placed against us. From the beginning Mama was right to treat me as she did. Mama was strict with me because she loved me–Is it a wonder then I'm being the same with my own offspring!"

"Listen, Child" counseled the victor of the *Battle of Heidelberg*. "You're a genius! I know that's a word so bandied-about it's hideously debased. But you're a *genius*–in the real sense! True, your formal education was sorely neglected. However, with your original, independent, penetrating, naturally-analytic mind, a lack of formal education might actually be an advantage! Your genius won't be saturated with outdated, disproved, dead-white-male bullshit. No corrupt, self-promoting, shameless political prostitute-selected textbooks will be doping-up, fatally softening, your piercing little brain like pseudo-intellectual morphine!"

"Please forgive my bad language," apologized Mattie. "But reality, whether we like it or not, is still–*reality*. You can't destroy *the Old Order* until *the Old Order* first lets you slip through its gates. If you're going to live in France, you must–let me repeat *must*–obtain a Baccalaureate! Never attending school can't legally prevent you taking the examination. Winning a Baccalaureate will also do much to speed-up your naturalization."

"But preparing for it, Mme. Matilda?" asked Pascale, anxious. "Not having attended school, I'll be hopelessly behind in many areas. How can I prepare, even know *how* to prepare?"

"Don't worry Sweetheart" assured Brendel's Daughter, releasing friend's shoulders, addressing her now in welcoming, sheltering voice; stern look changing to warm smile. "Don't fear Cherie. I'll tutor, drill, prepare, you for the examination, personally! I'll get you ready for it, personally! I'll personally make sure you pass the *Baccalaureate* in triumph!"

Pascale searched for appropriate words but couldn't find them.

"What can I do to reward all your kindness, Mme. Matilda?"

"No need doing anything. Simply be yourself a—*genius*. As Mama told me—'My happiness is your happiness. Your triumph, mine. Go forth and be all I know you are!'"

FIREBIRD

....

"*P*raise to the Virgin!" exclaimed the proprietress of *La Nouvelle Heloise*, making heartfelt-Sign of the Cross over protégée standing loyally beside. She kissed the religious medallion on end of silver necklace bearing image of St. Therese of Lisieux. "Praise to the Little Flower, too! Let's not forget the Little Flower!"

"Ooh! Ooh!" squealed Véronique, her long cherry-blonde hair covering pretty face. "My precious own darling, own miniature-scholar just won a *Bacho*, a *Bacho*!"

Up-and-down Véronique jumped. Up-and-down, she jumped. "Ooh-we! Ooh-we!" Unlike Matilda, always in heels, Véronique currently wearing indoor flats, was better able performing leaps, gyrations. At last, hair still disheveled, she carefully placed the valuable certificate with accompanying cover-letter back into the manila folder the postman delivered this morning. Atop the folder was printed **To: Marie Castellane, From: Ministry of National Education.** Just as Matilda promised, her little friend passed. In fact, the score she achieved placed the girl in the top 1-percent of all taking the baccalaureate examination this year across the entire country and all its overseas possessions.

"I couldn't have done it without Professor Eisenberg's help!" pleaded Pascale/Marie, straightening her bobbysocks. "It was only at Professor Eisenberg's insistence I took the examination at all. Professor Eisenberg donated so much of her valuable time to coaching and tutoring me, advising me. She supplied me resolution, courage, when I was nervous, scared. It would be impossible for me to succeed without Professor Eisenberg's guidance. My success is really her success, I—"

"Hush-up!" she was swift admonished. "Madame permits Child no *Witless Woman*-foolishness!"

Véronique retied the huge red satin bow crowning surrogate-offspring's ever-more voluminous jet-black hair. "Modesty is essential for our sex to be *proper,* Marie. I knew you possessed far more than adequate modesty from the moment Darling first appeared at the hotel front desk. A young lady endowed by God with superb gifts of creative talent and personal character is most striking when exhibiting these attributes with refined feminine grace, when looking *proper.*"

"Yes, Mme. Castellane"

"However, there's no reason *Cherie* denigrate herself, either."

"Yes, Mme. Castellane"

"There, that's better." Completed work on the huge red satin bow in her ward's ever-more voluminous jet-black hair, Véronique's voice became protective, shielding. She gave charge a loving, maternal kiss on forehead. "My pocket-sized darling is a *giant*-proportioned scholar! Your result places you in the top 1-percent of all the children taking the examination in the entire country and all of France's overseas possessions!"

Many things were in progress at *La Nouvelle Heloise.* "None, anywhere near as important as this, however!" insisted the hotel's proprietress. "Nothing in the universe possibly matches receiving the news my protégée won a *Baccalaureate.*" Since Napoleon introduced this academic degree, winning a *Bacho* is crucial, often determinant for teenagers obtaining success as adults in modern secular French society. "No doubt about that, Child!"

"The diploma is so impressive to look at!" further bubbled Véronique.

"Yes indeed, Mme. Castellane".

It's wording inscribed in elegant, antique script printed on thick parchment-like paper, bearing official symbol and motto of the Fifth Republic atop, signature of the Minister of National Education at bottom—this greatly-cherished, much-sought-after document was inspiring to view. On the papered-wall behind hotel lobby front counter hung glossy framed photographs of Richard and the siblings' late-mother Chantal Castellane.

"We'll hang it—*here*" chirped Véronique, motioning in chosen direction. "That's where it belongs! Right beside Richard and Mama! That's just where Child's *Baccalaureate* will be placed henceforth! I'll place it right next to my pictures of Mama and Richard. I'm going to get the certificate framed and hung here for the world to see! The entire world will and must learn Little Giotto has a *Baccalaureate*! And what a *Baccalaureate*! Besides a brilliant artist, you also rank in the top 1-percent of all children taking the *Bacho* examination in the entire country and all its overseas possessions! What a smart, gifted, talented, unique, priceless, Christian-darling my Marie is!"

"If so you say, Mme. Castellane."

Distinguished teenager directed gray-green eyes at waxed, dark-brown wood floor. She shuffled in place, left shoe come unbuckled. Her entire four-foot-ten, nicely developing adolescent feminine body squirmed in demonstration of intellectual, emotional unease. As heartfelt as was her benefactress's praise to hear, Marie wasn't quite sure it truly earned.

"Don't be embarrassed" counseled Véronique. "Be proud of your studious, God-fearing self! I'm indescribably proud of *you*. Top 1-percent in the entire country and all its overseas possessions! A great artist too! Instead of *a Scatterbrained Female* you're a tribute to all Christendom! Sister Claire and Sister Genevieve are coming over to *La Nouvelle Heloise* for lunch tomorrow. They'll be as delighted as I am when seeing the *Bacho* my Sweetheart earned through her diligent, God-fearing endeavors. Your test score placed you in the top 1-percent in the entire country and all its overseas possessions!"

"Thank-you for your kind words, Mme. Castellane. You're always so concerned for my welfare" replied Marie/Pascale grateful but not thoroughly convinced she possessing the brilliance others claimed.

"Sister Jeanne Navarro wishes meeting you when next she visiting Paris, Sweetheart" informed Véronique, broad smile of maternal pride on moist, red painted lips. "She's heard so much from Sister

Claire and Sister Genevieve about how: 'Mme. Castellane adopted a miniature genius!' How did Richard describe you? Oh yes, 'Marie's a Rembrandt-in-bobby-socks.' Sister Jeanne was told how Richard gave you permission to paint a mural of *The Nativity* on one of the walls of our church. *The Nativity* according to your own interpretation! Sister Jeanne hears about: 'the magnificent prodigy creating murals of the same artistic quality as Giotto, Rivera, Orozco or Siqueiros.'"

Teenager flushed.

"Sister Genevieve faxed Sister Jeanne photos of the mural" Véronique continued, again fiddling with the huge satin bow she insisted be ever worn in Marie's multitudinous jet-black hair. "Sister Jeanne found the photos most impressive. 'It appears Mme. Castellane has better taste in art than the average *Scatterbrained Female*' she must've remarked. Anyway, Sister Jeanne was so delighted with the photos she's called a temporary halt to her hectic schedule in order she might make a special trip to Paris to see 'the Divine Child's' mural with own eyes. So I'm inviting her for lunch along with Richard and the two good sisters."

"Ooh, mercy!" giggled Véronique. "I'm so excited about your future, Little Marie! You're on the way to setting a grand, brilliant Christian example to the entire world." She held protégée close to bust with both arms, soon began gently rocking the pair back-and-forth, two become one. "I'm confident you'll set the entire world a magnificent Christian example."

The rambling *Baroque* townhouse with adjoining subdivisions and *British Style* garden behind high red brick enclosing wall today known as *La Nouvelle Heloise,* was constructed in the early-Eighteenth Century as a Duchess's private residence. After the 1789 Revolution, the complex served until the mid-twentieth century: first, as a government ministry, next, as foreign consulate, later still, as discreet address for a statesman's *Kept-Woman.* Upon her death, it reverted to foreign consulate. Charming, historic, multipurpose, this palatial estate only assumed its latest manifestation in 1958 upon the second coming of General de Gaulle.

In truth, *La Nouvelle Heloise* was as much an aristocratic rooming-house as Five Star hotel. On the second and third floors were located the most expensive and largest suites of rooms for rent. In size and luxury, they exceeded accommodations found in any urban mansion or stately rural residence in Europe. Each apartment was elegantly furnished and decorated, boasting priceless art work hung on cork-lined walls, atop polished floors, found under glass, or seen high above on *Rococo* fresco ceilings. Each apartment was provided a: dance floor and dining hall with chandeliers, movie screen, *CD/Internet* set, weight-machines, a library containing first edition copies of great world literature. Kitchens and bathrooms possessed the most up-to-date amenities. *French Windows* opened on colonnaded sandstone balconies offering unforgettable vistas of Paris.

Sorry. They're long ago snatched-up. The suites have been occupied by the same: Marquis and Marquise; identical world-renowned diplomat and famous general, the latter two's common-law wives; ever since Chantal Castellane was proprietress. The identity of which distinguished guest occasionally shared her bed, fathered her children, Chantal took to grave, divulging truth not even to the great gentleman's offspring. The boy and girl soon lost interest in subject, both coming to assume parental arrangements at *La Nouvelle Heloise* no different than any other family.

In contrast to most single-mothers, Chantal experienced no legal difficulties, financial strain, or time concern. Nor was she target of neighborhood gossip or recipient of unsolicited-advice. Chantal's life as an unwed-mother was quite the opposite. Her coterie of aristocratic, well-healed, well-connected lodgers arranged and paid for her son to be educated at France's best private schools and later at the nation's most prestigious medical college. When Richard exhibited singular skill as a physician, the grandees happily employed their influence with the powers-that-be to advance his career. They also promoted the young man's burgeoning reputation as an imminent archeologist and scholar of the ancient Middle East. All devout Roman Catholics, the lords and ladies weekly attended Mass at Richard's church in the 5th Arrondissement. They insisted all their grandchildren be christened by the much-noted physician/priest/researcher whose patrons were pleased to say they knew, treasured him since birth.

Chantal's daughter Véronique inherited ownership of the highly-profitable family business. If she never attended school like her golden boy-brother, Véronique received a valuable informal-education serving as beloved mascot of *La Nouvelle Heloise's* elite guests. The globetrotting-diplomat and the famous general each regarded the girl as "a priceless, incomparable jewel." Both showered her with hugs and kisses, cuddles and strokes. Both adults sometimes found themselves nearly in a *tug-of-war* to place the child on own separate gentlemanly-lap. Ambassador Lefebvre taught Véronique to read and to acquire an appreciation for great poetry and drama. From General Rochambeau, she learned to become an excellent swimmer, markswoman and alpinist.

Their own daughter—Renée—dying of leukemia when only four, the Marquis and Marquise de Beaufontain developed a particular attachment to Véronique. Soon, they regarding her as a surrogate-daughter. Nothing was morbid, predatory, in the affection the two nobles eager and daily provided. They didn't try making her wear Renée's clothes or adopt Renée's voice, physical comportment. They didn't address Véronique by an absent-loved one's name. Nor, once did they exert emotional-blackmail attempting to win the child's allegiance away from her natural mother. *Treasure* wasn't merely a proxy. She was a special little soul to be cherished for her own sake.

As over time Renée inevitably receded from parents' immediate thoughts, Véronique unconsciously took her place in the Marquis and Marquise's heart. They showered her with hugs, pets, and kisses, enjoyed brushing and tying her hair, placing her on lap, telling her stories, teaching her poems and songs and stories. Véronique was purchased an entire wardrobe of pretty dresses along with dozens of elegant chapeaux.

The Marquis de Beaufontain was an art connoisseur. He frequently took his little favorite along to museum and to gallery openings where child developed a deep, lasting love of fine art. The nobleman's personal tastes were decidedly more conservative than the modernist ones of Véronique. Nevertheless, instead of many adults in similar position, the Marquis didn't wish altering the opinions of this young, impressionable girl to merely reflect his own. The Marquis possessed no interest in Véronique serving as a dainty sounding-board. Knowledge he successfully awakened in her an equivalent attraction to the fine arts, was for, the Marquis enough influence exercising over his special junior-friend.

When Véronique was home at *La Nouvelle Heloise,* no museums or gallery openings to attend, the charming Marquise de Beaufontain trained her to perfection at—*Chit-Chat*; correctly exiting a car; properly taking a gentleman's arm; sitting down and rising again as a lady should; making a refined mile, cough or laugh; at pouring tea in a genteel manner. The Marquise was careful her mascot displayed faultless ability at performing the role, exercising the duties of a garden party hostess and estate chatelaine. She also taught the girl flower arrangement and horseback riding.

Véronique was enabled by the Marquis and Marquise to receive dance, piano and drawing lessons from tutors normally restricted to daughters of the aristocracy. The lord and lady's pet, cuddly treasured toy, soon demonstrated striking talent for each of these three traditional feminine *Accomplishments.* Unlike daughters of families with documented-pedigree of nobility receding into the mists of the Middle Ages, this thoroughly bourgeois, shop-keeper girl of uncertain parentage was capable of far more than bounding ungainly across the floor singing out of tune, playing *Chop-Sticks,* or drawing stick-figures. When hearing warm approval for her latest picture, vigorous applause at the completion of her own newest graceful stage performance or rendition of a famous work, the five-year-old received these compliments for more than politeness sake.

Above all, Chantal's daughter displayed exceptional aptitude for ballet. A gift made even more impressive through her ability not just to exquisitely reproduce steps designed by others, but her increasingly skill at inventing leaps, spins, dips and other delicately artistic motions purely the little girl's own. She possessed tremendous potential not only as a dancer but also as a bold, innovative choreographer. Should she dedicate her life, commit all her time and energy, strength both mental and physical to fully honing this magnificent potential, Marie-Therese-Véronique Castellane would in a relatively brief time both capture and retain the well-deserved reputation as her generation's finest ballerina.

She might even prove the finest dancer in a century. Chantal and all the aristocratic lodgers of *La Nouvelle Heloise* uniformly pressed the child to follow that path.

"*How nice it would be to have a great dancer in the house!*"

"*What a conversation stopper it would be to say 'I know a prima ballerina!'*"

"*Her baby the finest dancer in Europe, nothing could make a Mama prouder!*"

"*My sister is the greatest prima ballerina of them all!*"

"*If he were alive now, Degas would eagerly ask to paint you practicing!*"

What a remarkable child you are! Just to bask in your own glory is enough satisfaction for any mere gawky, clumsy mortal!"

"*Remember, David danced for God in the tabernacle?*"

All these fond hopes expressed by the members of Véronique's nontraditional tight-knit family soon appeared fast on the way to fulfillment. Where once the world spoke of *The Great Pavlova,* it looked abundantly clear it soon might too discuss as frequent and with perhaps still higher sincere admiration of *The Exquisite Castellane.*

"*No Child! Do it again but faster, gentler!*"

"*Yes, Monsieur*"

"*Then get to it, time's a-wasting!*"

"*Is that better this time, Monsieur?*"

"*A bit better Child but still far from good enough. Do it again!*"

During succeeding years as beloved daughter, cherished mascot, special junior-friend grew from childhood into puberty, then adulthood, Véronique devoted nearly her entire waking life, to ballet. The girl was permitted no choice. Talent can on occasion be as much a cross to bear as a blessed advantage. She devoted to it as much as fourteen hours of relentless, diligent, repetitive, all-consuming mental and physical practice daily. Day in, day, out.

"*No Child, that's not fast, gentler enough!*"

"*Sorry, Monsieur, I meant to do it exactly as you told me.*"

"*If you're really sorry you'll perform the move as I told you!*"

"*Sorry*"

"*I said get-to-it!*"

147

Nevertheless, as time passed, Véronique's harsh instructors were also each of a steadily and speedier increasing distinguished reputation. The greater and greater severity with which the young dancer was treated, the progressively more rigorous, uncompromising higher demands placed on her ability to perform was equaled, unbeknownst to her, only by the way her martinet instructors fought one another cats-and-dogs, tooth-and-nail to win the privilege of being selected to shine in the little ballerina's own glory. As said Isaiah: "Rise, shine, thy light has come and the glory of the Lord has risen upon thee."

"Repeat it Child! Better now! No! That's not good enough, do-it-again!"

"Is that better, Monsieur?"

"That's still not good enough little girl, do-it-again!"

"Did I do it better that time, Monsieur?"

"Yes indeed you did Child but still not easier, swifter enough."

"What about that time, Monsieur?"

"Still again, Child but this time faster, swifter and easier, graceful!"

"Have I done it correctly, Monsieur?"

"Yes, at last Child, Excellent. Now, do it in the opposite direction!"

Not infrequently, Véronique received biting smacks with stick.

"Do the move faster and easier Child or you'll instantly feel even harder smacks on your bottom!"

"Yes, Monsieur, I must do it faster and easier or I'll feel ever harder smacks on my bottom."

"It's all for your own good Child. One like you requires a strong hand."

"Yes. Monsieur, one like me requires a strong hand."

"One day you'll be grateful, Child."

"Yes, Monsieur, one day I'll be grateful I'm treated with a strong hand."

"Now get to it little girl! Do the motion again just as fast, easy."

As painful, repetitive, exhausting, often humiliating, demeaning as this training might be, it appeared more than worthwhile. Véronique rapidly bloomed. Her name and the artistry it embodied, spread. Newspaper and magazine reporters asked the girl for interviews. Reliable stories about her mounting ability, predictions about her glorious future, soon caught the attention of major cultural and social circles across the continent. Famous ballerinas, current or retired when provided an opportunity to see the newcomer perform, unanimously endorsed her *exceptional* and likely *historic* potential.

Chantal and her aristocratic lodgers studiously kept the child's growing fame in their own firm adult hands, were meticulous the youngster wasn't exploited by self-promoting outsiders. Chantal and her aristocratic lodgers controlled all access to Véronique. No one was permitted speaking, even seeing the girl, without first rigorously vetted by her protectors. From a purely business, promotional angle, this strategy made perfect sense. Like the Medieval Caliph of Baghdad—mystery, enticing rumor, strict restriction of access—serve to infinitely enhance the isolated one's influence, fame and prestige.

The only individual beyond *La Nouvelle Heloise* granted free-contact to Véronique, was Cardinal Casimir Blanchard. Archbishop of Paris, president of the Council of French Roman Catholic Bishops, he also served as papal nuncio to the *United Nations*. A brilliant intellectual with *Old World, Mitteleuropa* education, His Eminence was fluent in multiple foreign languages. Renowned poet, painter, composer, recipient of the Legion d'Honneur, he was elected one of the just hundred lifetime members—"Immortals" of the *Académie Francaise*.

Superb journalist and social critic, Cardinal Blanchard's ever-insightful, illuminating, witty, always fun reading, syndicated column appeared in both secular and religious newspapers twice weekly. Where, it was enjoyed by millions of fans on three continents. He was as well an avid patron of similar creative minds. Many likened the great prelate to *Renaissance* pope Julius II—soldier/diplomat/art connoisseur who selected Michelangelo to paint the *Sistine Chapel*.

Given a private exhibition of Véronique's unique abilities, the Great Man was more than pleased. So impressed was he with the child's performance, so moved in fact, this Prince of the Church leaped from chair and jumped up-and-down in place, clapping until his hands grew sore and breath was out.

"Marvelous, your daughter is still even marvelous **more!**" exclaimed Cardinal Blanchard to Chantal in impressive baritone voice, upon he at last returning to chair to rest exhausted lungs. Ecstatic happy tears raised the prelate's worldly-wise cheeks; he grinned like a little boy receiving a much yearned Christmas present.

His Eminence addressed these particular members of flock by intimate *Tu*. A spirit in his learned, cultured, experienced mind whispered listener just privileged witnessing a watershed in western cultural history. "What a precious, uniquely blessed creative soul you are, my Dear! You're *Dance* made manifest! *Dance*, itself! You're art in its purest, clearest, surest, form! You're going to be 'The dancer of an Age!'"

Depend on it, Cherie" prophesied Cardinal Blanchard after setting Véronique on his distinguished lap. "Just keep to your exquisitely-delicate, ladylike-revolutionary, gently-overwhelming path, Divine Child. In a century people will speak of you in the same breath they do of Pavlova! 'Pavlova and Castellane'—no, no, please accept my heartfelt apologies, no, no '*Castellane* and Pavlova.'—This is a watershed in history!"

"It's not only a watershed in history" he added, "a watershed in history like the Battle of Marathon or Hastings, the Storming of the Bastille in its own far more lovely, feminine, dainty way of course. It's also a watershed in history allowing me to say: 'I was there! I saw it happen!' Just ask Uncle Casimir, he was on the scene, he'll be able to give you an eyewitness account!" He sighed reflectively before kissing the ballerina tender, protective on forehead. Pressing the girl close, His Eminence rocked the pair gently back-and-forth, two souls become one. Years of unfulfilled paternal affection at last provided opportunity to be expressed. "I promise you're going to be a star."

Stunned, unsure exactly how best responding, Véronique burst into sobs.

"No reason to cry, *Little One*" assured the Great Man. "Uncle Casimir knows his Cherie will become a star!"

For all: gifted but unpublished-writers; aspiring, talented yet unrecognized visual artists; young stage and concert performers—winning the support of Cardinal Blanchard was of immeasurable value. Among Europe and America's: clubby, exclusivist, doctrinaire intellectual spheres; jealous, avaricious, restricted art communities; powerful, self-appointed arbiters of public good taste—endorsement by Cardinal Blanchard guaranteed any heretofore unappreciated-outsider swift passage to fame and easy navigation through critical acclaim's otherwise eternally-locked gates. This favor wasn't bestowed lightly, however. Nor, was such esteemed-patronage granted to the lucky recipient without representing *The Master's* full personal conviction. Across the planet, His Eminence was revered in the eyes of tens of millions of art and music lovers, countless readers of fine literature, attenders of the theater, as the "critic of critics," "scholar of scholars," "expert of experts."

Cardinal Blanchard's endorsement provided a talented novice immediate acceptance by all Europe and America's normally: bestseller-driven publishing houses; only dependable big hit-theaters; renowned ballet and opera companies, concert halls. None of the era's already-famous ballerinas received *The Master's* lofty favor as young as did Véronique Castellane.

Cardinal Blanchard suggested Véronique debut her professional career with Stravinsky's *Firebird.* Most people, the Great Man advised, were expecting she open in a more traditional work like Tchaikovsky's *Nutcracker Suite.* The more daring conception by Stravinsky, proposed His Eminence, would make a swifter impression. The ballet-appreciative public would in this way better and swifter recognize Véronique's exquisite individual, pioneering style of dance.

"Glorious *Little One*" assured the Great Man, "you possess more innovative talent, greater gift for demonstrating your chosen art upon the theater stage than probably you know yourself! This God-given innocence I see in you so well makes your performances infinitely more beautiful still."

Cardinal Blanchard wasn't disappointed.

One graceful triumph on the stage followed yet another rousing appearance in a still more illustrious theater. Commentators not easily persuaded to champion newcomers over the established ballet royalty fast joined the ranks of the brilliant girl's ever increasing legion of admirers.

Many on the political/cultural Left, notably Sister Claire, Sister Genevieve and their Order of nuns, were long at odds with Cardinal

151

Blanchard. They bitterly resented his numerous, sometimes quite undisguised-forays into national and continental affairs. Indeed, Blanchard was an unabashed living-replica of earlier time. However, so approachable, learned, charismatic, engaging, was His Eminence compared to all of contemporary Europe's usual mediocre, boorish male party hacks and pandering office-seekers, he reaped his political ambitions as no French churchman since Cardinal Mazarin. Thoroughly *apolitical* teenager Véronique might have easily fallen victim to her mentor's protracted and very public feud with the Left. Yet as further evidence of the girl's skill, her stage career was universally praised.

"No one can deny this singularly-gifted child possesses an other-worldly, blessed, God-given innocence" declared the traditionally anti-clerical press, unconsciously adopting religious terminology. "There is a perfect, unassuming grace exhibited in each and every unique step of Mlle. Castellane's superb and unprecedented performance. No reason exists communion with this matchless virgin can ever be smudged by association to politics. She likely doesn't even know what politics are! This holy child dwells far above all tawdry, back-biting, self-interested mortal affairs. She's a dancer, the finest in decades, a good chance for even longer!"

In fact, when Véronique first performed *Gisele* at the Paris L'Opera, newspapers and columnists most hostile to Cardinal Blanchard's secular aspirations proved the most warm and fulsome celebrating his new protégée, the prima ballerina. When she next performed *Firebird* with a personal interpretation so magnificent, so boldly new, so truly unique, spell-bound audiences just couldn't get enough of it.

For weeks, no sooner were tickets for additional performances printed than they were immediately snatched-up.

Hawkers made near fortunes.

One evening, the young star needed to come out and deliver the frantically-adoring audience a gracious curtsey ten times.

At the close of each performance, she was covered in bouquets of white roses.

There soon followed Véronique's first international tour. It accompanied now by not simply praise from France but acclaim for her mastery of ballet from across the planet. She won the hearts of even the worst skeptics at Moscow's Bolshoi and the Kirov/Kandinsky in Leningrad/Petersburg, at Lincoln Center in New York, Covent Garden in London, in Rome, Vienna, Lisbon, Amsterdam, Geneva, Tokyo, Bueunos Aires, Sydney, Cape Town and Los Angeles.

She once more danced superbly her own bold, truly unique interpretations of *Firebird* and *Gisele*. And in addition performed to equal perfection: *Swan Lake, Cinderella, Sleeping Beauty, Bayadere, Don Quixote, Nutcracker, Romeo and Juliette, Les Syhlphides.*

No surprise it was to Cardinal Blanchard that historic comparisons were made. Once returned to France, Véronique repeated her finest performances to nightly packed audiences, not only at the *l'Opéra* in Paris but after repeated demands from those outside the capital, in Lyon, Bordeaux, Rouen, Marseilles, Monte Carlo.

Véronique's image appeared on the covers of many prestigious magazines. She was interviewed on television (reporters first needing to pass her protectors' strict vetting process). She was, invited to see the Presidents of France, the United States and of Russia, the Queen of England, King of Sweden and the Emperor of Japan. She was given a private meeting at the Vatican with the Pope, on another occasion a personal chat with the Dalai Lama. A new perfume was brought out with her name. *DVDs* were sold hotly to preserve her image on the stage for eternity.

The nonfiction tale of Jeanne d'Arc—seeming-nondescript teenage peasant shepherdess who one day believes angels summon her to liberate her country from foreign conquerors, then eagerly obeys what she is sure her divine mission. In short order through her display of selfless idealism wins first the trust of a cynical king, next, confidently casting aside the strategy of defeatist male generals, the teenager personally leads the armies of France herself to victory after victory, soldiers uniquely inspired to follow Jeanne's mystical girlish spirit. Until eventually, being judged no longer necessary for the success she alone inspired, alone created, she is callously abandoned to her enemies and left to close her brief life in heroic martyrdom. Hers is a martyrdom which has for centuries occupied a special and always vibrant place in the human imagination. If the story of Jeanne d'Arc was recorded in noted pieces of drama, it never became the subject for ballet.

At last, a contemporary composer and choreographer decided producing the long overdue piece. Both had in mind a specific ballerina to play the central role. The two's fervent desire for her debuting it enabled both men to craft a ballet of far higher artistic quality than either ever dreamed himself capable.

When *La Pucelle* debuted in Paris at the L'Opéra, Véronique in main role, it proved a ballet as boldly new, revolutionary and influential in style as was earlier *Firebird*. Once more at the close of the performance, this ballerina was covered by her adoring spectators in flowers. Already acknowledged incomparable executing classical roles from the Nineteenth Century, recognized as no less splendid on the stage in Stravinsky Modernist works, Véronique now eliminated any lingering doubt she might not too be the unchallenged performer in contemporary dance.

She took *La Pucelle* around the world.

Soon the public came to visualize the dancer and The Maid of Orléans as one-in-the-same. "Look Mama, look!" cried a child in Zurich, tugging parent's arm to summon attention on by chance seeing Véronique at the airport. "Look Mama, look! There goes Jeanne d'Arc! Is Jeanne d'Arc going to be traveling on our plane, too?"

Soon, Cardinal Blanchard felt obliged hiring a team of bodyguards to shield the prima ballerina from her more overly enthusiastic fans. Yet, one of the most enterprising of the *Door-Johnnies* still managed eluding the escorts. As occurred similarly to Sarah Bernhardt, when this devotee begged an autograph but idol lacked a pen, the fan instantly slashed own arm with a sharp instrument and suggested Véronique provide her signature written with fan's own blood.

In Boston, New York, London, Rio de Janiero Milan and Tokyo, Véronique was mobbed at airport by ardent little girls all wishing to follow her path in life. She was often asked to deliver speeches at schools, cultural societies in churches, on television. Companies of all kinds begged Véronique to let her name and image be attached to products from sports cars to toasters. In all these cases, she graciously declined.

Assuring the little girl there were many, many far more constructive ways for a woman to leave her mark on the world than just as a ballerina.

Instead of delivering speeches, she provided exhibitions of her skill with all receipts going to charity. She avoided getting involved in business or politics. Rather than leaving the impression she was aloof, haughty—"one of those artsie-fartsie types"—Véronique's refusal to exploit her skill born of true ability not self-promotion, her refusal or to adopt positions on controversial issues, served only making her a yet still more attractive figure to the General Public.

The dancer's pretty face appeared on two stamps on two separate continents.

Both a grand boulevard and a famous heater were renamed in her honor.

Véronique became the inspiration for three still wildly popular *Rock* songs.

Then abruptly, when only twenty-six, she just returned from fifth and most renowned international tour—performing *La Pucelle, Firebird, Swan Lake, Bayadere, Sleeping Beauty, Romeo and Juliet, Gisele, Cinderella, Nutcracker* for a fifth consecutive sold-out season at the Bolshoi and the Kirov, in similarly sold-out theaters in Warsaw, Helsinki, Budapest, Prague, Milan, Berlin, Copenhagen, Stockholm, Oslo, Madrid, Lisbon, Athens, London, Tallinn, New York, Chicago, Montreal, Mexico City, San Francisco, Tokyo, New Delhi and Beijing—*Midsummer Night's Dream, Copellia, Rossignol* added to repertoire of unique personal interpretations dazzling both critics and audiences–Véronique slit her wrists.

Although surviving, the world's new Jeanne d'Arc never appeared on stage, again. Why try commit suicide, destroy the incomparable beauty she entrusted by a grander, higher dimension? Even today the answer remains one of the nagging mysteries of modern art. Strict, regimented, single-minded, blinkered, narrow, Spartan, Véronique's existence as a prima ballerina, unquestionably was. But such it is for any first rate classical pianist, violinist, opera singer, champion tennis player, *Olympic* ice skater. So too, for a number of other artistic, athletic professions requiring unstinting commitment for even the most talented continue performing at top ability. If Véronique never heard the American phrases—"Use it or lose it," "No pain no gain," No guts no glory"—she followed these same principles since the age of five. If mentally arduous; physically painful; repetitive; unbending, at times personally humiliating, following them since age five obtained for her all those remarkable victories, achieved for her so young a career of historic, decisive significance in chosen field of artistic creativity.

From the outset, Véronique uncomplaining adjusted to the enclosed, structured life of a prima ballerina. She soon learned to comply with all the harsh discipline. She did what she was told, never talked back. She blossomed for the entire world through subjecting herself to all the heavy demands made upon her. Blossomed, to an extent far more uniquely beautiful than any of the martinets, petty-dictators with their sticks even dared dream possible. Requirement to follow others' commands was also the only existence she knew or understood. Still, at just twenty-six and nowhere near reaching apex of her career, she chose ending it. And almost herself as well.

Why?

Véronique still refuses revealing: "what turned me into a *Scatterbrained Female?*" Perhaps she's not herself sure the reason.

Was it fear or sudden lack of resolution? Of course no!

Waning interest in ballet? Don't be stupid!

Boys intruding? Chantal, the Beaufontains, Ambassador Lefebvre and General Rochambeau saw to it no passionate *Stage Door Johnny* ever came within ten feet of their impressionable prodigy, made sure the virgin wasn't slipped a single message by male admirer.

Was it a *female-plumbing* problem? No, unanimously-agreed gynecologists brought in to make examinations.

Psychologists too failed detecting origin of girl's dilemma.

Recruited in capacity of spiritual adviser, Cardinal Blanchard was no more successful.

Nothing could be done.

If events traveled a different direction, millions today around the world, even those with no particular interest in ballet, would easily recognize Véronique's name. Instead, she manages a pension. It's a splendid establishment, one possessed of many historic connections. All the same, instead of dancing *Firebird, Swan Lake, La Pucelle, Sleeping Beauty, Gisele, Romeo and Juliet, Cinderella* or *Nutcracker* at the Kirov, Bolshoi, Paris l'Opéra, London's Covent Garden, or New York's Lincoln Center, she manages a pension. Decade elapsed since her unexpected retirement, length of General Public's memory being what it is, the vast majority of people don't know the century's greatest, most uniquely interpretative prima ballerina ever existed.

II

Dozens of magnificent, framed, eight-by-ten-inch, glossy, black-and-white photographs decorate the papered-walls of *La Nouvelle Heloise*. These beautiful camera shot-images record the progress of Véronique's triumphs at the Bolshoi and Kirov; at Covent Garden; at the L'Opéra; Lincoln Center and all the other most prestigious cultural venues around the world. Any mention of her tragic, near-fatal and still inexplicable early withdrawal, however, is strictly taboo. Nevertheless, even following decade of enforced silence and the twentieth century's greatest prima ballerina outwardly receiving the warmest, fondest, most affectionate regard from her nontraditional family, a residue of mutual bad-feeling persists. It's made at once apparent by observing the painful, uneasy glances *La Nouvelle Heloise's* permanent lodgers cast one another whenever a temporary guest chances to indirectly mention the sad issue.

No sooner is the taboo raised than one pair of still young brown feminine eyes (Véronique's) swift interlock with several other familiar sets of older gray, green or blue eyes, some male, others female. On each such blessedly rare occasion, the same sorrowful message issues from Véronique's gaze. It is a confession of abiding personal shame, of self-loathing, an acknowledgment of failure she believes easily avoided. Rather than offering love, understanding and sympathy, the other sets of eyes respond uniformly delivering the conviction of having once been unforgivably betrayed, heartlessly abandoned.

157

So distressing for all involved is this exchange it never lasts more than a couple moments. Often, the, outsider accidentally raising the subject is unaware he or she provoked these harsh visual confrontations. A minute later, relations between all members of this nontraditional family were as normal; remaining no less warm, chummy, loving, cherishing until another outsider's idle comment.

It was during these terrible episodes, passages of actual time lasting just seconds but in Véronique's consciousness, infinitely longer, that she desperately yearned for her next rare opportunity to visit Cardinal Casimir Blanchard, archbishop of Paris. She knew: "His Grace, like every great statesman in history is a busy man. Leadership of a country, the crafting of international diplomacy, responsibility for deciding on matters of war and peace are not professions taken up by idlers, their successful accomplishment done by lazybones."

"Often" feared Véronique, "His Eminence is on the verge of being mentally, physically overwhelmed by the massive duties required of him to best fulfill all the titanic responsibilities, seeming countless obligations, he consented to take on alone." Cardinal Blanchard she declared "is a great man. A *statesman* concerned with assuring the betterment of all humanity into the following century! He's not a whorish *politician* only interested in soliciting for votes in the next election."

Earlier, sponsor and protégée were in almost daily contact. Since the prima ballerina's retirement, this was no longer possible. "Nonetheless" she confided "even today His Eminence is meticulous to reserve some of those all too short and seldom interludes in his hectic schedule, to let humble me cry on his august shoulder."

In stark contrast to the unspoken animosity Véronique still received intermittently at *La Nouvelle Heloise*, Cardinal Blanchard remained her all protective, shielding, understanding, compassionate surrogate-father. Still asking "my precious girl" to sit on his lap, still holding her close, rocking her in his arms, two souls, become, one. "All that unending talk on the Left about His Eminence being a *Smooth Operator*, a *Pied Piper*, a 'Shameless self-promoter'" grimaced protégée "is—well I won't use the unladylike term. If anyone doubts His Eminence is a good Christian they need only observe how he 's so comforting to those in distress."

Once, she seated upon Cardinal Blanchard's lap, held close in protective arms, Véronique almost confessed the reason for withdrawing from ballet. At very last moment her resolution failed. Cardinal Blanchard didn't press the issue, then or later. He felt he was already granted enough honor. It was more than enough understanding that of all the people on earth, he alone was judged worthy to even approach learning the eternal mystery.

Véronique was deeply grateful for receiving *Uncle Casimir*'s undiminished paternal affection. His love was a tender, shielding, never-failing, all-forgiving one. A pure love, Véronique increasingly feared she wasn't truly deserving.

If she too became a highly-creative girl's benefactor, Véronique often mused, she'd, make sure raising her gifted ward into an adult freely dedicating all her tremendous artistry to The Virgin. This was surely, Véronique reasoned, what Cardinal Blanchard originally intended for his own "Divine Child." For a decade, these plans went no further than fondest daydream.

Then, one morning, Pascale arrived.

THE DIVINE CHILD

....

"*Excellent*, excellent, Sweetheart!" exclaimed the noted priest-physician-archeologist-lecturer, clapping vigorously, tears of happiness running cheeks, voice choking. Like his motherly, possessive, extrovert younger sibling invariably mistaken as elder of pair, Richard Castellane too, had a deep parental affection for the adolescent he and sister were praising. One, unforeseen events abruptly made the distinguished cleric and the prima ballerina's ward. And far was this from a run-of-the-mill teenager! This evening, her legal guardians and close friends convened to celebrate the girl's brilliant, self-trained artistry.

Richard wore a red, white and green ermine and silk cassock elaborately hand-embroidered with cloth-of-gold, enveloping his entire body. He also wore blue alpaca gloves. A large, ornately carved ivory Byzantine cross was suspended on his weak chest from a heavy gold chain around his narrow shoulders. Yet further impressive and museum-quality, religious chains, emblems, medallions each crafted by a royal goldsmith or elite silversmith centuries dead covered his 100-pound, five-foot-five-inch figure. He appeared so much more robust, powerful, even literally taller than he really was under all that grand imposing clerical attire.

Normally, when he on visits, trips, outings, at cocktail or dinner parties with intimates, Richard dressed in "civilian clothes," or "secular outfits" as his sister enjoyed calling "my erudite dear's garb." He did the same when operating the neighborhood clinic, delivering lectures, naturally, while excavating Biblical sites in Turkey, Syria, Jordan or Iraq. This current event, however, was occurring within a chapel of his historic church in Paris, the surging spires of Notre Dame visible above orderly, undulating-waves of *Mansard* roofs. Given the venue selected, the reason get-together held, above all the particular individual for which it was to celebrate, Richard arrived in full Easter Sunday morning Mass regalia.

"My brother this evening is going to be—awesome!" predicted Véronique, strapless. She bubbled with all schoolgirl excitement. Her bare shoulders, arms and back were fetching to behold. "No, Richard-dear" she chattered, unconsciously adopting guest of honor's favorite phrase, "you're going to be *really* awesome! And remember Richard-dear, our Sweetheart Little Marie is a young lady. No young lady on earth can ever resist a gentleman in uniform! Tonight's going to be awesome—no it's going to be really awesome!"

A month was elapsed since Pascale Kedari—now *Marie Castellane* according to newly-acquired French passport—won a coveted-*Baccalaureate*. Won it so grandly too, just as Matilda Eisenberg promised. The score the professor's little friend achieved (both on written and orals) placing her in the top 1-percent of all adolescents (girls *and* boys) taking the examination that year throughout France and in all its overseas possessions! Dare it be ventured hers was the top examination score of *all*. No wonder people coming in close contact with "this Divine Child" insisted she emitted an aura! Or that they all wished being included within that glow's so comforting diameter!

Since then, this girl attained an infinitely higher distinction. One, which no amount of formal schooling can compensate for lack of personal artistic talent in achieving. She was brought this evening by her mentors to their *Romanesque-Gothic* church on the Left Bank in the 5th Arrondissement so they might officially recognize, celebrate Pascale/Marie's undeniable artistic genius. Much was changed for the better since she leaped with despair from the Pont Neuf to be just barely, unwillingly fished-out of murky Seine.

Her fresco of *The Nativity* was finished. Ten meters wide, four-and-a-half-high, located on a chapel wall three meters above granite floor, this near-life-size mural is impressive to say the least. Unlike traditional representations of the subject portrayed in strong or bright colors and shades, Babe in cradle or on Virgin's lap exuding kingship and optimism, promising glory and triumph to come, surrounding figures in picture just ancillary, the event as depicted by Pascale, is quite dark, somber in color, shade. More involved and active, too, is the pictorial narrative. No reminder of long-desired presents soon unwrapped is evoked. *The Nativity* as represented by Pascale is far from a purely joyous occasion. The unmistakable warning shown to viewers is that terrible menace lies ahead, not easily guaranteed victory.

That newly-born Christ will later struggle, this picture leaves no doubt. That He is going to suffer, often be rejected, persecuted, before consenting to die for the sins of many still twisting, misinterpreting the true and wider significance of His sacrifice also is abundantly clear. Pascale demonstrates the life of Christ isn't simply a movie, a theme put to music, or morality tale with happy ending for hero already known.

Rather than fanciful manger in faraway, imaginary, long ago, never truly existed-Bethlehem, here, *The Nativity* is set in a crowded, contemporary, all too familiar urban bus terminal. Prostitutes, Midnight Cowboys, drug addicts, transvestites and similar unsavory characters take the place of reverent angels, Magi, shepherds and docile farm animals. Once again, viewers are starkly reminded the life of Christ wasn't just a comfortable idealized fable, nice Sunday school lesson, or set of words of liturgy described in aloof, antique grammar. Nor will journeying that same path be simple for those wishing to follow His teachings. Being a Christian is a struggle despite what politicians, plutocrats and others seeking to manipulate faith for own personal ends, often promise.

Pascale also far from romanticizes the Virgin and St. Joseph. In her portrayal of history's most famous duo, both are without dispute non-Anglo-Saxon teenagers. Perplexed, unmarried, ragged, they're either Turk, Kurd or Roma, possibly too, illegal alien refugees. Left alone together in a hostile world, neither child suddenly confronted with responsibility for raising another child appears at first anywhere near emotionally-mature enough to successfully handle the grave-difficulty.

The kids' illegitimate Babe, now needing to be changed, exhibits no hint of future greatness. The legal minor, penniless, unwed Holy Family is currently being approached by unsympathetic emigration police, not awe-struck, shielding angels, Magi. No written words, however, do justice to this magnificent piece of visual art. That Pascale modernized the scene, clearly making this ancient birth as equally significant, applicable, relevant today, is but one reason her picture so profoundly moves viewers—Christian and not, believer or not. Another reason is that in her fresco, the Virgin is no aloof, vapid, two-dimensional figure without breasts. Instead, she is a real girl. One, her observers might actually meet, or perhaps even already know. A real girl endowed with all a real girl's needs, wants, all a real girl's ambitions, fears, strengths and weaknesses. As for the Babe, it is an actual infant not a two-dimensional symbol.

The flesh-and-blood human observer quickly finds that this picture ostensibly made of paint and plaster located on a medieval stone wall, is in fact as alive, vibrant as he or she. Not merely alive, vibrant but for each separate pair of eyes observing it, becoming his or her individual and intimate companion. Once more no written words can do the great visual art work and its ability to commune with its audience proper justice. To be fully appreciated and understood the fresco must be seen.

Brendel's Daughter, wearing earrings and necklace of natural pearls; lovely parakeet blue dress, chapeau and high heels; white hose—abruptly fell on knees before the fresco. Falling off her shoulder, *Coach* tote-bag scattered makeup, schedule book and other contents on the dark brown, gray, medieval granite floor. She crossed herself several times fervently.

With teary eyes clinched-shut, bust palpitating, sculpted hands clasped tight at smooth, strong chin in prayer, moist red painted lips recited desperately, each succeeding time in faster, more penitent, supplicant voice "*Je vous salue, Marie, pleine de grace, le Seigneur est avec vous—*"

Only after reciting the *Rosary* six ardent times did Matilda halt sudden demonstration of apparent newly-restored faith. "Jesus Christ! I've not rattled that mumbo-jumbo since leaving St. Clothilde!" she whispered, terribly embarrassed.

Matilda looked about furtively, concerned she'd become target of derisive glances, object of snide comments. Instead, her devout companions were delighted. They much pleased observing the avowed-agnostic's unexpected show of deep piety. "Thank God my colleagues from the University aren't here!" professor muttered, scrambling back on high heeled-feet. Urgently, she brushing ancient dust from short parakeet blue dress, re-adjusting necklace and angle of chapeau.

"What's wrong Mme. Matilda? What's wrong Mme. Matilda?" begged Pascale, scurrying to retrieve friend's *Coach* tote-bag, collect all its scattered contents. "Are you ill?"

"No, no, Divine Child" assured Matilda. She gave Pascale a kiss on right cheek in show of grateful thanks for help in recovering *Coach* tote-bag and contents. "No, no, Dear. I was just so overcome with admiration for your fresco. Gazing at it so intently I was overcome with emotion, my mind recalling passed times and passed things I thought sadly gone forever—I guess looking upon all great works of art can stir such feelings in a viewer."

Pascale looked away embarrassed.

"Excellent, excellent, Sweetheart" repeated Richard, master of ceremonies to this evening's guest of honor. "I'm positive, songbird," he continued, pointing to the other walls in large chapel with forty-foot ceiling, these other walls and ceiling as yet covered only in white plaster. "I'm positive Songbird! Your friends have only seen tonight the very first of what will prove many splendid pictures you're going to create for the world. Splendid pictures which, I know will be honored and looked to as an inspiration for future artists far beyond this parish, city and nation for centuries to come!" His words echoed down *the Nave* from *Narthex* to *Chancel*, leaped *Vault*. "Ladies, I wish to announce" he informed Sister Claire, Sister Genevieve, Professor Eisenberg, "that Mme. Castellane and I arranged—"

"It's going to be another Arena Chapel! Another Arena Chapel!" burst-out Véronique ecstatic, clapping ladylike, chapeau fallen off, long thick cherry-blond hair obscuring pretty face. She jumped up-and-down in-place as furiously as high heels allowed. Melody of refined feminine enthusiasm echoed the *Nave* from *Narthex to Chancel*, filling *Transept*, leaping the *Vault*. "It's only to be expected from her—only right and proper she now be given the responsibility, the glorious task—my little Christian genius should—*our* little Christian genius—should be given the chance and means by our church to properly honor the Virgin and Her son!" She crossed herself fervent, eyes gazing pious above.

Véronique solemnly promised her brother could make the announcement. Richard after all was shepherd of this congregation, sister, just one of his flock. Still, the grand project the siblings assigned Pascale and her completion of what Véronique decided was only first in a long cycle of narrative images crafted by the "Divine Child," ultimately made it impossible for the prima ballerina to resist breaking news her genteel self. "It's going to be like the new Arena Chapel! It's going to be the *new*-Arena Chapel!"

The Arena Chapel, as Véronique and her fellow art connoisseurs well-knew, is the ultimate masterpiece of Giotto. The great Florentine painter is chiefly responsible for liberating western visual art from a millennium of rigid imitation of the unrealistic, openly propagandist Byzantine style. Giotto, is the painter chiefly responsible for propelling western visual art on its own independent and far superior, infinitely more creative aesthetic path. During the *Fourteenth Century* Giotto covered the walls of the Arena Chapel in Padua with 64 beautiful, moving, highly expressive, and above all for each succeeding observer, personally engaging, intimate, almost living frescoes. They narrate the life of Christ, of the Virgin and present a depiction of the Last Judgment.

Ironically, as Sister Claire (dressed fetchingly in lapis-lazuli) is always meticulous to remind, this matchless example of late-Medieval painting was commissioned by the Scorvegni family—the most notorious usurers in the Italy of their day. Brutal, heartless, exorbitant-interest rate money-lenders, they stopped at nothing to make sure borrowers paid-up on time and in full. The clan's patriarch, Enrico Scorvegni, appears in *The Divine Comedy,* situated by Dante at one of the lowest and fieriest circles of Hell.

"Ah! Like another Arena Chapel!" the collective-gasp of Sister Claire, Sister Genevieve and Professor Eisenberg echoed down the *Nave* from

165

Narthex to *Chancel*, encompassed *Transept*, leaped *Vault*, resounded off the *Chancel* and returned to original place of utterance.

Moments later, each spectators' breath recovered, heart again beating normally, all fixed their eyes on painter in collective expression of immense emotional awe, intellectual admiration.

Save for signature huge red satin bow in voluminous jet-black hair, Pascale was *The Girl in White*—white chapeau; necklace of natural pearls, birthday present from Véronique; short, sleeveless dress beneath unbuttoned white Kashmir cardigan, white bobbysocks and high heels; gripping white purse with both hands in white gloves. The compliments received made her feel terribly embarrassed. She turned away, finely developing four-foot-ten adolescent body squirming with anxiety.

She grimaced as if in severe physical pain, clinched shut gray-green eyes.

"Yes, the darling created the frescoes all by her own pure, virginal self!" announced Véronique, beaming with maternal pride. "And just like the original Arena Chapel in Italy, this new one will also possess sixty-four brilliant, immortal frescoes! All created like Giotto by my darling alone!"

"Ooh! Our child really will, Mme. Castellane?" her friends asked excitedly. "Our *Angel* will paint us sixty-four frescoes?"

"Yes *really* ladies! Yes *really*! Our Divine Child is going to make Giotto frightfully jealous! Frightfully jealous of our miniature genius! I promise by the Virgin's womb!"

Richard glowered, clearly annoyed being snatched what was earlier agreed to be his opportunity taking announcement. Observing her brother's sour face, Véronique was seized with guilt. She instantly released Giotto's rival and rushed over to shower Richard's face with penitent maternal kisses. She was about to embrace and hold him tight, rock him back-and-forth in maternal arms before deciding that might damage the Easter Morning Mass regalia she was so insistent her brother wear for this occasion.

"Please forgive me Richard-dear? There your *Scatterbrained Female-*sister goes again! First doing all she can to arrange everything properly—doing all she possibly can to serve you. Doing all that's best for you, get everything prepared for you—convincing herself she knows exactly how all the arrangements to assure your success are set in motion—being is a dutiful, supportive sister to her brilliant brother—and then ruining it all for you by revealing she's in the end just a typical *Witless Woman*. Please, please, please forgive somehow find it in your noble heart to forgive silly me? I promise, *really* promise, this time, to do all I can to avoid this catastrophe in the future."

"I forgive you, dear"

"Imagine trying to put-up with a *Nothing-between-the-ears; Knock, knock, nobody Home*-character like me, as your sister?" opined Véronique rhetorically, while supplying sibling further endearing kisses. "Well Richard—I should say *Father*—I can go-on about my idiocies," she halted to recover breath, "endlessly."

"No worry" brother chuckled. "Granting forgiveness—providing the penitent is *sincere*—is one of my primary jobs."

"Bless you, bless you my long-suffering, all-understanding Richard!" gratefully answered Véronique, strapless. "Being willing to endure a pestering *Scatterbrains* like me is no better proof you're such a true Christian, a true servant of our, Lord!

"What a matchless darling you are, Little Marie!" extolled Sister Genevieve. Tonight, she and Sister Claire dressed in traditional black habits. "What a splendid little creature our Sweetheart is at only the very start of her grand career! Fly high above the clouds Christ's winged-messenger! I know you can and know you will."

The pint size winged-messenger was further embarrassed, the little dove's feathers were now all totally matted, confused, in disarray.

"Wait! Wait! Wait! I must capture that priceless image of the Divine Child and preserve it for all eternity!" gushed, Véronique, restored to lovingly-overbearing, kindly-dominating self. Pushed long cherry-blonde locks from attractive face, she took a complicated Japanese gadget from *Hermes Birkin* handbag to frantically snap an entire roll of film. "Oh! Ooh! Ooh! The Virgin, be praised! I must capture that glorious image and preserve it for all eternity!"

Snap, snap, snap, snap, additional frantic, ladylike camera snaps.

"Richard honey, get-up close to our Little Marie!" commanded Véronique. Speedily refilling complicated Japanese gadget, she delivered desperate, not to be challenged instructions with motion of her Roman head, sculpted neck. "Get close to our Sweetheart, Richard, so I can recall both my Beloveds for all eternity! Now hold the child's right hand and look down at *Firebird* with a protective, 'I'm-so-proud-of-my-little' smile." Her brother instantly complied.

Snap, snap, snap, snap, still more zealous, ladylike camera snaps.

As on all occasions when touched by any man other than Father, a *The Creeps* infinitely creepier than *The Creeps* shot through his daughter's entire body and soul. *Chere Petite* clinched her eyes and jaws, made fists, her heart and lungs throbbing speedy, stomach nauseous.

"*There. Perfect!*" cried Véronique. "Maintain that pose." She merrily snapped-off a third roll of film while humming the most famous theme of *Swan Lake.*

Snap, snap, snap, snap, additional passionate ladylike camera snaps.

At last, following what for tormented Pascale seemed endless time, Father Richard released her. Yet no sooner he doing so, than Sister Genevieve requested he clutch the artist again so she too might take photographs.

Snap, snap, snap, snap, additional genteel camera snaps.

"'Our Little Marie is another Giotto,'" wrote Sister Genevieve in the latest bimonthly report she dutifully wrote to her parents back in Rouen. "If our Little Marie were from Mexico and this an earlier time in history I would call her another Rivera or Orozco or Siqueiros! The pictures our Little Marie creates are so moving, so real, so personally engaging, friendly and welcoming to the eye of each separate individual man or woman, boy or girl, scholar or day-laborer. The figures in our Little Marie's frescoes are nearly alive! They make the viewer, every succeeding viewer, each for his or her own different but equally legitimate and worthwhile reason wish getting inside the canvas or fresco wall with them. The characters in the pictures make the viewer cry or laugh or sing with them, shout, run, jump, wonder or dream with them!'"

"'Come on inside with us!' the figures in our Little Marie's painting instantly say to the viewer," further wrote Sister Genevieve to her parents back in Rouen. "'We're your friends. Come and be with your friends. Love us, since we love you, cherish you. We want to protect and guide and shield you! Even though we look like pictures we're real people with lives and souls.' I know all this sounds rather silly. No written words exist to properly and justly describe visual art. You must find some opportunity to come to our church in Paris and see this splendid art. Miss Preston and I promise you won't be disappointed!"

To bolster assertion, Sister Genevieve dispatched with her latest bimonthly report to Papa and Mama Fauré a series of color photographs their daughter personally took of the new frescoes emerging on chapel walls. "'I hope these photos give a small example of our Little Marie's artistic brilliance. And she is dedicating all her immense, incomparable creative talent to the Virgin! I won't be surprised if the child is a saint!'"

"I hope I prove worthy of your hopes and dreams Mme. Castellane, Father Richard, Mme. Matilda, Sister Claire and Sister Genevieve," pleaded young painter. The warm, heartfelt praise she received this evening making her terribly uneasy. "I hope my art proves worthy of the Virgin."

"No fear, Sweetheart" promptly assured the duchess and nanny.

"No fear" seconded the prima ballerina and the distinguished priest.

"Don't worry for a moment, darling" promised Matilda. "You're the greatest painter in centuries! There's no way you can't succeed."

Sister Claire and Sister Genevieve each patted her protégée on shoulder with a loving, protective, wise older sibling's hand.

"Leopoldine?"

"Yes, Mary?"

"Was it Wordsworth or Goethe who said—'I knew the world when she was in her springtime, I was there at the morning of the, world.'"

"I'm not certain, Mary. Wordsworth, I think but don't mortgage your soul on it."

Sister Claire readjusted the huge red satin bow atop *Chere Petite's* ocean of jet-black hair. "Whoever made that famous quote Leopoldine, I can be absolutely sure of one thing. It's that—we too will know that glorious 'springtime.' We too will know 'the morning of the world.'"

INNER SPIRIT

···

A month passed.

"I'm indescribably—moved—awed—overcome—by what you can paint, Sweetheart! I wish I could put into precise words—accurate phrases—how much your latest creation touches me!" pledged Sister Claire haltingly, apologetic. She and gifted teenage friend were alone together in the chapel. Tears ran the nun's unblemished, soft cheeks. She sniffled. "What did Therese of Lisieux write? Ah, yes. 'There are things the heart feels but which the tongue and even the mind cannot express.' I'll leave it at that. If a great saint underwent sublime experiences she found no accurate words to describe, who am I supposing I'll do better."

Sister Claire only spoke after gazing silently for several minutes, eyes transfixed upon Pascale's next completed fresco. As Véronique was fond of repeating, "My ever-so-talented ward is the next Giotto! Just like Giotto, she's going to paint 64 frescoes in one chapel. And this time, in Paris! In addition, each of *Little Thing's* murals will be a priceless piece of art! Guaranteed! My Divine Child will craft the second Arena Chapel! Guaranteed!" That was an exceptionally bold and daring promise for anyone to make. Politicians after all, only promise the moon. Nevertheless, as swiftly, steadily mounting and irrefutable evidence demonstrated, Véronique—ever the *proper* lady—was proving as good as her genteel, refined word.

"So thought-provoking your picture is, Sweetheart," commented the nun.

"Thanks, Sister Claire" replied the artist. "I wish to be thought-provoking."

"It's an inescapable reminder to our parish, don't you think, Little Marie? Just because a number of people we both know prefer not talking about certain decisions they each freely and without slightest compulsion once made, doesn't mean those same voluntary decisions and unforced-actions have gone away, or their consequences, diminished in significance! What's done can't be *undone*. Nor can those same people we both know, forever avoid at least moral and historical condemnation! They cannot escape responsibility simply through pretending it all never happened! Or, legitimately claim—'I didn't know' or, 'I thought it was resettlement in the East.'"

"In fact," she added, following additional contemplative gaze at Pascale's newest fresco, "a number of people we both know, secretly realize they'll soon confront the day of at least moral and historical judgment! As much as they dearly want it to be so, Truth i*sn't* confined by time and space!"

Sister Claire eagerly pranced the chapel in boxer's stance. She threw a strong right hook at imaginary opponent. Next, threw a left; again, a right.

Pop, pop, pop. Knockout!

"Little Marie? What did Joe Louis say about Billy Conn?"

"He can run but he can't hide."

"I don't expect you becoming a prize-fighter, of course. All the same, you deliver splendid 'knockouts' of another sort. My Little Marie is the artistic-Joe Louis!"

Pop, pop, pop. Knockout!

Like *The Nativity*, this fresco too. is painted in deep, expressive, often melancholy shades of color. As so it should, considering both the grizzly episode recorded in Matthew and its modernized-portrayal are chosen to pronounce unmistakeable judgment on the darkest period in Twentieth Century French history. It was a shameful era, one many still alive vividly recollect. A time, as Sister Claire's words indicate, during which more than a few members of the current parish conducted themselves less than honorably.

In this depiction of *Slaughter of the Innocents*—the flunkeys sent to murder all the Jewish male infants in Bethlehem in order to eliminate the unidentified child Roman-stooge Herod is warned might challenge his collaborationist regime, wear 1940s-era Paris police uniforms. These are the same outfits worn by officers of the force on July 16-17 1942 when the French—not the Germans—arrested much of the capital's lower middle and working class Jewish population for deportation on French trains to Auschwitz. In her fresco, Pascale depicts the many local witnesses of the atrocity exactly true to life. Painting them either as morbid voyeurs, as people who "just don't-want-to-get-involved," or, as individuals heartily approving of the crime but meticulous to avoid direct personal association.

"Superb!" exclaimed Sister Claire. "Superb! Of course critics will inevitably jabber—'Little Marie never went to art school.' But then, Giotto didn't, either!"

Pop, pop, pop. Knockout!

Like a fresco on the same subject by the great medieval Florentine muralist, this later work too is intensely expressive, almost in motion. Viewers immediately seem to watch, even hear the bloody and shameful event transpiring. Rather than looking upon collections of inanimate paint strokes frozen on a plastered wall, viewers even before realizing it, honestly sense themselves placed amidst living, breathing human beings. Audacious, striking, compelling, magical to behold, this is a superb picture. Just as Pascale/Little Marie wished it to be. Written words however cannot do adequate justice to visual art. To fully appreciate, it must be seen.

"Why did you choose portraying the scene as you did?" queried Sister Claire. After a moment she ventured uncomfortably: "Besides recording the *Holocaust,* does the picture also depict what you saw occur in your own country during its recent upheaval? If that's terribly wrong, out-of-place and dreadfully-intrusive of me asking, please forgive me."

"No forgiveness required Sister Claire" answered Pascale, enveloped in paint-smeared overalls and apron designed for someone much taller. "I wasn't present. I didn't know at the time but Father suspected revolution was about to break-out and sent me abroad. For months-upon-months,

I asked Father for permission to visit Paris. He firmly refused, saying "little girls belong at home.' Then, only a day after refusing yet again, Father suddenly announced he wished me going to Paris. I should've guessed something unusual was-up. But of course I was just a silly-head then."

"How do you get inspired to paint?"

"A voice, a spirit inside me is my trusted-companion, Sister Claire. She's been inside me, been my trusted-companion as long as I recall. Her voice, her spirit inside me, begins by saying—'Paint *this*.' Next— 'paint *that*. Don't forget more blue *here*, a touch of yellow *there*.' I'm just an average girl with nothing special to recommend me. I'm no different than any girl you meet daily in the street, on the bus, on the *Métro*. I'm simply doing as the voice, the spirit, companion inside me instructs."

"Like the Holy Ghost?"

"Why in all creation my blessed inner voice chose me as her instrument, I've never understood, Sister Claire. The reason is hopelessly above my uneducated-head. —But so be it. —I'm so grateful to be chosen. I'm so grateful that of all the girls in the entire world, many far smarter, better, more religious, humble than me, I was chosen to follow the spirit's voice, I was chosen to be God's vehicle."

Miniature Artist surveyed the wall opposite where her next fresco was to appear. She paused to open a new can of azure paint while at same time casting protective, big feminine sibling an anxious glance.

"I hope what I just said doesn't make me sound nutty, doesn't make you think I'm a crackpot, Sister Claire. This chapel shouldn't be decorated by a crackpot."

"I don't think you're 'nutty' or a 'crackpot'. Not at all *Precious*, not, at all!"

"Truly you mean that, Sister Claire?"

"Indeed, I mean it darling! I pledge on my soul I do! With your encouraging special voices you remind me of Jeanne d'Arc! With your encouraging special voices showing God's way, you remind me of Jeanne d'Arc! What our Europe of capitalist, money-grubbing, exploiting, self-absorbed atheists really needs today isn't some new computer software.

173

It doesn't need yet another fancy gadget. What our Europe, what humanity needs today is a new *Maid of Orléans*!"

The Duchess of Airandel couldn't help finding it paradoxical that one of her own ancestors ordered Jeanne d'Arc burned at the stake.

She stroked her singular protégée's voluminous jet-black hair lovingly, cherishing.

"This time though I'll make sure *The Maid* isn't abandoned by those owing her everything. I'll make sure this time *The Maid* isn't burnt at the stake."

The huge satin red bow atop her mane again come undone manifested exactly how Pascale felt at this moment—embarrassed, ashamed. So embarrassed, so ashamed at the thought someone as trivial as herself could be mistaken as Jeanne d'Arc material.

"I do my best, Sister Claire. I do my best for my pictures to honor the Virgin."

The Duchess of Airandel pondered the fresco anew, soon breaking into song. She doing so, not in French but in her native *BBC* English.

Charlie Chaplin went to France/So he could teach girls to dance

Echo of melodic voice meandered down the Nave, up the Vault.

First the heels, then the toe/Then the splits and around we go—

The viewer's continued meditation of the fresco restored to immediate consciousness some of the fondest, most cherished memories of her childhood. Irreplaceable, priceless recollections Mary Preston's busy adulthood permitted scant opportunity, even less time, to savor.

Charlie Chaplin went to France/So he could teach girls to dance

Hop, hop, hop—the young British peeress in nun's habit skipped merrily in-place. She moved up-and-down at single, steady rhythm. Her arms and legs revolved in circular motion as if she jumping rope. Eagerly singing a song her nanny Mrs. Anderson taught. One, designed precisely for such occasions.

First the heels, then the toe/Then the splits and around we go—

Hop, hop—she merrily jumped in-place singing a song, as if skipping rope.

Charlie Chaplin went to France/So he could teach girls to dance—

After passage of playful, happy time, deep brown eyes still riveted pensively on new fresco, the Mary Preston of long ago halted her song, dropped imaginary skipping-rope and rushed hurriedly off, feet still in-place. Concern on this child's un-meddled-with face, agitation in her yet-to-be-disillusioned heart and lungs indicated she might be late for an important meeting she pledged on the Bible to attend. If now physically in mid-twenties, living in the 5th Arrondissement of Paris, while contemplating the fresco, Mary Preston was in vivid-spirit, active-consciousness if not in body, returned to the mountains of southern, coal-producing Wales.

Bubbling with joyous, triumphant enthusiasm, yearning to contribute her *all* and far more, to the glorious cause—Sister Claire sensed herself again the child who scrambled up the scaffolding's steps to reach rostrum. She at last arriving, nearly out of breath. A rostrum whose top the little girl could only reach after a union brother first lifted her atop a heavy wooden barrel.

"Thank-you ever-so-much Mr. Rees!" that same child with fiery-red hair repeated aloud, now far from mountainous Wales, her merry, innocent voice echoing the *Nave*. "I've come to show the workers not all aristocrats are oppressors! Believe me Mr. Rees, the Duchess of Airandel is on the workers' side! The Duchess is as our lord Jesus Christ instructed she must be, at-one with the proletariat! I'm so grateful to be invited here by your union. And please Mr. Rees, call me Mary or Mary Alice not—*Your Grace.*"

Today, in France, her inquisitive hands running through abundant burning-red hair, adult Sister Claire again felt her tresses expertly wound by governess Mrs. Anderson into braids reaching near waist, tied with bright-colored ribbons. Searching fingers racing body head-to-feet, Sister Claire was just as before clothed in corn-shade chapeau; frilly white blouse; Royal Stuart tartan and monogrammed-navy blue jacket, feet in white bobbysocks and flat shoes. As before, a gentle, soft, encouraging breeze stroked her legs. Temporarily setting fun-and-games aside, the radical junior Duchess prepared to address the picket line

Gazing upon Little Giottto's newest fresco, Sister Claire again heard the same warm, lengthy applause she once received from the

175

crowd of rough, dusty, unshaven but all welcoming, protective, Welsh coal miners. She actually felt once more the miners' tender, shielding, fatherly hugs and kisses. A moment afterward, this young warrior for justice would pledge on all that's holy she was on the side of the workers; again, she be carried on the strikers' shoulders; declared, honorary union chairman. Making a fist with right hand, she clearly sensed the touch of the new skipping-rope the miners gave their mascot.

Charlie Chaplin went to France/So he could teach girls to dance
First the heel, then the toe/hen the splits and around we go

Finally, emerging from confines of her deepest, most dormant memory, sentences never spoken twice, ones, she unaware still remembering after passage of twenty-five eventful years–now abruptly issued from adult lips. They burst forth today with the same, original, precocious nine-year-old's fervor. Echoing down the *Nave* from *Narthex* to *Chancel,* crossing *Transept,* the words leaped *Vault.*

"'Be not afraid' comrades! Our cause is a pillar of fire! Ours is the voice thundering from the burning bush! The bush that burned but was not consumed! Righteousness is our guide and protector! Blessed are they who do hunger and thirst for righteous sake, for they shall be filled.—'Be not afraid' my comrades, co-believers. Ours is not but a voice crying in the wilderness—it's The *Good News!*—Know the truth and the truth will set you free!'—Let my people—sorry, I mean: our people go!—For though the Lord is high He regards the lowly and the haughty He knows from afar.' We now go forth to spread the *Good News* of our lord Jesus Christ to all the lands high and low, near and far—We'll make it so that one day all countries and all peoples will profess in all languages, believe in all minds, hold dear in all hearts a common loyalty to socialism! The first shall be last and the last shall be first—Put not your trust in princes—So out-with-the-plutocrats! We 'll drive the money-changers from God's temple! The Pharisees, we will scatter! The veil shall be rent.—'The truth shall set you free!" Hear the message! Socialism is *The Good News* of our lord Jesus Christ who lay down His life for the workers! Socialism is the path to the city upon a hill shining forth eternally as the guiding beacon of hope, the light unto all the nations!—Socialism, we follow, socialism we teach! Socialism will triumph! *True Socialism!*"

If slightly nuanced, tinkered-with along the edges to adjust for grownup realities—the spiritual message enunciated by the nine-year-old in pigtails and the one shown living witness today by a nun from the 5th Arrondissement of Paris were essentially unchanged. *"Blessed are they who do hunger and thirst for righteousness sake,"* she again quoted **Matthew** while gazing upon the fresco. Sister Claire's voice today was as fervent and sincere as the little Duchess of Airandel addressing the Welsh coalminers. *"'Blessed are they who do hunger and thirst for righteousness sake for they shall be filled.'"*

Small wonder conservatives accuse her of being: a Communist, a lesbian, a heretic, or all three at once. No surprise she remains "an undesirable alien" banned entry to the United States under the *McCarran-Walter Act.* No consternation another on that prestigious blacklist—Sister Jeanne Navarro—considers this fellow religious, her own most trusted and able lieutenant.

"Little Marie, Sweetheart" remarked Sister Claire haltingly, at last weary from reliving twenty-three years of life experience standing in place.

Yes, Sister Claire?"

"Your frescoes move my soul! They take me at least in spirit to a nigher, loftier dimension, to a better time and place! Your frescoes transport me to a world in which each and all of us can truly fulfill those words of **Micah**—*Do justice, love mercy and walk humbly with thy God."*

Pascale once more emitted a brilliant, transcendent, deeply compelling aura. A supernatural personal glow all the more captivating through the fact girl possessing it hadn't the slightest inkling.

"Please forgive me not explaining myself properly, Sweetheart" apologized Sister Claire, flustered. "I'm so overcome I can only blabber like a *Scatterbrained Female.* I hope you gather at least a hint of what I wish to tell you."

"Yes," Pascale comforted. "I understand what you're getting-at."

As earlier, the Divine Child's magical shine expanded steadily outward until at last bringing one of its only handful of privileged observers completely within otherworldly light's own sheltering, loving diameter.

"It all confirms precisely what Leopoldine and I suspected about you from the beginning" explained the nun, anxiously fiddling with meddle crucifix around her slender neck. "Sweetheart?"

"Yes, Sister Claire"

"You're the Songbird, Christ's Messenger!"

I

Another month passed.

"Sweetheart, you're a truly sublime, primal, universal, unbounded, elemental, creative force of Nature" gasped Professor Eisenberg as the pair were alone together in the chapel.

"I try my best" answered Pascale modestly, shuffling feet, clasping hands behind back, directing gray-green eyes to dark brown stone floor."I try my best, Mme. Matilda."

Matilda gazed with awe upon the third completed fresco. Today, Sister Claire was elsewhere, supervising the children scrape yellowish, cracking old plaster off corridor wall in nursery school. Once that task was done and energetic, *do-it-yourself*-Sister Genevieve (father, uncle, brother plumbers) repaired leaky pipe fixtures, provided new plaster, the corridor would be graced with a mural by Pascale. The nuns requested on this occasion artist use bright, optimistic colors. The subject selected, was a modernized-version of Christ blessing the children. If any youngsters so disposed, they could receive as reward for all their current eager, industrious help serving as models in new picture. As she was engaged at plumbing repairs near ceiling high atop ladder, one boy was far more excited at the opportunity provided him to look-up Sister Genevieve's skirt.

Mattie Eisenberg, Socialist—declared the words on the corsage of bright blue, white and red flowers attached to left lapel of candidate's tweed sports jacket. *Liberté Egalité Fratenité*—shouted the tricolor cordon crossing the party standard-bearer's shapely feminine torso, from left shoulder to right hip.

"If I was old enough to vote" pledged Little Giotto, "you could depend on receiving mine, Mme. Matilda!"

"Yes, Sweetheart, I know I could."

"When I'm old enough to vote, Mme. Matilda, I'll vote for you in every election you stand! One day I'll be able to say—'I'm best-buds with the President of France.'"

"Before I make history in the Chamber of Deputies, Sweetheart, first let me succeed in becoming a backbencher."

"If you'd like, Mme. Matilda, I'll paint a mural for your campaign."

"So I know you gladly will if I ask" acknowledged friend, tightening huge red satin bow in Pascale's voluminous jet-black hair. "However, this Divine Child I only met by sheer accident on an airplane from Frankfurt has a higher mission than making political campaign pictures!"

"If you say so, Mme. Matilda"

"So I do! That lofty mission you've been called to perform has in fact already begun! Ask Sister Claire if you don't believe me."

"That kind of a *mission* sounds a little bit scary, Mme. Matilda."

"Don't worry, darling. You wouldn't be selected to perform this great mission unless you possessed far more than sufficient ability accomplishing it." The longtime religious skeptic abruptly quoted from Matthew. *"Blessed are the pure of heart for they will see God."*

A new, far bolder, infinitely more meaningful era was opening in the professor's life. Following years of she casting erudite-judgment on the troubled, anxious world from behind the safety of lecture hall parapets, conference auditorium fortifications, pontificating in learned-quarterlies only her colleagues knew even existed, she publishing scholarly unread tomes now gathering dust on library shelves, the moment was come. Mattie recently decided to leave the academic-convent, renounce the learned bystander's-veil.

"If you sincerely support, honestly endorse them" Auschwitz-survivor Brendel Eisenberg often admonished her child in Silesian accent, "you must demonstrate your convictions with action! You must bear *Witness*."

"Our predatory, bigoted, materialist, anti-intellectual, closed-minded, worshiping-capitalism-like-a-pagan-idol species can only be saved from its willing self-destruction by deeds not mere words!" Brendel, *69509331*-tattooed above left wrist, often enjoined child. "Only saved through action, not still further gutless, spineless, cocktail party-jabber!"

Just days earlier, following weeks of ever-mounting nationwide labor strikes, massive street demonstrations by teachers, university and secondary school students as well as heretofore reliably pro-government business owners and office workers, President Thomas Belanger's long-dominant conservative bloc lost a key budget vote. The critical defeat compelled new elections for the Chamber of Deputies. All polls indicated the approaching vote might produce a historic redrawing of the political map.

After fourteen years devoted, tireless, invaluable, if largely unsung-labor in the *SP*-Leban's vineyard as—all-around militant; stenographer; fundraiser; campaign pamphlet-writer; contributor of pro-*SP* articles in newspapers; local party club chairwoman; even babysitter, escort— Brendel's Daughter received at last, if not Rachel, an equally-desired, long-coveted reward. The *SP* asked if it might come waltzing Matilda to a reliably-left-wing National Chamber of Deputies seat in either Paris, Lille, Rouen, or Caen.

She leaped at the opportunity. Especially, when discovering the Paris constituency offered, encompassed much of the 5th Arrondissement— already long her personal and career stomping ground. Each day this lapsed-Roman Catholic couldn't resist several times crossing herself and casting periodic grateful kisses toward a loftier dimension. From where, she was confident, Mama looked down both lovingly and with immense satisfaction on her only offspring.

"There's no limit to your artistry!" pronounced the *SP* candidate gazing upon newest fresco with rapture. Under a tweed sports jacket with corsage and tricolor cordon, Mattie wore a blouse of parakeet blue, white skirt, crimson hose and heels. The *Coach* tote-bag with strap slung over shoulder was full of campaign fliers. Currently inside a church, however she deemed it inappropriate distributing the literature. Even though, as Mattie remembered from university, the clergy were never shy promoting its own political agenda.

"So kind of you, Mme. Matilda!" gratefully answered Little Giotto, again enveloped in paint-smeared overalls and apron designed for someone much taller.

Pascale's third fresco portrays *The Flight into Egypt*. It also, painted in dark, brooding colors. The teenage, penniless, clearly non-European Holy Family earlier found in seedy urban bus terminal is now interned at a crowded, unruly, rat-infested UN refugee camp enclosed by razor wire. Mary and Joseph, however, are no longer so overwhelmed by the many responsibilities suddenly thrust on their too young shoulders and immature minds. Despite the tremendous odds initially set against the pair's survival, these kids still somehow managed to muddle through. They aren't hopelessly become lost attempting to navigate the complicated maze of adult society.

Christ's parents no longer confront life's peril as total ingénues. All the same, viewers of the fresco can detect the famous duo still require additional anxious time and painful experience before fully mastering their lot. Christ, in the midst of a furious tantrum, is certainly being less than helpful. Joseph is busy checking the *Holy Family*'s ID papers in order they can receive some of the thick, dark-brown, unappetizing slop a UN sign designates: "high nutrient food." The Madonna, far from her traditional sexless, vapid, submissiveness—is instead portrayed wearing short skirt as she engages in a bitter argument with another teenage mother grasping her own child. Some of the language the Virgin employs in her cat-fight over the tiny space available to each refugee in overcrowded camp, isn't immaculate.

"Awesome!" cried Mattie, following several additional minutes gazing silent upon her unique friend's newest mural. "No, no, it's *really* awesome! The gossipy, holier-than-thou, irredeemable-boor, old crones aren't going to approve at all," she giggled. "They'll accuse your version of the story as looking 'too modern,' 'not traditional enough.' They'll accuse you of making *The Holy Family* appear too human! Christ, the Virgin and St. Joseph, they'll say, 'appear too much like real people.' They're 'too approachable,' too easy for mortals to identify with."

"The same accusation earlier old crones leveled against Manet when depicting Christ taken down from the cross!" chirped Pascale, triumphant. "'Oh blah'—I say, Mme. Matilda! Oh blah'—I say! If the former collaborators don't like my version let them come forward and produce a better one themselves! Those former collaborators who filched Jewish art collections, 'purchased' Jewish businesses and property, wore sable coats, drank *Romanée Conti* wine, ate caviar and fresh oysters, obtained free gas for their sports cars during the *Occupation* can go to—" she caught herself "—can go to where collaborator, stupid, vulgar anti-Semitic, dark roots crones belong!" *Chere Petite* paused again before chortling as do children when observing adults unawares doing something stupid.

Together, bathed in one of the two's glorious aura, compelling glow visible only to privileged handful, the friends irrupted into furious, protracted-giggles.

The sound of' merriment echoed throughout the *Nave* from *Narthex* to *Chancel*, encompassing *Transept,* leaping, *Vault.*

"What's the subject of your fourth fresco, Dear?" queried Professor Eisenberg when at last regaining composure. She scooted around as fast as high heels allowed to recover all the campaign fliers which during her furious giggles fell out of *Coach* tote bag and scattered on the granite church floor.

"I've not completely made up my mind, Mme. Matilda" answered Little Giotto, washing paint brushes in large canister of water.

"Well, whatever it's going to be, I know it'll be grand. It can only be grand! After all you're the messenger."

"*The Messenger,* Mme. Matilda? That's what Sister Claire too says I am."

"Yes, honey. You're the *Songbird.* You're the *Messenger.*"

MAMA

....

*P*ascale awoke with a fierce start.

She lay in an oak, *Queen Anne* canopied-bed at *La Nouvelle Heloise*. A month was elapsed since her conversation with Matilda. Unlike Richard's church in the serpentine *Latin Quarter*, *La Nouvelle Heloise* was located several miles to the west, beyond the Trocadero. Pascale's heart raced, lungs throbbed, teeth chattered. *Goose Bumps* covered her jittery arms and legs. Thick, soupy blackness enveloped the room whose shape and dimensions were impossible to surmise. Pascale was in the midst of that kind of darkness so impenetrable one can walk aimlessly in circles without being in the least aware. Only sense of touch provided any indication her body and the mattress it lay upon even existed. Opened gray green feminine eyes possessed no better a view of the world than when closed.

Pushing her massive shawl of jet-black locks back from pretty face, the teenager gazed restlessly about; finally, locating a hazy beam of ivory projecting anemically through the enveloping, thick, soupy night. This feeble sliver of ivory constituted the narrow opening between chintz curtains drawn over a window at the foot of the bed. That French window looked out upon the townhouse's inner quadrangle paralleled by Moorish arcades. At the quadrangle's center was a splendid if currently invisible gated garden roughly 13-meters in circumference constructed in the *British* style.

Here, Richard grew every plant mentioned in the Bible. For months, Pascale affectionately-tended the over-1000 different species of flowers, shrubs, fruits, vegetables and trees, as if she was each one's doting-parent She had in her loving charge not merely the familiar *Rose of Sharon* and *Lily of the valley*, the well-known grape, fig and olive, common mustard seed, pear, cedar tree, but also a number of exotic and anything-but-household word-named flora. No similar example of applied botany existed in France.

At this hour, the garden was lost in soupy darkness. A sliver of anemic light issuing from the narrow space between drawn chintz curtains over French window gave no hint if dawn was either just ahead or still hours to come. Few vehicles originating from central Paris entering this upscale, semi-suburban neighborhood even in daytime, the present lack of traffic sound meant nothing in particular.

The girl's newly awakened hand groping steadily leftward at last touched what was in daylight a museum-quality *Chippendale* walnut chest-of-drawers with brass shelf handles. Hung on papered-wall immediately above, if, unseen in soupy blackness, was a framed-photograph of nineteen-year-old Véronique performing *Gisele* at the Bolshoi in Leningrad. Inquisitive hand groping now atop furniture–"oops"–it in process knocking a hairbrush on to am intricately-woven, ornate, multicolor design Bukhara carpet, Pascale at last snatched-hold of a plastic, battery-operated clock whose arms glowed in the dark.

3:15 AM.

"Goodness gracious! It won't be light for hours! Even if I get up early to assist Mme. Castellane with the hotel chores, 6:30 is still hours away! And during the night time is so dreadfully slow. It even seems to stands still. Better I try getting more sleep. What does Mme. Castellane say? 'My Little Marie needs to receive the proper amount of rest in order for her to completely develop as she was intended both in as well as body.'" Pascale's voice was still hoarse from all the ecstatic, joyful nonstop screams emitted two nights ago at campaign headquarters when it became clear Matilda was elected to the National Chamber of Deputies.

"In both mind as well as body"—softly repeating those motherly, protective words directed solely to her, always brought a humble, grateful smile to *Chere Petite's* face. Now pulling the covers up high, her body in long hand-embroidered nightgown knitted by Véronique, curling into a fetal position, her eyes clinched shut, Pascale attempted drifting back to sleep. Normally, a nightmare, *anxiety dream* was more accurate description of recent experience, didn't swiftly return.

"Perhaps it's because you're an artist" counseled Father on similar occasions, motioning daughter climb into his own bed for the rest of night. "Your exceptional creativity at times gets the upper-hand, *Chere Petite*. At least your anxiety dreams are unique, interesting and highly imaginative, though. They might be the drawings of John Tenniel."

After an indefinite length of time, Pascale once more awoke with a start.

John Tenniel was an apt comparison. The same: curious, teasing, unique images possessed of deeper political significance earlier troubling young sleeper, again invaded teenage feminine mind. Pascale might as well be Alice having tea with the *Mad Hatter, March Hare* and the *Door Mouse*; Alice, playing croquet with a flamingo as mallet; she, too, observing the *Cheshire Cat.* Pascale was confronted by the *Queen of Hearts* and the other more unnerving inhabitants of *Wonderland* and *Through the Looking Glass.* Even in unconsciousness, she stayed true to her modernized-style of traditional subject portrayal. While Alice, shares a train compartment with a gentleman illustrator John Tenniel unmistakably makes Benjamin Disraeli, Pascale is accompanied on her ride by Margaret Thatcher.

As before, her groping atop the chest of drawers enveloped in thick, soupy blackness she grasped the clock.

3:40

"Just as it happened before, just as it happened before!" lamented Pascale. She well remembered when last suffering protracted bouts with alternating anxiety dreams and insomnia, persistent rapid heartbeat, throbbing lungs; *Goose Bumps* on jittery limbs, chattering teeth. It happened with gathering intensity during the two weeks leading up to her two suicide attempts.

"I thought my *Scatterbrained Female*-behavior was over-and-done-with, at last at! My *Witless Woman, Knock-knock nobody Home*-conduct, is supposed to all be behind, me at last!" Pascale scolded herself. "I thought that shameful, shameful carrying-on was permanently ended when I dedicated my life to art—was over, after Sister Claire and Sister Genevieve selected me to paint the walls of the nursery school and playground—after Madame—I mean now *Deputy* Matilda helped me obtain a *Baccalaureate*—after I was provided a French passport—after Mme. Castellane and Father Richard selected me to redecorate the old chapel! I thought that shameful, shameful, *Chicken-with-her-head-Off* foolishness was over. I thought I was finally a smart, responsible girl?"

Girl paused.

"Likely, the next time I decide jumping-off the Pont Neuf into the Seine, I won't get fished-out! Or, even if I still do, Father Richard will be unable finding a magistrate willing to release me from the nut-house. Maybe the nut-house is where I belong! Considering too how angry Mme. Castellane will be with me this time if she gets me back, I'll now *want* to stay in the nut-house!"

Pascale yanked the thick covers over her agitated head, curled round-and-round, moving restless this way and *that*. So small on this huge canopied-bed, she could travel considerable distances at alternating speeds without even once loosening tuck of the sheets. In fact, her continued presence was detectable only by a meandering bump rising from the bedspread.

In time, this meandering bump came to a halt. Here, it remained motionless until Véronique entered the room at mid-morning to place new red tube roses in a bronze Persian vase and pull-back the chintz curtains over a French window. Through the newly-scrubbed panels of glass, a 13-meters in circumference botanical garden at the center of the Moorish quadrangle was on splendid display in all its multicolored, exotic, fecund glory. No longer enveloped in thick, soupy darkness just brief and intermittently pierced by feeble slivers of anemic moonlight, girl's combination bedroom and study was instantly bathed in bold sunbeams.

"Time to get up darling" instructed Véronique. "Madame permitted you to stay in bed longer than usual because se's got something of particular importance to explain."

"Yes, Mme. Castellane" meekly answered bump on bedspread.

"Did you sleep well?"

"Oh yes indeed Mme. Castellane!" pledged bump on bedspread. "I slept very well. I hope you did as well, Mme. Castellane."

In truth, the deferential bump was quite drowsy. If it remained near-motionless for hours, the bump experienced not a minute of deep, dreamless, recuperative sleep. Achieving only short, intermittent drifts into semi-consciousness providing a worried soul no more mental or physical rest than when fully awake.

The Messenger; The Songbird; Jeanne d'Arc of Socialism; Divine Child whose brush strokes are the voice of a new and greater age; Precious One who crafted a second Arena Chapel; Secular Saint; Giotto-in-a-skirt; Picasso-in-bobbysocks; Tiny-Turner—"That's quite a reputation for me to live-up-to!" reflected Pascale lying on the huge, canopied bed under heavy embroidered covers. Contemplating how to reach such a life's goal set for her entirely by others agitated the insomniac teenagwerl minute after minute, uneasy adolescent hour after hour. As her body rested until mid-morning apparently fast asleep, her mind was in heated, self-debate. "It's quite a reputation to live up but somehow, I must do it!"

Failure was only an option if Pascale took a better leap into the murky Seine. All those in her new existence in France she loved and knew loved **her**, all those who befriended, nurtured, protected, guided the helpless, *Scatterbrains* when she blundered unexpected on to their own paths—Mme. Castellane, Sister Claire, Sister Genevieve, Professor Eisenberg, Father Richard (though he strenuously insisted he'd done nothing special), a few kindly others too—were all placing so much hope in the success of their protégée's artistic career. An artistic career, their protégée was convinced, only her benefactors made possible. Pascale had the sacred obligation to fulfill their expectations.

"Above all I, must do so for Mme. Castellane! Anything and everything positive which has, or is, or ever will occur for me in France, ultimately comes from that awesome lady! Mme. Castellane is far more my Mama than my blood-Mama! I've no right disobeying or disappointing Mme. Castellane! She's far more the one giving me birth, responsible for making me who I am than my blood-Mama!"

Unfortunately, Véronique the's surrogate-daughter made no progress in the last month. Following Little Marie/Pascale's explosion of exceptional creativity, she producing in rapid succession—*The Nativity*, *The Slaughter of the Innocents* and *The Flight into Egypt*—*the painter* now found herself temporarily exhausted of further artistic inspiration. A month passed and "The New Arena Chapel" projected to be decorated with 64 masterpieces still boasted just three. The walls of that corridor in the nursery school were also today stubbornly blank. Church plumber and girl-on-a-ladder Sister Genevieve was yet to be compensated for boys looking-up her skirt.

For weeks, the four-foot-ten creatrix with ocean of jet-black hair now descending to knees, racked her singular childlike brains to discover how she might again seize Emptiness by the throat, master the Void, give Space no alternative but submission to this teenager's will. What was the solution? The answer continued elusive.

Gazing remorseful, ashamed, at so many coats of blank plaster at last became so discouraging, *The Messenger* abruptly lost her way, the hushed-*Songbird*, unhorsed-Jeanne d'Arc of *True Socialism* didn't enter the sanctuary. If Véronique permitted—and she certainly did not—Pascale would have stopped attending Mass. Still, her sudden block in further inspiration couldn't be escaped just through physically avoiding the geographic spot the problem first arose and where its stubborn refusal making-way-for-a-lady was so clear and sore to a pair of gray-green eyes. The troublemaker with whom Pascale never wished or provoked a confrontation pursued her far beyond the walls of Father Richard's medieval church in the 5th Arrondissement.

Before arriving in France, at least two hours of *Chere Petite's* daily schedule were assigned exclusively to drawing. Véronique nsisted this practice now continue. She immensely enjoyed showing her surrogate-daughter's completed sketchbooks (all elaborately-bound) to both the regulars of the aristocratic pension and to its distinguished visitors. Véronique invariably gushed and bubbled with maternal rightful pride as she heard those looking through the pages always express great admiration for the drawings the sketchbooks contained.

"Nurture" the prima ballerina often explained, slightly rewording a popular American phrase, "is even more important than Nature!" *La Nouvelle Heloise* being the cultured, elite, learned, Old World institution it is, these high estimations of all the pictures done in pencil, chalk or crayon are of tremendous critical value. Yet in the last month the same creative block currently obstructing work on The New Arena Chapel, expanded sphere of negative influence to sketchbooks. Their unfilled pages became as discouraging to see as the blank plastered walls. This sanctuary too the artist no longer entered.

"Sometimes mediocre people with nothing at-all recommending, themselves, live so well, so content and happy," reflected Pascale beneath the covers on the huge, oak, Queen Anne canopied bed. "Great talent can on occasion be a terrible burden, especially for a girl! Especially for a girl who's yet to properly thank those who've made all she's accomplished possible."

"Come!" summoned Véronique after placing new red tube-roses in a Persian cast-meddle vase. "Come sit on Madame's lap!" She took off her halter-top brown apron covering a Royal Stuart tartan, white blouse, white hose and pair of flat brown shoes. Tossing the apron into one chair, she sat in an adjacent seat. "Come out from under the covers and sit on Madame's lap!"

Little Marie/Pascale emerged from under covers. Still in her nightgown, she climbed on the designated lap. Though no hint existed of anything to fear, she couldn't help feeling a sense of foreboding.

"Yes, Mme. Castellane? You've something important explain to me?"

Véronique didn't answer immediately. Instead, she first held the miniature artist close. She first rocked her beloved one back-and-forth silently for a couple of minutes.

"Yes, Mme. Castellane?" asked her ward in time. "You've something important to explain to me?"

"Little Marie, you're the exact same matchless, Christian, loving, Sweetheart with incalculable artistic gifts today as when I first met you" began Véronique in responsible, protective, maternal voice. "Being the one given a chance to be your guardian is the greatest, most fulfilling experience of my life. It's impossible to ever put into words the honor, grace, blessing it brings at being provided this unexpected opportunity."

"It's been an AWESOME experience knowing *you*, Mme. Castellane."

"That's so nice of you, Little Marie."

The Kindly Lady kissed protégée's unblemished cheeks. Pensive, steady, deliberate, cadence of her words immediately indicated they prepared. "I want you to always remain that same loving, Christian Sweetheart who gives the world so much beautiful and irreplaceable art. I don't want the artistic gift you received from God ruined, spoiled, stunted as the result of unwarranted emotional pressure received from others, myself very much included. Even when—what do the Americans call them—oh yes, *Back-seat-drivers*—mean the best."

"No not from you, Mme. Castellane!" insisted teenager loyally, too aware the opposite, correct. "I never receive emotional pressure from you, Mme. Castellane!"

"No need being diplomatic, Sweetheart. I'm guilty most of all."

Pascale felt immense relief the Truth was out but didn't know exactly how to respond.

Véronique relieved her of that need.

"Little Marie, those well-intentioned harpies who mean you only well, who, aren't really trying to seize-control for themselves but sincerely believe they're offering help—are the worst pests of all! It's very difficult telling someone wishing to come to your aid to 'Shut-up and go away.' Is it not?"

She paused:

"It's especially hard to say 'Shut-up and go-away' to a person who treasures you more than all else in the entire world!"

The two linked eyes knowingly.

"I'm chiefly responsible, Sweetheart" confessed Véronique. "I'm chiefly responsible for your sudden inability over the last month to create more splendid paintings and drawings."

Although knowing it to be true, Pascale loyally, shook her head in denial.

"Don't deny it, Cherie" replied Véronique. "Don't be frightened acknowledging it's true! Your legal guardian is responsible. Because of all Madame's—*Witless Woman* pestering; behaving as if she knows best, how to advance your own career—Madame has instead only stymied it. Madame created a situation where her junior-Michelangelo is more preoccupied wondering if her paintings are enjoyable to her silly guardian than concerned with being a masterful artist."

She again stroked the magical girl's ocean of thick, soft, smooth, jet-black hair descending to the girl's knees. If mere sight and touch of those glorious tresses was enough to capture the admiration of the first woman in France with an opportunity encountering them, Véronique was also the first one granted the privilege to kiss and brush those heavenly locks. Her words also shifted into intimate **First Person.** "I now understands that no matter how good-intentioned I was, well-meaning in—as the Americans say *Back-seat-driving*—I've absolutely no right to interfere. I now realize my continued meddling with your God-given, just once-in-only-many-centuries artistic ability, will lead only to the most disastrous results. You're suffering this terribly block in further inspiration because me. It's all my doing. I'm not merely supposed to be your legal guardian, the guardian of your physical and economic interests. It's my responsibility to be the guardian of your genius. As such I've recently been far more than lax on my obligations."

"Oh, Mme. Castellane?" begged Pascale. "I'm the one who's been terribly lax in my responsibilities, obligations to *you.*"

"Nonsense. Any *obligations,* you long ago repaid by letting me take care of you!"

"Come to me now!" Lifting Pascale on to her own welcoming, maternal lap, Véronique gently stroked her rotégée's splendid mane. Mother and child swayed in silence, two souls become one.

"What did you wish telling me this morning Mme. Castellane" queried younger of elder at last. "You let me stay in bed late because of something you wished to say?"

"I'm sending you away."

An unnerving, metallic cold shot instantly through Pascale's young body.

She experienced precisely the same abandoned, impotent, naked, hungry sensation when the telephone link with Father broke-off.

"You're—*sending me away?*"

"No, no, my own junior-Rembrandt!" quickly assured Véronique, applying the girl's face warm, maternal kisses. "Don't fear! I should've chosen different words. It's not *that kind* of—'sending you away!' Rather, I'm sending you temporarily to live under the care of my best friend, Rose. Rose lives just one mile distant. You and she actually twice met! First, in the Place de Vosges, then again along the embankment. Both times, Rose came across you sketching."

"She did, Mme. Castellane?"

"Yes!"

"I'm sorry I can't recall, Mme. Castellane."

"Don't worry, *Cherie*. Considering it occurred just days before those dreadful events in your birthplace, it's not surprising you don't recall. Rose vividly remembers, though. She was deeply impressed both with your brilliant artistry and no less sweet character. You spoke to her of how your family decided you were—'Accomplished' and of how each time visitors and public figures came for dinner—'I was always trotted-out to show what I can do.' Rose said you told her that since you were now—'the family artist' it was incumbent on you—'not to make my relatives look *silly.*' All kinds of things can serve as successful motivation, can they not?"

"So they can, Mme. Castellane."

"Rose like Sister Claire, is an intellectual," elaborated Véronique. "Rose possesses a fine art collection. One, you'll greatly admire. It might even provide ideas for your own splendid work. Rose is the ambassador for *UNICEF.* Ever since her appointment, she's been hoping to find a companion for her two daughters. The children always remain behind whenever their Mama is dispatched to dangerous, troublesome places abroad. Rose isn't looking to hire a nanny. Rather, she's searching for someone not that different in age from the girls—Someone, the girls can look upon not as a chaperon but as a close, intimate, caring friend—A special buddy, who the girls might even in time regard as their sympathetic, understanding, protective-Big Sister. You're perfect for the assignment, Marie. In addition, joining Rose's extended family is a far better home for a teenager than remaining at eccentric *La Nouvelle Heloise.*"

Out in the quadrangle, morning was clearly arrived.

"I'm confident" promised Véronique "that you, Rose and her daughters will all soon become the best of lifelong friends. Living removed from Mme. Castellane's daily *Witless Woman*-pestering, alleviated from her constant *Scatterbrained Female*-meddling, you'll be able to reach your own free and independent decisions as to how best express the marvelous gift for art God gave you! That nasty, badly-mannered Creative-Block refusing to step aside to let a lady pass, will, I predict, soon vanish."

Véronique brought Pascale to welcoming bust. Two special friends—younger, atop elder's lap, swayed gently as, one. "However, I do expect weekly progress reports from you, Little Marie. I'll be ever-so flustered without hearing regular news from my daughter."

"Yes. I promise *Mama.*"

www.ingramcontent.com/pod-product-compliance
Lightning Source LLC
Chambersburg PA
CBHW020636110726
47899CB00002B/788